THE COLOUR OF SUMMER

VICTORIA CONNELLY

Cover design by The Brewster Project
Photos copyright © Depositphotos

Author photo © Roy Connelly

Published by Cuthland Press

ISBN: 978-1-910522-18-9

To Kate with love and thanks for being there!

CHAPTER ONE

There is a house that sits high up on the Sussex Downs. Its name is Winfield Hall, but the locals call it The House in the Clouds. With its golden Georgian façade and huge sash windows which wink in the light, it really is something to behold no matter what the season. Spring brings wild flowers in yellows, violets and gentian blues; summer blesses it with light and warmth; autumn colours swirl and dance right up to the doorstep; and winter silvers the downland tracks and slopes with rime.

On clear days, if you walk up on the downs, you can glimpse the sea between the hills and catch the softest of salty scents from the waves. And this is something that one of the owners loves to do.

Abigail Carey had been at Winfield for two years and the place still enchanted her on a daily basis, which made for rather a wonderful life, she thought, because enchantment could be hard to come by sometimes. Ever since the house had been put up for auction, it had found a place deep within her heart, even though she hadn't made the original successful bid. That had been Edward Townsend's privilege. But, during extensive renovation work, a couple of cruel twists of fate had befallen Edward and he'd made the decision to contact Abi, selling his underbidder half of Winfield.

Abi still couldn't believe all that had happened in the last few years. She'd sold her successful design company, left her London home, bought half an historic house, let two apartments, and also had a misguided romance with Edward's brother, Oscar, which almost ended with her being driven off a cliff into the sea. It all left her quite breathless when she thought about it, but Winfield had a way of helping a person to heal – no matter what life threw at them – and she couldn't have been more content with her new life.

Abi hadn't seen Oscar since the accident. He'd texted a couple of times, checking that she was okay, but Abi really hadn't known how to respond. How should you react to the man who'd stolen flowers off somebody's grave before almost driving you over a cliff, leaving you with a broken arm and nightmares for months? It hadn't come as any surprise when he'd been fined and banned from driving.

As she left the table where she'd been choosing some mounts for her latest prints, she walked towards the French doors and gazed out into the walled garden. It was a breezy May day. A few autumn leaves, which had escaped raking, were now swirling among the late spring flowers. The yellow and white tulips Abi had planted in October had put on a fine display, but the last of their petals were being torn from their stems by the downland wind, reminding her of the continual passage of time and how important it was to stop every so often and just look around and note the changes. That was something she'd rarely been able to do when running her company. Time had always eluded her, but she'd claimed it back now, enjoying her art once again and making time to walk, cycle and swim.

Back in October, after her cast had come off and she'd had some time to experience life with two working arms again, Edward had reminded her of the swim he'd promised. He'd then taken her to a small lake on a private estate where one of his clients lived. The water was deep, cold and silky, and Abi regretted her decision to venture in as soon as she'd dipped her first toe. But she'd done it, encouraged by Edward who'd promised her lunch in a pub afterwards where they'd thawed out by the fire. But now, even though it was late May, they were yet to have their first swim of the year. The weather, up until this point, had been so erratic. But it was warming up now and Abi was hopeful it wouldn't be too long before their first outing together.

Opening the door into the walled garden, Abi picked up a couple of terracotta pots that had blown over in the wind and popped them in the greenhouse. She looked back at the hall. All four apartments were let now. Abi had leased her first one to Aura Arden, a yoga instructor and healer, and her second to Tim Becker, a writer. She hadn't seen much of him, she had to admit. He had the apartment at the back of Winfield and he very much kept himself to himself as she guessed most writers did. She'd advertised the flat back in August and word had spread fast about the low rent and Abi had been inundated with applicants. She'd decided to do preliminary interviews online and only invited shortlisted candidates to Winfield. Tim was the clear winner with his quiet manners and assurance that he'd disturb nobody.

He was in his forties, loved old buildings and seemed to own a lot of waistcoats – all with holes in the pockets where he kept sharp pencils. He'd been a schoolteacher until four years ago, and had been writing all his life, but had only recently become a novelist when a big publisher had signed him up. Unfortunately, they had paid him badly, not promoted his book and then dropped him. Then, instead of securing another deal for him elsewhere, his agent had also let him go. Tim had been devastated and was having to start all over again while writing freelance pieces for newspapers and magazines.

Abi had read his book and had loved it. It was full of humour, charm and perception and she hoped he would keep writing and that he wouldn't have to go back to teaching the unruly children at the school he referred to as 'The Zoo'. Perhaps Winfield would work its magic and be a source of inspiration and calm to him just as it had been for her. She hoped so. She liked him a lot. He reminded her of a Beatrix Potter character, but she wasn't quite sure which one. Peter Rabbit or Samuel Whiskers perhaps. Someone sweet and endearing. Anyway, she was glad he'd found Winfield.

Edward Townsend couldn't have been happier with Harry as his neighbour. He was a quiet young man, dedicated to his work with a local B corporation, and he was friendly without being intrusive. Just what Edward liked.

If only it had been as easy finding a suitable tenant for the new apartment. He'd first let it out at the beginning of September to Miss Bradley, a sales rep working for a large international company. But, in mid-March, Miss Bradley had decided she needed a more central location and moved to Leeds. Edward had then had to go through the whole advertising and interviewing process again. Luckily, he'd found a replacement quickly, but he had yet to make his mind up about her although he'd liked her initially.

Samantha Everett had arrived for her interview punctually, she'd been neat and tidy in appearance and absolutely charming. In short, she'd come across well and Edward had been happy to offer her the apartment, but the truth of it was that Edward was having his doubts now. Shortly after she'd moved in, litter had started to appear in the hall and driveway. It wasn't anything much: a chewing gum wrapper one day and an empty tube of sweets the next, but it did show a lack of care that annoyed Edward. Was it deliberate? Or did Samantha genuinely not know she'd dropped these bits? For it surely was her, as litter had never been an issue before.

Then there was the radio. Edward had been in a Zoom meeting when he'd first heard it coming through the walls. He'd winced at the noise. It was some dreadful pop band whose song had the kind of chorus that could send the mind into madness within seconds. But, not liking a fuss, he'd ignored it, hoping it was a one-off. After all, everyone was entitled to make a bit of noise once in a while, weren't they? It was just unfortunate that it hadn't been a one-off.

He was just pondering this thought when there was a knock on his door.

'Abi,' he said with a smile as he answered. It was always a delight to see her.

'Hi Edward.' She looked anxious.

'Everything okay?' he asked.

'I'm afraid Tim's been complaining,' Abi said. 'About the noise.'

'You mean Samantha?'

Abi nodded. 'Their walls join at the back of the hall, you

see, and he's trying to write and the music – well – it's been quite loud lately.'

'Oh, dear, not again.' Edward said. 'I'll have to have a word with her.'

'If you wouldn't mind. Tim's been wearing ear plugs, but isn't very happy about having to.'

'Of course not.' He sighed. 'I'm not sure I'm cut out to be a landlord. It's all very well when things are going smoothly, but it's something else entirely when they're not.'

'I'm so sorry.'

'It's okay. It's what we signed up for, isn't it?'

'But we've been so careful to make sure the people we choose are right for Winfield,' Abi pointed out.

'I guess you don't really know someone until you're living with them.'

'I guess not,' Abi agreed. 'Listen, let me know if you need any back up.'

'Do you think I might?' Edward said, panic in his voice.

'Well, I meant emotionally,' she said, smiling. 'I'm hoping we won't have to physically throw her out. At least, not yet.'

'No, of course not,' Edward asked, scratching the back of his neck anxiously.

'Edward – don't worry!' Abi stepped forward, placing a hand on his arm. 'You're simply reminding her that we like it quiet here at Winfield. She knew that when you agreed to her tenancy, right?'

'Right.'

'And she won't want to jeopardise that, will she?'

'I guess not.'

'Then you've nothing to worry about.'

He took a deep breath. 'I wish I had your confidence.'

'It'll be fine. You worry too much.'

'Very likely.'

'Let me know how it goes, okay?'

He nodded and watched Abi cross the hallway back to her own apartment. He was truly on his own in this, wasn't he? There was nobody else to sort it out but him. And he supposed that he should get it over and done with and then treat himself to some time outside. Maybe he'd go for a walk and let the wind from the downs blow away some of the dread and anxiety. But first...

He made his way to Samantha's apartment. He could clearly hear the music in the hallway as he knocked on the door and waited. And waited. He knocked again – louder this time. Finally, the door opened.

'Samantha? How are you?' he began with a smile.

'Edward!' she said, looking surprised to see him as she ran a hand through her short dark hair.

'Can I have a word?' Edward asked, raising his voice slightly above the radio which was still blaring.

'Everything all right?'

'It's about the music.'

'What about it?'

'It's too loud.'

'Says who?' Her forehead creased into a frown. 'That old bore next door, is it? Tim whatshisname?' She gave a brittle laugh.

Edward wasn't sure how to respond, but he didn't like her flippant tone. 'You can hear it everywhere, I'm afraid.'

She continued to frown and Edward shuffled his feet awkwardly. 'It is a condition of your tenancy here that peace and quiet is maintained at all times. That was made very clear, I believe?'

Her face changed suddenly. 'Yes, of course,' she said,

obviously realising she was at fault. 'I'm so sorry. I'll turn it down right away.'

She closed the door in his face and, a moment later, the music was no longer audible. Well, it was a result. Of sorts. Edward grimaced. He felt uncomfortable after the encounter. This spiky individual was most certainly not the young woman he'd interviewed. Where had that sweet, pleasant woman gone? Had it simply been a front to get the apartment? She'd also told him she was a full-time manager at a hotel in Eastbourne, yet here she was at home in the middle of the day blasting music. What was that about? Did she do night shifts and, if so, surely she should be resting now rather than winding up everybody else who was trying to work from home.

He shook his head. He wasn't going to fathom it out today, was he? And the music had been turned down so the problem had been dealt with. Still, as he left the hall and bent to pick up a chocolate bar wrapper from the driveway, he couldn't help wondering if he'd made a terrible mistake letting Samantha Everett into Winfield.

CHAPTER TWO

The last week in May brought warm sunshine to Winfield and there was a real feeling that summer was just around the corner, and Abi thought she'd go in search of that very corner. Her bicycle had had a quick once-over and the ebony metalwork was looking shiny and in need of an adventure, so she tied her hair back, popped her helmet on and hopped on and was soon freewheeling down the country lanes, the sun full on her face. It was a glorious feeling and really helped to shake off the dark images that had haunted her through the night, waking her up in the small hours, her bed sheets tangled around her feet and her skin hot with fear.

It had been the same dream – or rather nightmare. Once again, she was a child, creeping down the stairs of her old family home – the one where they'd lived with their mother before Aunt Claire had taken them in – the one she only had vague and hazy memories of. But she remembered those stairs. She seemed to be forever stuck on them, neither up nor down. Half-way. Suspended between the hall and her bedroom in a place she shouldn't have been so late at night.

Then there'd been that awful, hollow feeling of dread as strange voices broke the silence of the night. Her sister was shouting at her, telling her to go to her room and Abi could feel the hot sting of tears. And that's when she'd wake up, her cheeks streaked with tears once again.

Abi could almost feel them again now, but being out on her bike helped to blow away the memories of the night, replacing their darkness with the light of the spring day and she did her best to focus on that . Live in the present, she told herself, shutting out the shadowy pain that could so easily threaten the beautiful day around her if she let it.

As was her routine whenever she headed out on foot or on her bike, she found her way to Ronnie's cottage in the tiny village on the other side of the downs. The unmetalled road had her teeth rattling and body vibrating and she decided to get off and push before she cycled right into a pothole.

A moment later, she was wheeling her bike through the open gate into his garden, breathing in the deep scent of fresh honeysuckle. She leaned her bike against the wall of the cottage and took her helmet off. What was it about Ronnie's place that made her feel so relaxed within seconds of arriving? It wasn't as though she loved it more than her home at Winfield, but this little downland cottage had quite a different hold on her heart. It was small and intimate. It was cosy and cute. And it was wonderfully loose around the edges in a way that the rather grand Winfield could never be, and the artist in Abi liked that a lot.

Peering in through the open window to the living room and finding it empty, Abi cast her gaze into the garden. Where else would Ronnie be on such a day?

'Hello!' she called, following the brick path which crumbled lazily into an unkempt lawn where daisies jostled with dandelions.

'Abi?'

Abi frowned. She could hear her friend, but couldn't yet see him. 'Ronnie? Where are you?'

'Behind the viburnum.'

Abi panicked. Which one was that? She'd been doing her best to learn about shrubs, but she still had a long way to go. Luckily, Ronnie's teddy bear face peeped out from behind some large white blooms.

'Smell that,' he said, beckoning her over to the plant.

Abi dunked her nose into the domed flowers and inhaled. 'Lovely!'

'One of my Emma's favourites,' he told her.

'I can see why. It's glorious. I should get one for Winfield.'

'I'll get you some cuttings.'

'Oh, thank you!'

'Not now, of course. In the autumn.'

Abi nodded. She still had so much to learn. 'Come and see the garden some time, Ronnie. I'd love to show it to you.'

'And I'd love to see it. Got your car, have you?'

'No. I came by bike today.'

'Ah. I'm afraid me and bikes don't really work anymore.'

'It's okay. We'll arrange something another time.'

'I'll look forward to it.' He waved a hand. 'Tea, I think – yes?'

'Yes please.'

A few minutes later they were sitting under the dappled shade of an ancient apple tree, mugs of sweet tea in their hands.

'You've been having nightmares again, haven't you?' Ronnie said without any sort of a preamble.

Abi looked at him in surprise. Since befriending him, she'd told him more about her personal history than she'd ever told anyone, and that included the nightmares she occasionally fell prey to. Still, it caught her off guard that he was so perceptive to her feelings.

'How did you know?' she asked him.

'You have that pale look about you that no amount of sunshine can chase away.'

'Do I?'

Ronnie nodded. 'You okay?'

'I'm not sure. I mean, I feel fine now. A bit shaky, perhaps. But I don't really remember much. It's all just feelings from my childhood, really, and vague images of me coming downstairs and there being strangers in the house and lights flashing and my sister yelling at me. I don't remember any more. I never do. And I can't tell if it's real or not. Did that all happen or is it something I've made up? And is it something to do with my mother's death? I think it must be.'

'Have you talked to your sister about it?'

'Not really. Her mum's death seems to be one of those taboo subjects and it happened such a long time ago now that it seems strange to want to revisit it.'

'But not that strange if it's still affecting you today.'

Abi sighed and gazed deep into the greens of the garden, her gaze softening slightly and a little of the tension she was feeling slipped away.

'Surely, if it is a memory, it'll fade with time,' Abi reasoned.

'Well, it hasn't yet, has it?' Ronnie said. 'Sounds to me like it's festering.'

Abi winced at the ugly word he'd used. 'Oh, don't!'

'Sounds to me like there's something that needs to get out.'

Abi sighed. 'I'm not sure I like the sound of that.'

'Maybe not, but it could be good for you. You might feel –

what's that word?'

'Closure?'

'No. *Release!* That's the word they use, isn't it?'

Abi nodded and she had to admit that it sounded pretty good to find such a thing and yet the thought terrified her too. Wouldn't she have to confront something locked deep inside her in order to get to the release part? And what if that thing didn't want to be unlocked?

Sipping sweet tea on a sunny bench beside her friend, it was fairly easy to ignore the horrors of her nightmares and just hope and pray that they wouldn't return.

Abi's sister, Ellen Fraser, was having a nightmare too – or rather a bad day. But, then again, she couldn't remember the last time she'd had a good one. She stood at the bottom of the stairs and tried not to look at the filthy skirting board or the peeling wallpaper. There wasn't time to worry about such things on a school morning.

'Girls – come on! I don't want to be late!'

Honestly, she was sick of raising her voice and heaven only knew her daughters must be tired of it too. But the morning had been full of woes from Rosie spilling her breakfast to Pugly tripping her up which had caused her to bang her elbow on the corner of a kitchen unit. She rubbed her elbow now as she yelled up the stairs.

'I won't tell you again!' She grimaced at the empty threat. What exactly would she do if they didn't appear after she'd said that? *Not* take them to school? It was a very silly thing to say and yet, up and down the country, parents were threatening their children with *I won't tell you agains*.

Of course, Douglas wasn't around to help when she needed him. He never was. He left in the blessed peace of the hours before the rest of them got up, leaving just enough crumbs and unwashed dishes to let her know he'd been there.

'Finally!' Ellen said as her two girls thundered down the stairs and pulled their shoes on by the door. 'Rosie – straighten your uniform.'

Rosie tugged at the skirt. 'It's too big.'

'No it isn't.'

'It is, Mum! It keeps slipping down.'

'Then do your belt up tighter.'

'I don't like belts.'

'Well, you won't have to wear it when you grow bigger.'

'I'm never going to grow bigger. I'm going to always stay small.'

'Don't be perverse,' Ellen said.

'I really think she is,' Bethanne chimed in as they all headed out to the car. 'She's a titch!'

'Am not!'

'Yes you are!'

'Well, you're lanky!' Rosie said and giggled. She'd just learned the word and couldn't get enough of it. 'Lanky, lanky, *lanky!*'

'Shut up!' Bethanne retorted.

'Girls, please! I'm getting a headache.'

The three of them got into the car.

'You're *always* getting a headache!' Rosie said.

Ellen glanced behind her, but chose to ignore her younger daughter's comment. 'Do your seat belts up.'

'We have, Mum,' Bethanne told her.

Ellen started the car. She really was getting a headache. She could feel it pushing and pulsating behind her left eye. Maybe she could slip back into bed when she got home and catch up on the sleep she'd missed out on the night before. She'd have to walk Pugly first, mind, then put a load of washing on. The kitchen floor needed mopping too after the breakfast spill and heaven only knew what else that had been thrown or dropped onto it since she'd last done it.

Of course, the traffic was against her like everything else that morning. Thinking quickly, Ellen took a road that would mean a longer journey but slightly fewer cars and she couldn't help smiling as she pulled up outside Bethanne's school. It was hard to believe that Bethanne was at secondary school, but she was twelve now and a very mature twelve at that. All her teachers said so and Ellen had to agree that Bethanne had been born mature. If Ellen was one to believe in old souls, then that's what Bethanne was, for she behaved as if she'd completed a few lifetimes already.

'You've got chess club after school tonight, haven't you?' Ellen asked, looking at her daughter in the rear-view mirror.

Bethanne nodded from the back seat, but didn't say anything.

'She's not going,' Rosie said.

Ellen frowned. 'What?'

'She doesn't go.'

Ellen turned around and saw Bethanne elbow her little sister in the ribs.

'Don't do that, Bethanne! And what does she mean?'

'Nothing,' Bethanne replied, looking out of the window. 'She's a tell-tale, that's all.'

Ellen frowned. 'You *are* going to chess club, aren't you?' She paused, waiting for her daughter to reply. 'Bethanne – look at me when I'm talking to you.'

Bethanne's wide-eyed glance told Ellen all she needed to

know. She might be capable of hiding information from her mother, but she would never be able to tell her a direct lie.

'I don't like chess,' she said simply. 'So I've not been going.'

'But you've been in school?'

Bethanne gave a little shrug that was all awkwardness.

'What are you doing with yourself if you're not in chess club?'

She answered in a very small voice. 'I go to the library.'

'The school library? It's still open then?'

'No. The public library.'

Ellen gasped. 'You *leave* the school premises?'

She nodded.

'Bethanne!'

'It's safe, Mum. There are lots of people around.'

'That's not the point. I thought you were at school. What if I'd needed to contact you? What if nobody could find you?'

'I wasn't far away and I went back in time for you to pick me up.'

'That's not the point.' Ellen sighed in frustration. 'What are you doing there anyway?'

'Just reading. The librarian keeps books aside for me.'

'What sort of books?'

'*Boring* books!' Rosie said with a giggle.

'Bethanne? What sort of books?' Ellen asked again.

Bethanne hesitated. 'Art.'

'You mean picture books?'

'Well, they've got pictures in them, but they're about the artists.'

'So, not only are you missing chess club, but you're wasting your time reading about artists?'

'I'm not wasting my time. They're interesting to me, and

Miss Hughes shares all her favourites too because she loves art as well.'

'Oh, does she now? Well, I can see that I'm going to have strong words with this Miss Hughes.'

'Oh, Mum! Please don't!'

'You're a child and she should know you shouldn't be there on your own.'

'But I'm not on my own! There are lots of people there.'

'Yes, but you shouldn't be one of them, should you?' Ellen could feel her blood pressure rising. It was so hard to get through to her daughter sometimes and the older she got, the more wilful she became.

'I hate chess,' Bethanne suddenly blurted. 'I never wanted to go in the first place. It was *your* idea!'

'Pardon?'

'I *hate* it! It's dull and I don't see the point of it.' Bethanne unclipped her seat belt and reached for the car door. 'I'm going to be late, Mum.'

'This conversation is not over, young lady!' Ellen called after her as she got out of the car and walked away.

'Is she in trouble, Mummy?' Rosie asked, taking a little bit too much pleasure in her sister's predicament.

'She most certainly is. And you will be too if you're late for school.'

After having stern words with Bethanne after school, Ellen told both girls to go their rooms.

'That's not fair!' Rosie complained. 'I didn't do anything!'

'Get upstairs now, Rosie!' Ellen said, wagging a warning finger at her. A moment later, she listened to the angry thumps of her daughters' footsteps and found herself alone in the kitchen with Pugly. She sat down on one of the kitchen chairs and noticed that there was something strange in Pugly's basket. Something that looked suspiciously like a crisp packet. An empty crisp packet.

'Oh, Pugly!' she said, but it was useless to reprimand him. The deed was done.

She got up, pulled the crisp packet out from under Pugly as well as a chewed-up ruler one of the girls had obviously left lying around. Honestly, they should know by now that Pugly was a thief and a chewer. She put both in the bin, grimacing at the smell that emanated from it before pulling the liner out and taking it into the front yard. Nobody else would do it, would they?

When she came back in, she washed her hands and then got to work preparing dinner for the girls. Just once, wouldn't it be wonderful if somebody prepared dinner for her, she thought, as she scrubbed the organic celery she'd pushed the boat out buying. She'd recently read an article about the dirty dozen foods one should really try to buy organic if possible because of the risk of pesticides, and celery was one of them. Perhaps she should try growing some. If she ever got a moment to herself to tackle the garden. Heaven only knew that the house, the girls and the dog took every ounce of energy she had.

Douglas came home as she was preparing the salad.

'Sneaked away early,' he said, kissing her cheek. 'God, you look exhausted!'

'Thanks a lot!'

He rested his hands on her shoulders. 'Shall we get takeaway? Save you cooking?'

'God, Douglas! Are you kidding? Getting the girls hooked on that rubbish! And think of the cost.'

'I am – to your happiness. You're obviously shattered.'

'Well, I am, but that doesn't mean I'm going to compromise on the health of our daughters, does it?'

'No, of course not. What can I do to help then?'

'You could lay the table.'

Douglas got to work and Ellen took the opportunity to tell him about her day and the fight she'd had with Bethanne.

'Don't you think you're overreacting?' Douglas said. 'I don't think you can come to any harm in a public library and it sounds like this librarian has taken Bethanne under her wing.'

'I knew you wouldn't understand, Douglas. You never do!'

'Okay, then tell me what it is I don't understand.'

Ellen hunted for the words to describe what she was feeling, but drew a blank. Instead, she flapped her hands in the air at him.

That evening, after dinner, she rang Abi, hoping for some words of comfort from her sister at least.

'You can't fight it – art is obviously her passion,' Abi said.

'I should've known you'd side with her,' Ellen said, disappointed not to have at least one person backing her up.

'I'm not siding – I'm just pointing out what's in front of you.' She heard Abi sighing. 'Ellen – remember how much you loved netball at school? Any chance you'd get, you were out on the court, weren't you? Well, just imagine if you'd been told you couldn't do that and that you should – I don't know – join the woodwork club or something.'

'You're being ridiculous!'

'But just imagine how you'd have felt to be dragged away from the thing you loved most and told to do something you weren't interested in. Imagine what a huge waste of time that would feel because you'd know it was never going to lead anywhere or become a passion. And that's what I'm saying, I guess – you can't force a passion on someone because that comes from within them.'

Ellen pinched the bridge of her nose. She was hearing Abi, but she couldn't help but feel that nobody was listening to *her*.

'I've got to go,' Ellen said at last. 'My head's thumping. I need to take something.' She hung up.

Douglas had put the girls to bed and she went in and kissed them both good night. Bethanne rolled over, turning her back to her and Ellen could feel the waves of resentment rising from her.

Standing at the bathroom sink a few minutes later, gazing at her reflection, she noted how odd everything seemed to feel. It was as if the colour had drained out of life and she felt like she was spiralling deeper and deeper into herself to a place where nobody could reach her. Sometimes, life seemed muted and yet too loud at the same time and she had the urge to run away – to find a little corner somewhere and just close her eyes against it all.

That night, she lay awake for hours after Douglas had fallen asleep and, staring up at the bedroom ceiling, she felt the hollow ache of loneliness. Even though her house was filled with people who loved her and whom she loved, she still felt isolated. Nobody was helping her, were they? Perhaps because she'd always been perceived as strong. She didn't need help. Well, that's what people thought.

For one crazy moment, she thought about waking Douglas up and telling him her fears, but she didn't. She couldn't. She knew how hard he worked and how much he needed his sleep. Instead, she continued staring at the ceiling, hoping sleep might claim her for at least a few hours before the alarm clock sounded and the day would begin all over again.

CHAPTER THREE

Edward was aware of a vague sort of rumbling noise, but he was on a conference call and so put it to the back of his mind. However, when the call finished and he got up to make himself a cup of tea, he could still hear it. It wasn't quite rumbling, he decided as the kettle boiled. It was more of a thumping. And there weren't any builders in anymore, which meant only one thing. It was the base of a stereo. He sighed and then sipped his tea. He had two choices. He could knock on Samantha's door and have words with her – again, or he could go out.

He walked towards his French doors, which he'd kept shut all morning for fear of being distracted when he was working, and glanced out at the fine spring weather. It wasn't the sort of day to be indoors anyway, he thought as he finished his tea. The sky was the colour of forget-me-nots. But then again, he really needed to sort this business with Samantha.

With that in mind, he left his flat before he could talk himself out of it, and marched across the hallway with determined strides and knocked on the door a moment later.

When she answered, Edward smiled politely.

'Do you fancy a swim?' he asked.

Abi laughed. 'Now?'

He smiled. 'Why not?'

She smiled right back at him. 'Why not indeed?'

'I'll see you out the front in ten minutes, okay?'

'Okay!'

He returned to his flat and got changed into his trunks and a lighter pair of trousers. It was much too nice a day to face the reality of frustrating tenants, he told himself. Besides, he hadn't spent any quality time with Abi in a long while, despite promising himself that he would. Ever since the accident she was involved in with his numbskulled brother, he'd told himself he'd make the most of time – only he hadn't. Seeing Abi in hospital that day and knowing how much worse things could have turned out had shaken him to his core. Life was so very fragile and fleeting and you really had to grab every opportunity that came your way and not waste a single minute. If there was something you wanted to do, you should do it; if there was something you needed to say, you should say it. Only he hadn't. He hadn't told Abi how he felt about her. Whenever he'd tried to summon up the courage, the words just died in his mouth. The truth was, as soon as Abi was out of danger and able to take care of herself again, life had gone back to the way it was before.

He cursed himself as he thought about it. Why was it so hard for him to just tell her he wanted to be more than friends? Over the long months since the accident, his feelings hadn't changed. If anything, they'd grown and he'd spent many a sleepless night wondering what he should do about it.

His good friend Stephen had run out of patience with him.

'Just bloody tell her!' he'd yelled at him the last time

Edward had confessed his feelings and his inability to move forward with them.

But people like Stephen found that sort of thing easy. They were natural communicators and Edward – well, Edward wasn't.

Of course, he and Abi were still friends, and a good friendship was not to be taken lightly, he knew that, but he couldn't help yearning for something more.

Leaving his apartment, he walked out of the hall. Abi was standing by his car, gazing up at the downs, the warm May breeze blowing her long fair hair back from her face. She was sporting freckles already, he'd noticed, adoring the way they crowded around her nose and cheeks. He took a moment to look at her as she stood there.

Abi. Abigail. She had come into his life so unexpectedly, brought to him through her love of the house they both now called home. How funny life was. He had cursed her in the auction room that day, making him bid more and more for Winfield Hall. Then he'd cursed the endless repairs that the builders had uncovered once he'd purchased it, and then he'd despaired at being made redundant. And yet all those things had meant that Abi had found her way here and was now standing before him.

She turned towards him. 'There you are!'

'Ready?' he asked.

'If it's horribly cold, I'll never forgive you.'

'Yes you will – once you acclimatise and get that buzz.'

'You're probably right.'

They got into the car together, Abi dropping her swimming bag in the footwell.

'Were you working when I called?' he asked as they drove off.

'Yes. Well, kind of. I was messing about with colour. I'm not sure you can really call it work.'

'You're an artist – I think messing about with colour absolutely constitutes work.'

'How about you?'

'I'd just come off a very long and dull conference call and decided I needed a break.'

'Sounds like you've earned it.'

'I needed to get out anyway. Before I stormed over to Samantha's.'

'Oh, dear! What's happened now?'

'Loud music, I'm afraid. Didn't you hear it from yours?' he asked.

'Mercifully not although I can hear the thump of the bass when I'm in the garden sometimes.'

'God, I'm sorry, Abi.'

'It's okay. It's not all the time.'

'Have there been any more complaints from Tim?'

'I've not seen him to be honest. I think he's got his head down working on his novel.'

'I'm going to have to have a word with her again and I'm dreading it.'

'Oh, poor Edward,' she said, and he caught her gaze briefly as he stopped at a junction, her face full of sympathy.

'Maybe we shouldn't have let any of the apartments. Maybe we should have kept Winfield all to ourselves.'

'You can't mean that!' Abi said, sounding genuinely horrified. 'We'd never have met Harry and Aura and then they wouldn't have got together!'

'No, you're right.'

'Samantha just needs to be reminded of the ground rules, that's all.'

'Yes.'

'I'm sure she's a perfectly reasonable person. After all, she impressed you when you first met, didn't she?'

'She was absolutely charming, yes,' he said, pulling out of the junction.

'And no alarm bells went off, did they?'

'None at all.'

'Then don't worry. It'll work out.'

He smiled. 'You're always so optimistic, Abi.'

'Am I?'

'Yes, it's one of the things I love about you,' he said, and then he swallowed hard. Had he really just said that? He glanced at her again and saw her bright, wide smile.

He cleared his throat and turned his attention towards the road, feeling the heat of embarrassment flooding his face. It was a good job he was about to take a cold dip in the sea.

'How's your sister?' he asked, keen to change the subject.

'Oh, you know – stressed, tense, full of the woes of life.'

'I'm sorry.'

'Don't be. It's her default setting. Although...' Abi paused.

'What?'

'I don't know. I feel that there's something more going on recently. She's behaving differently.'

'How?'

'Well, I rang her this morning to check in on her. She'd told me something about my niece Bethanne the other day and I probably wasn't as supportive as she wanted me to be. You see, I have a habit of defending Bethanne as a fellow artist and Ellen doesn't always like that.'

'Oh, dear! That must be awkward for you.'

'It really is,' Abi confessed, 'because I want to be there for both of them and that usually means I end up offending

Ellen.' She sighed heavily. 'When I spoke to her this morning, she seemed a bit odd. Odder than normal, I mean. Like her head was somewhere else and she wasn't really listening to me.'

'I guess those girls keep her busy.'

'Of course. I know she's always worrying about them.'

'Motherhood's a big responsibility.'

'Yes.'

'Still, you must feel like a mother to them sometimes,' he said with a smile.

They'd reached the beach car park now and Edward parked, glancing at Abi as he did so. She was staring straight ahead, her face pale and suddenly very sad.

'Abi? Are you okay?' She didn't say anything. Panicking, Edward unclipped his seat belt and reached across to touch her shoulder. 'Abi?'

She shook her head. 'I'm okay.'

'No. You're not. What is it? Do you feel ill?'

'No.'

'What is it, then? Is it something I said?'

'It's nothing.'

She started to shake.

'Hey! It's okay!' he told her, rubbing her back and feeling utterly helpless. What the hell had he said? 'It's okay.'

She started breathing heavily. 'I... I...'

'Slow your breath down, Abi!' he said, worried that she was hyperventilating. Luckily she did as he told her. 'That's it,' he encouraged. 'Breathe slowly now.'

She took a few moments before her breathing returned to something approaching normal, but her face was deathly pale and she was trying to speak.

'I... I was a mother,' she whispered. 'I was going to be a

mother. But I lost the baby. I lost it!' There were tears in her eyes now. 'I wanted it so badly.'

Edward froze, unsure how to respond. What could you say to someone who'd revealed such a tragedy? Words felt somehow inadequate. But he had to say something, *do* something and tears were coursing down her cheeks now.

'I'm so sorry, Abi. I'm so sorry.' He pulled her towards her, bringing her close across the awkward space of the car, feeling her slim shoulders under his hands. She felt so fragile and vulnerable – like a little bird, he thought. A beautiful, terrified bird.

'It's okay,' he kept chanting, half aware of the passers-by in the car park and the strange feeling of other people's lives going on when there was somebody falling apart just feet away. But his focus was Abi. He couldn't bear to see her in so much pain. He wished there was something he could do, but maybe just holding her was enough. And so he did that until the shaking and the tears stopped and a calm descended.

He reached in the glove box and pulled out a pack of tissues. Abi took one and mopped her eyes and blew her nose.

'I'm sorry,' she said. 'I didn't mean to blurt all that out. I don't know what happened. My emotions seem to be so close to the surface at the moment.'

'There's no need to apologise.'

'But there is. I feel awful. I don't want to bother you with all my angst.'

'It's fine. Really. I'm glad you told me.'

She looked up at him, her blue eyes rimmed red now and he wanted to hold her again and take all the pain out of her. 'Are you?'

'Of course I am. It's good to – you know – be open.'

She blew her nose again and nodded. 'Yes.'

'Even if it hurts.'

There was a pause when Abi seemed to be considering this. 'That wasn't all,' she told him. 'I kind of had a bit of a breakdown after that. It's one of the reasons I gave my company up. Everything was suddenly too much. Work, life, my partner.'

Edward frowned. 'What happened to him?'

'I broke up with him,' she said. 'It was clear he didn't want any sort of commitment and the thought of a baby terrified him. He actually thought it was for the best when I lost it.'

Edward shook his head. He didn't know what to say. That such people existed – and that such a person had been close to Abi and treated her like that – was abhorrent.

'And then you found Winfield?' he said gently.

'Yes!' She gave a small smile. 'Winfield was my saviour although some flash businessman stole it from right under my nose.'

Edward grinned. 'Sorry about that.'

'It's okay. I'm just teasing you!'

'I hope so.'

They held each other's gaze for a moment, exchanging gentle smiles.

'Listen,' Edward said at last, 'do you want to go and get a drink or something? We don't have to swim today.'

'But we came here to swim.' Her eyes flashed with a determined light.

'Are you sure?'

'Absolutely.'

He watched in surprise as Abi got out of the car with her swimming bag and walked resolutely towards the beach, and then he quickly followed her, still shaken by the things she'd told him. He'd always seen her as such a happy person. She gave the impression that she didn't have a care in the world. He'd had no idea she was carrying such a weight of grief.

You could never tell what somebody was hiding from the world, could you? And he should know better than most because he was hiding secrets from her too.

CHAPTER FOUR

The large open-plan living room in the barn conversion was perfect for meditating in. The wide wooden floor, the large windows with their far-reaching views, the space, the ambience, it all seemed designed for someone like Aura Arden. She'd been coming here weekly since last summer when Harry's father, Leonard, had been brought home from hospital having suffered a heart attack. He was the very last person she'd thought would respond to her teachings, but he'd quickly become attached to the crystals she'd given him and had learned to use them to meditate and slow down, which pleased his wife Maria no end.

'As we close our eyes, just focus on the sense of sound. What can you hear outside this room? Are there birds in the sky?' Aura paused, giving them time to listen. 'Then bring your attention to the sounds in the room. Be aware.' She listened herself, hearing the gentle tick of a clock and the whirring of the fan Maria had switched on just before their session.

'Now, bring your attention closer. Listen to yourself – to the soft sound of your breath as it comes in and as you let it go. To the quiet but vital sound you make as you swallow. Feel it. Hear it. You are alive! You matter. Listen to yourself – to your physical being.'

She let her words hang as they took several rounds of breaths and then she led them into some gentle yoga stretches before settling down on the mats again for another round of breath work.

'And slowly blink your eyes open,' Aura said at last, her words slow, her voice calm. She opened her own eyes and smiled at the three people surrounding her on their yoga mats. Each had their own now: Harry's was sky-blue, Leonard's was a buttercup yellow and Maria's was sunset pink, while Aura's was lime green. They looked so jolly in this corner of the open-plan barn conversion, by the window with the wide view across the river valley. She liked the way that Maria had made a feature of this space with meditation in mind. There was a low wooden table against the bare brick wall. It wasn't referred to as an altar, though. Maria called it her 'Inspiration Table'. Aura smiled as she looked at it now. With its large salt lamp glowing a warm orange, its crystals and its candles, it looked suspiciously close to something Aura would create in her own home.

Maria had yet to adopt the barefoot approach to life, but she was slowly getting there. She did the yoga and meditation sessions barefoot, her nails painted a pale lilac because full-on purple was way too mystical for her conservative tastes. But Aura had noticed she was wearing sandals more – very expensive sparkly ones.

'Our home always feels so peaceful with you here,' Maria confided in her as they all stood up and stretched.

'Thank you!' Aura said graciously. 'And I feel peaceful being here.'

'Some tea, I think?' Maria suggested. 'I've picked some sage from the garden.'

Again, Aura smiled at the new Maria Freeman who would never have made her own herbal tea concoctions a few months ago, but was sowing, growing and harvesting herbs like a pro now. She was getting confident making her own blends, although Leonard had drawn the line at nettle and dandelion, declaring it tasted like ditchwater and that he'd go back to PG Tips if she didn't make something more pleasant.

Maria had also been very generous in spreading the word about Aura's gift and, as a result, she'd been much in demand, teaching weekly yoga and meditation classes in the Freeman's local village hall as well as being booked for private sessions by three of Maria's close friends.

'That was a truly relaxing experience,' Harry told Aura now, kissing her cheek before rolling up everyone's mats and stacking them neatly in the corner by Maria's Inspiration Table.

'Yes,' Leonard agreed. 'For a moment there, I thought I was about to drop off, but then I wiggled my toes to remind me to stay in the moment.'

'You and your toes!' Maria teased and then smiled at Aura. 'I've never seen so much of his feet before. They seem to be all over the place these days.'

Leonard guffawed at his wife's declaration and Aura smiled.

'Bare feet is a great thing to discover,' she told them. 'It's so freeing.'

'Of course, I did step on a slug the other day while trying to commune with nature,' Leonard confessed.

'Yes, you were definitely taking your communing too far *that* day!' Maria admonished, but she was smiling, Aura noticed.

'Are you having a cup of sage tea, Lennie?' Maria asked.

'No, thank you, dear. Actually, Aura, I want to get your

input on something in the garden. If I may steal you away from everyone for a moment?'

As soon as Leonard and Aura were out of earshot, Maria caught her son by the arm and whisked him into the kitchen.

'Mum!' Harry cried, wondering what on earth was happening. But it wasn't until they were in the safety of the kitchen that she spoke.

'So?' she said.

'What?'

She slapped him on the arm. 'How's it going?'

'Work?'

'No! Not work. Aura, silly boy! How are things with Aura?'

'Oh, good. As you can see.' He motioned towards the garden and, through the window, saw his father sitting on the grass with Aura. It was an endearing sight.

'Well, it's almost a year, isn't it?' his mother went on.

'Since what?'

'The summer solstice.'

Harry smiled at the thought that his mother should know when something like the summer solstice was approaching. 'That's right.'

'And wasn't that your big date?' she continued. 'The picnic?'

'Blimey, Mum, you've got a good memory. *Too* good!'

'Only for the important things in life.'

Harry picked up an apple from the fruit bowl, red and rosy, sniffing it in appreciation.

'A whole year,' his mother added. 'Makes you think, doesn't it?'

'Does it?' Harry bit into the apple. 'I suppose it does.'

'I mean, someone like Aura – someone with her sweetness and beauty – she's probably got dozens on men vying for her.'

'I don't think so,' Harry said.

'And how do you know? Do you attend all the classes?'

'Of course not.'

His mother gave him a look which seemed to suggest that he should be concerned.

She picked up the kettle and took it to the sink. 'All I'm saying is that someone like Aura is bound to be snapped up sooner rather than later.'

Harry swallowed hard. He loved that his mother was using phrases like 'someone like Aura' to denote a very special person. It wasn't so long ago that she'd been adamant that her son should have nothing to do with her. How she had changed her tune, he thought, and thank goodness for it because Aura was the woman he wanted to spend the rest of his life with.

He gasped as he realised that. If he truly wanted to spend the rest of his life with her then what was he waiting for? He glanced out of the window again. His father was now doing some kind of crazy yoga move and was laughing while upside down with his legs in the air as Aura's gentle hands steadied him. It was quite a sight. She was the most amazing person Harry had ever met and she'd quite literally turned the whole family upside down.

'You're right, Mum,' he said. 'I should... well, I just should, shouldn't I?'

She put the kettle down and walked towards him. 'Yes,' she told him, kissing his cheek. 'I really think you should.'

～

It was the half term before the summer holidays and Abigail was in auntie mode, with Bethanne and Rosie staying for a sleepover. But not just any sleepover. The weather was going to be warm and dry and she'd promised the girls a night in the walled garden. Ellen always found half term to be a frazzling time and Abi was more than happy to take some of the pressure off her. The girls, too, seemed to benefit from some time away from home and it would give Ellen a chance to tackle the house properly, decorating the landing and the main bedroom.

'Because it's quite clear nobody else is going to do it!' Ellen had sighed down the phone.

Like Ellen, Abi was also planning to paint, but she had a feeling that hers would be a slightly more joyous experience and, watching her two nieces sitting at her large wide table now, the French doors open into the garden and a mass of colour on each of their pieces of paper, she realised just how much she loved teaching. Not that she was doing anything so formal as organising a full lesson. That would be ghastly. But she loved communicating her passion to the girls, encouraging them, showing them how to use the tools of the trade and advising them if they asked for help.

As she was musing on all this, she noticed that Bethanne had a puzzled look on her face and was staring out into the garden.

'What is it, Bethy?' she asked.

'Why do some painters paint the same pictures over and over again?'

'Who were you thinking of?'

'Monet. Do you know him?'

'Well, not personally. He died some time ago.'

'I know that!' Bethanne said with a smile.

'But I know of some of his work. It's glorious, isn't it? Do you like it?'

'I've been looking at it a lot and I really love it.'

'So, why do *you* think he paints the same subjects again and again?'

Bethanne looked very serious for a moment. 'I don't know.'

'Well, I think there are a number of different reasons,' Abi began. 'For a start, the light changes all the time. Have you noticed that? If you stand in one place and gaze out into a field or a wood, the light will slowly change. Maybe the weather will change too. Clouds might build up. It might rain and then the sun might come out and there'll be a rainbow. Or maybe it's windy and the grass and leaves are blowing. Or maybe you move your easel just to the left or just to the right a little and, suddenly, everything's slightly different and you need to capture that.'

'But wouldn't it get boring?'

'I don't think so. Are you ever bored when you paint?'

Bethanne shook her head. 'No. Not yet anyway.'

'And if you have a scene, a view, or a subject that fascinates you – like Monet's haystacks or his pond at Giverny – it could never bore you. Because, don't forget, that an artist is exploring themselves just as much as their subject. Each time they start a new painting, they've evolved slightly, haven't they? They're growing and learning all the time.'

Bethanne listened, wide-eyed, as Abi told her about some of her favourite artists and how they painted their favourite things over and over again.

'Do you think I'll have a favourite subject?' Bethanne asked at last.

'Maybe.'

'My favourite subject is pink,' Rosie declared, obviously paying attention to their conversation.

'Pink isn't a subject,' Bethanne declared.

'It is, isn't it, Aunt Abi?'

'Colour can actually be a subject, yes.'

Rosie stuck her tongue out at her sister, thrilled to be right.

'Picasso was fascinated by blue for a number of years. And the French artist Yves Klein was obsessed by it too. There's even a blue paint colour named after him that's still used to this day.'

'Really?' Bethanne asked. Abi nodded.

'Will they name a pink paint after me?' Rosie asked earnestly.

Abi smiled. 'Well, Rosie Pink definitely has a nice ring to it, doesn't it?'

'Everyone will want it!' Rosie said. 'Everything will be painted pink – buses, schools, dentist's waiting rooms – everything!'

'That sounds heavenly!' Abi agreed.

Later, once they'd cleared their paints away after a morning of creativity, they made a loose sort of lunch from early garden salad served with a fresh baguette and sweetcorn fritters. Abi had made a trifle and, in an attempt not to feel guilty about it, they all took a long walk up on the downs afterwards.

The real fun began once the sun had set. Abi had been longing to spend a night under the stars. Aura had sometimes slept in the walled garden and Abi envied the ease her tenant obviously felt in nature. Perhaps Abi would feel less odd about it with her nieces as companions. They were certainly as excited as she was about the upcoming adventure and insisted on packing their overnight bags even though they were only crossing the lawn.

Abi had borrowed yoga mats from Aura in lieu of camping

mats, but had plenty of bed linen for padding and warmth, and pillows for comfort. Three fine beds were soon made on the near the round border Abi had planted with white roses, and the scent from the flowers at dusk was intoxicating, their pale blooms floating in the air like little ghosts. She'd checked the weather report and it promised to be a clear and balmy night.

How wonderful it was to snuggle up to her nieces in the comfort of the walled garden. It was sheltered enough to feel safe and yet open to the elements to give that feeling of adventure. Abi positioned herself between Bethanne and Rosie and, for the first few minutes, the three of them stared up at the star-packed sky as the evening darkened from indigo to black. The only light came from the back of the hall where Samantha's flat was, but it didn't bother them.

'I feel like I'm falling into the sky,' Bethanne said as they all continued to watch the heavens.

'I think I have fallen,' Rosie said.

Abi laughed and tickled Rosie, making her giggle. 'No! You're still here on Earth!'

'How far away are they?' Bethanne asked.

'The stars? I don't know,' Abi said honestly.

'I can touch this one,' Rosie said, stretching her right hand above her head. 'It's ticklish like me – look! It's twinkling!'

'I didn't know you twinkled when you're tickled,' Abi said and Rosie giggled again. Abi loved the sound. Rosie must get her giggles from Douglas, she thought, because she'd never heard Ellen giggle like that.

'I think we should probably try and sleep, don't you?' Abi suggested at last, hearing a yawn from Bethanne.

'Good night, Aunt Abi,' Bethanne said.

'Nighty night,' Rosie said.

'Night, girls.'

For a little while, Abi continued to stare up at the stars, so clear and bright and perfect and then her eyes slowly closed. The scent of the roses swirled around her and the gentle breathing of the girls lulled her like the ocean until she drifted off.

Abi wasn't sure if the noise that woke her was laughter or shouting, but it was loud and very sudden and, when she opened her eyes, she realised it was still dark. She sat up, looking around the walled garden and then she heard it – the thump, thump, thump of music.

'Oh, no!' she whispered, seeing that Samantha's light was still on and hearing voices from her apartment. She was obviously having some kind of party.

'What's that noise?' Bethanne asked, her voice drowsy.

'It's so loud!' Rosie added from somewhere under her bedding.

'It's just a bit of music, sweethearts. Go back to sleep now.'

Abi snuggled back down under her duvet, but the music seemed to fill the whole of the walled garden. She took a few deep breaths. It wouldn't last forever surely. It was late. Samantha would realise that any minute now.

'I can't sleep, Aunt Abi! It's too noisy,' Rosie whined after a few minutes.

'I know it is, darling. Shall we go back inside?'

'But we won't be under the stars then,' Bethanne said.

Abi sighed, frustrated that their special night had been disturbed.

'Listen, I'll go and see if I can get them to turn the music down, okay?'

Abi got up from her bed on the grass and walked across the lawn back to her apartment where she pulled on a jumper and ran her hands through her hair. She glanced at the clock in the living room. It was just after midnight. She felt awkward and self-conscious about approaching Samantha's so late at night, but she couldn't let the noise continue anymore. Who on earth started a party after midnight? Surely Samantha must know that it wouldn't go down well with the other residents. Tim would no doubt be wide awake in his apartment and Edward would probably be able to hear the noise too.

Taking a deep breath, she went out her front door and crossed the hallway, knocking on Samantha's door a moment later. She could hear the thud of music and the sound of chatter and laughter through the door and it took another round of knocks before somebody opened it. It wasn't Samantha.

'Hi,' Abi said.

'You here for the party, love?' the man said.

'No, I'm here *because* of the party,' Abi said, trying to hold her annoyance in check.

The man frowned at her. 'I'll get Sam.'

'Please do.'

Abi waited a moment at the open door, peering in to see at least half a dozen people milling about with glasses in their hands. This was not the vision of Winfield she or Edward had had when they'd agreed to let rooms out, she couldn't help thinking.

Finally Samantha appeared at the door. She was wearing a light summer dress, low cut with a gold belt tied around it, and she was holding a very large glass of red wine.

'Abigail? Are you joining us?' Samantha cast her eyes over Abi's attire as if assessing her party animal credentials.

'No. I was actually asleep.'

'Really?'

'It's after midnight.'

'Is it?'

'Yes, and I have my young nieces staying and they can't sleep because of the noise.'

'Oh!' Samantha said as if the lateness of the hour came as a complete surprise to her. 'We're finishing up in a minute, you know?'

'You are? I thought you must be as it is very late,' Abi stressed again.

Samantha nodded, seeming to understand and then she closed the door in Abi's face. Abi blinked in surprise and then heard a peel of laugher from the other side of the door. She winced, feeling like the unpopular girl at school whom the others were making fun of. Still, she'd got what she'd wanted, hadn't she? A promise that the noise would stop.

Only it didn't. Not for a good half hour at least. Luckily, Rosie had managed to fall asleep, but Bethanne was still wide awake, gazing up into the heavens.

'Why are some people so noisy and others so quiet?' she asked Abi when it was finally peaceful again.

'Because it makes life interesting,' Abi said.

'Do you think so?'

'Well, not at this moment in time. I'd rather everyone was nice and quiet like us. But imagine if we were all the same. If everybody was nice and quiet, I think things might get boring pretty quickly.'

'I don't think they would. I'd like it.'

Abi smiled into the night. 'Yes, I probably wouldn't mind either,' she confessed, thinking of how she'd lost herself for a little while when dating Oscar. They said opposites attracted, but they also self-destructed.

'I think the trick is to find your own group of people – those you really connect with,' Abi told her niece.

'Like you and Edward?' Bethanne said.

'What do you know about that?'

'Just what Mum's said.'

'And what's she said?'

'That you're really good friends and that you do fun things like swimming together.'

'Yes,' Abi said.

'And that she'd like to see you happy with someone like him one day.'

'Your mum said that?'

'I think she did,' Bethanne said. 'Or maybe it was me thinking it.'

Abi snuggled up closer to Bethanne and kissed her on the cheek.

'Do you like him?' Bethanne asked with a yawn.

'Edward? Yes. Well, he's hard not to like, isn't he? I mean, he's kind and sweet and generous. And I love how much he adores Winfield,' Abi said. 'He's a special person, don't you think?' Abi waited a moment for an answer, but quickly realised that Bethanne had fallen asleep. 'Good night, sweetheart,' she whispered and then she gazed up at the stars again but, instead of counting them, she found herself counting all the different ways that she liked Edward.

It was sad to be packing the girls' things away. Abi was always amazed at how quickly she got used to their bits and bobs scattered around her home, loving seeing their colourful toothbrushes, their little clothes and their dinky pink suitcases.

She wondered if she could keep them for an extra day, but Bethanne quickly reminded her that there was some kind of community party that Ellen was helping to organise and they were expected to take part in that.

So Abi dutifully returned her nieces home to their mother, telling Ellen about the starry night in the walled garden and the party that had woken them up.

'It all sounds rather dramatic for Winfield!' Ellen said. 'You should just evict her and be done with it.'

'I'm not sure it's that easy.'

'Why not?'

'Well, she's signed for six months.'

'But she's clearly flouting her agreement, isn't she?'

'I don't think Edward likes confrontation. I think he'd rather see the contract expire.'

Ellen, who was examining her nails, didn't seem to be listening anymore.

'You look tired,' Abi told her.

Ellen looked up, frowning. 'Why does everyone think they need to keep pointing that out to me?'

'Listen, let me put the kettle on, okay?'

'I really haven't got time to stop.'

'Yes you have,' Abi insisted. 'I'll make the tea and we can sit out in the garden and talk properly.'

She heard her sister groan, but she didn't protest further.

A few minutes later they were both sitting outside on plastic chairs, the girls playing with Pugly in the far corner. It felt strange sitting out in Ellen's garden. Abi had never done that before. Ellen really seemed at odds outdoors – uncomfortable, awkward. She really was an indoors sort of a person.

'You should come hill walking with me sometime,' Abi suddenly said before taking a sip of her tea.

'Walking – me!'

'Yes. It would do you good to get out and exercise more. Get some oxygen into your blood.'

Ellen winced. 'Sounds horribly clinical.'

'You look pale.'

'Well, you look freckly.'

Abi laughed. 'Yes, they've come out early because I've been walking and cycling a lot.'

'I do my best not to court freckles these days.'

'But you should get out more, Ellen.'

'I really haven't the time to go running off into the hills like you.'

Abi felt the barb, but chose to ignore it, as usual. But she wasn't going to ignore the thing that had been playing on her mind so she took a deep breath, knowing that she was risking her sister's anger by even mentioning it.

'I've been having these dreams,' she said without preamble.

'Dreams?'

'Well, nightmares actually.'

'What sort of nightmares?'

'About when we were children,' Abi said and, when Ellen didn't reply, she took it as her cue to continue. 'I'm on the stairs and you're in the hallway. There are blue lights flashing.'

'Stop.'

'And people in the house I don't know.'

'Stop it!'

'And something's happening in the living room, but you're shouting at me not to go in.'

'I said, *Stop it*, Abi!' Ellen cried, standing up so fast from her chair that it fell over behind her. The girls looked up from where they were playing, anxious expressions on their faces.

'Is it just a nightmare, Ellen?' Abi continued. 'Or is it a

memory?' Ellen was on the move now, walking towards the back door. Abi followed her. 'Ellen – please – I need to know.'

'I don't want to talk about this, Abi. ' Ellen stopped by the back door, turning round to face her. She looked pale – paler than normal – and Abi wanted to reach out and hug her, but didn't feel she could because there was such a wall of resistance around Ellen in that moment.

'It isn't fair, Ellen. We never talk. Not properly.'

Ellen gave her hair a flick as if dismissing Abi's notion. 'I'm very tired, Abi. I think it best if you go.'

'What's the matter, Mummy?' Rosie asked, propelling herself into her mother's arms while looking at both her and Abi in turn.

'Nothing's the matter. Aunt Abi was just leaving.'

Bethanne joined them, Pugly snuggled in her embrace. 'Is everything okay?' Bethanne asked, the question aimed at Abi.

'Yes, of course, sweetheart,' Abi said, bending to kiss her cheek and give Pugly a tickle. She then kissed Rosie and attempted to give her sister a hug, but Ellen pulled away, disappearing into the kitchen where she stood, resolutely, with her back to Abi. Abi's opened her mouth to say something, but she was at a loss as to what to say, and so she did what Ellen had asked and left.

CHAPTER FIVE

Harry was tired, but it wasn't the tired that he'd felt from his old job in advertising. This was a new kind of tired. Happy tired. Satisfied tired. Relieved that you were adding something valuable to society tired. He smiled at the thought of that. His old job had suited him for a number of years. He'd been young, ambitious and hungry to climb the corporate ladder, but he hadn't taken a good look around him, nor had he asked the sort of questions he should have been asking. Like what were the products he was helping to advertise? Did they add anything to the world? Or did they strip it, confuse it and add to the unstoppable beast that was consumerism?

Leaving his shoes by the front door, he sank into the chair that looked out over the downs, he sighed in relief at being home, and thanked Aura for the peace of mind and the stillness in his heart which he felt from his new job. Ever since he'd met her, he'd begun to see the world through new eyes. Not only had he learned how to question things and feel the benefit of being barefooted in a shoe-obsessed world, but he'd learned how to breathe again – to take time out, switch off and enjoy the world around him even if that just meant sitting in the garden with a cup of tea.

Now, Harry couldn't imagine his life without Aura in it and he'd been thinking of their future a lot lately. The summer solstice was fast approaching and his mother had planted an idea in his mind that he couldn't shake. Reaching into his jacket pocket now, he took out the little jeweller's box and opened it. There, on the deep blue velvet, sat a diamond ring. Harry smiled as it winked up at him. It was a vintage piece, from the nineteen-thirties with a central solitaire diamond framed by five smaller stones, all set in eighteen-carat white gold to look like a star. He'd looked at dozens of rings over the last few days, spending his lunch times going from jeweller to jeweller, but he'd known the minute he'd seen this one. Silvery and celestial, it had whispered Aura's name with its quiet, understated beauty and its simple magic. He hoped she'd love it. Well, he hoped she loved *him*! But what if she said no? What if he was taking her 'yes' for granted?

Suddenly Harry felt weak with nerves. What if, when he asked Aura to spend the rest of her life with him, she laughed? No, she wasn't the sort to do that. What if she froze and panicked? What if marriage was the very last thing she wanted? She was a modern woman, carving out a wonderful future for herself, wasn't she? And what if she didn't see marriage being a part of that? What if marriage was a horribly outdated thing in her mind?

Harry got up from the chair and opened the French doors into the walled garden, feeling the fresh air on his skin and remembering Aura's instructions to just breathe in times of stress. She wouldn't want him feeling like this, he thought. He looked down at the ring again and then closed the box, placing it safely in his jacket pocket. He was envisaging scenarios that might never happen, which was ridiculous. Even if Aura didn't want to get married, Harry felt sure of her love for him. So the ring would be a gift – a sign of his love for her, his commitment, and their joy at having found one another. Yes, he thought, feeling better now. No pressure – just love.

He looked down at his feet, realising he'd stepped outside still wearing his socks. Bending, he took them off and threw them back indoors. Ah, that was better. Bare feet. Who knew that life could improve so quickly and so simply by removing your shoes and socks and walking around barefoot for a few blissful moments? Harry had even introduced it to his new workplace. His colleagues had laughed themselves silly when he'd first suggested it, calling him an old hippie, but they'd realised he was in earnest and had stopped laughing as soon as they'd experienced the joy for themselves. Harry was quite evangelical about it now and was happy to spread the word about the benefits of bare feet. Perhaps he should go on some kind of crusade, downing tools and spreading the word on foot – barefoot, crossing the South Downs, venturing into the next county, ridding people of their prejudices and encouraging them to free their feet.

He smiled at the idea, knowing that such crazy thoughts wouldn't have dared enter his mind before he'd met Aura. Now, he felt no embarrassment at all in sitting on the grass with his eyes closed, taking deep lungfuls of downland air or rolling out a yoga mat for some life-enhancing stretches. It was all good.

Sitting on the grass now, he saw Edward walk out of the apartment next door.

'Hi there!' Harry called. Edward waved and came over. 'Take a seat!'

Edward smiled, looking slightly awkward as he bent to sit on the grass.

'How's the job going?' Edward asked a moment later.

'Good,' Harry said.

'Remind me – it's one of these new eco-friendly businesses, isn't it?'

'Yes. It's a B corporation. Eco party planning. We plan events for companies or individuals, linking them with venues and materials and accommodation that's all eco-friendly.'

'Sounds fascinating.'

'It is. I love it. It's a small company at the moment – there's just three of us in the office – but we're hoping to grow.'

'Well, you look pretty happy these days,' Edward told him.

'I feel happy,' Harry confessed, smiling broadly. 'Actually, it's not just the job that's making me happy.'

'Oh?'

Harry paused for a moment, his hand delving into his pocket. 'Oh, rats! I have to tell someone.'

'What is it?'

Harry brought the box out into the sunlight and opened it. 'I bought this today.' He showed the ring to Edward.

'It's beautiful.'

'Thanks. I was thrilled to find it, I have to say.'

'For Aura?'

'Well, I don't buy pieces like this for my mother, put it that way!'

Edward laughed. 'Aura will love it.'

'You think so?'

'Don't you?' Edward sounded surprised by Harry's doubt.

'I hope she does.' He closed the box, returning the ring to his pocket. 'But I'm a bag of nerves. I don't think I've ever loved anyone as much as I love Aura and I want to do the right thing.'

Edward nodded. 'So you're going to propose?'

'On the summer solstice. It's kind of a special time for Aura.

She loves celebrating the longest day of the year and it marks one year since...' he paused.

'Since what?'

Harry could feel himself blushing. He hadn't meant to open up like this, but found a kind of release in talking to Edward about his feelings for Aura. So he took a deep breath and continued.

'It's a year since I kissed her for the first time.'

'Wow!' Edward gave a long, low whistle.

'Yeah. A whole year. And now I can't imagine a single day without seeing her. Does that sound weird?'

'No. It doesn't.'

Harry smiled. 'I often wonder who I was before I met her. I mean, I thought I was happy then. Thought I had life sussed. I'd made the move from London and found this place – thank god! And I'd got my job in Brighton. I knew I was tired. I knew something wasn't quite working, you know? But I had no idea that what was missing was so fundamental.' He shrugged. 'But it was.'

'And now you've found it?'

'Yes. I think I have.'

'Well, I'm really happy for you, Harry.'

'Thanks.'

'Have you thought about what you're going to say to her? I mean, if you don't mind me asking.'

'No, I don't mind you asking. And, yes, I've given it a little thought. I should give it some more, really, but Aura's taught me that it's important to live in the moment and I think that's pretty good advice. And I want to keep things fresh. I don't want to sound over-rehearsed. I want to read the moment too. I'm taking her for a picnic – like last year. But if the moment's not right – if a big group of hikers is sitting in the next field, or it's blowing a

gale or if something's happened in our day to kill the mood –
well… it's got to feel right.'

Edward nodded.

'Here's what I think. We make our own rules and while
marriage might suit some, it might terrify others, and terrifying
Aura is something that's not very high on my agenda.' Harry
gave a laugh. 'So, if I go down on one knee or whatever it is I'm
going to do, and I can see she's about to freak out, we'll make it
work another way.'

'That sounds good.'

'I think so. I mean, we're really happy as we are. I have to
keep remembering that. But there's always room for
improvement, isn't there?'

Edward nodded.

Harry wiggled his toes in front of him, closing his eyes
against the sun. 'Anyone special in your life?' he casually asked.

'No,' Edward said quickly. 'I mean… well…'

Harry opened his eyes and glanced at Edward. His face was
set in a deep frown.

'If there is,' Harry began, 'if there might be, make sure you
let them know because, well, life's short, isn't it? The days pass,
the years roll into one another and things get left unsaid and
undone, and then it's all over.'

Edward turned to face him.

'Sorry!' Harry said with a self-admonishing shake of his
head. 'I'm not sure where that came from. Maybe it's having
this ring in my pocket.'

'It's okay.'

Harry was the first to look away, but he was aware that
Edward was still looking at him.

'I wonder if there's something in the air here,' Harry said.
'Some kind of magic, perhaps. Do you feel it?'

Edward glanced up at the great flank of the down. 'Yes. I think I do.'

'Well, I'll never be able to thank this place enough for bringing me and Aura together,' Harry said, getting up from the grass. 'I can't imagine our paths would have crossed otherwise.'

Edward got up too. 'Like me and Abi.'

Harry took in Edward's smile as he said this. 'You and Abi?' he prompted, wondering if Edward had more to say.

'I mean our friendship,' Edward said quickly.

'Yeah?'

Harry felt sure that he read something in Edward's eyes – something that hinted at more than mere friendship.

'I – erm – wouldn't have met her without Winfield. Like you and Aura.'

'But not quite like me and Aura,' Harry pressed.

'No, no – of course not. We're just friends,' Edward said, nodding his head as if in time to a very fast tempo.

Harry waited, but it soon became clear that Edward wasn't about to divulge anything more even though Harry suspected there might be something he was hiding. He watched as Edward continued to nod as if he was trying to convince himself about the whole friend thing perhaps. Or was Harry reading too much into it?

'I'll catch you later,' Harry said, deciding to put his landlord out of his misery.

Edward smiled. 'Right.'

As Harry went back to his apartment, he couldn't help feeling relieved that he knew exactly how he felt about Aura. Seeing Edward talking about Abi, Harry had noticed how insecure Edward seemed about his feelings. Or maybe Edward really wasn't harbouring any romantic feelings for Abi after all and Harry had been reading into it because of the great love he himself was feeling. He had to admit that he wanted the whole world to fall in love and share the same emotion. Either way, it made Harry realise how good he felt about himself. He adored Aura and he couldn't help wanting to share that feeling, as daft as that made him sound. He just couldn't help it.

Edward returned to his apartment, mulling over what Harry had shared with him. Harry was a man who made things happen. It was over a year since he'd first let Aura know how he felt about her and now he was planning on moving things forward, whereas Edward was still stuck in indecision. He silently chastised himself. He'd wasted so much time with Abi and, when she'd been injured in the accident, he'd vowed to say something to her then, but had lost his nerve. What was wrong with him? It was quite clear that his feelings for Abi weren't going away. If anything, they were getting stronger – the more time he spent with her, the more he learned about her. He loved being in her company. She just lit him up even if he didn't always show it. He did often wonder what she made of him. He always felt so dull and reticent beside her. And that's what he'd been admiring about Harry – he wasn't afraid to express his emotions. He actually seemed to be enjoying them. That felt something completely alien to Edward.

If only he could be more like Harry, he thought. If only he could make the decision to be – well – decisive. He could roll his shoulders and tell himself, *Today, I'm going to be bold. I'm going to express my feelings clearly and honestly. I'm going to approach the woman I love and tell her exactly how I feel about her.*

The woman I love.

Edward was startled by his own admission. Love was a serious business, wasn't it? One had to get things right. And yet Harry had seemed so unfazed by it all. Naturally, he was anxious about Aura's reaction to what he had planned, but he was also excited by it all, and that excitement had lit him up from within.

Edward thought of Harry and Aura up there on the downs, enjoying a picnic on the summer solstice, the sun warm and bright, lighting their future together, and their joy at being in each other's company. He couldn't help smiling at the scene, imagining his friend's proposal. If only he could do something like that. Well, maybe not the proposal thing – not just yet. But if he could only tell Abi how he felt about her. That would be a start, wouldn't it?

Pausing by the French doors, suddenly feeling out of breath and not only because he'd been pacing ever since he'd come back inside, Edward – in true businessman style – considered his options. What would work for him? What could he successfully plan and pull off between now and the summer solstice that wouldn't fill him with dread and make him feel horribly uncomfortable? He wasn't really the picnic on a rug kind of guy, but maybe the answer was right before him.

'The walled garden,' he whispered. Abi loved the walled garden, as did he, and what better setting to tell her how he felt than the grounds of the house that had brought them both together?

He took a deep breath, trying to imagine it, but then shook his head. It felt too scary even to imagine. He'd have to let himself get used to the idea for a little while. But he was going to do it. No more stalling. No more excuses. It was time to tell Abigail how he felt about her.

CHAPTER SIX

'She won't talk to me, Douglas,' Abi told her brother-in-law. They'd met in a small café in Brighton after he'd had a meeting for work. Abi had thought it better than inviting him to Winfield because Ellen had got upset when she'd learned Abi had seen Douglas there without her knowledge. Not that a meeting in a café without her knowledge would be any more palatable to Ellen, but Abi was at a loss as to what to do because there was never an opportunity to talk to him alone at the family home.

'Every time I try and ask her about the past, she just clams up. Well, worse than clamming up – she gets mad at me.'

'I'm so sorry, Abi, but you know what she's like,' Douglas said, spooning another sugar into his coffee as if to fortify himself.

'I do, but it's not good enough. I need to find out what happened when we were children. We've never talked about it properly.'

Douglas sighed. 'Why now? I mean, if you don't mind me asking.'

'Because I've never had the courage to ask before – not in any detail anyway,' Abi told him honestly. 'Perhaps I've been afraid to know. And life was always in the way – work, the girls – you know?'

'Oh, yes – I know.'

'And Ellen's never been the most open when it comes to personal matters. But it's these little barbs – these endless jabs she makes at me – I can't help thinking it's all tied in with what happened back then.'

'You mean when she calls you "the lucky one"?'

Abi nodded sadly. 'I think it goes beyond my professional success.'

'And you've asked her outright?'

Abi stirred her coffee, staring down into the milky swirls. 'Yes. I asked her what happened on the night I seem to remember. Although, to be honest, Douglas, I'm not even sure if it's a real memory or just a fabrication. But I keep dreaming the same thing and I want to know. I *need* to know.' She blinked back the tears that were threatening to spill as her emotions rose dangerously close to the surface.

'And you're sure Ellen will have the answers you're looking for?' Douglas asked.

'I'm not sure. But I won't ever know if she doesn't talk to me about it all.'

'Don't forget, she was just a child too when your mother died.'

'I know.' Abi looked out of the café window for a moment, watching shoppers as they walked by. She turned to Douglas, noticing the sadness in his face and realising that this whole situation with her sister wasn't just about her – it was affecting him too.

'Are you okay?' Abi asked, reaching a hand across the table to touch his.

'Yeah, I'm okay.'

'Are you sure?'

He took a moment before answering. 'I'm worried about her to be honest. She's been worse than normal.'

'Oh, Douglas – I'm sorry to hear that.'

'I really thought this house move would change things.' He gave a hollow laugh.

'Haven't things improved at all?'

'They did for a while. She seemed happy to have a smaller place to run. But you've seen the state of it.'

'Yes, but that's just temporary. You're getting there, aren't you?'

'I sometimes wonder...' He stopped.

'What?'

'If she needs help.'

'You mean domestic help?'

Douglas shook his head. 'No. Someone to talk to.'

Abi blinked, taking in the seriousness of his statement. 'You do?'

'Well, we're not getting anywhere with her, are we? And it seems to me like she's in pain, and I can't bear to see that. You don't see it like I do – and I don't mean that as a criticism; it's just what happens when you live with someone. It's all the time, you see. It doesn't switch off even for a minute. It used to. There'd be days when there wouldn't be a hint of it, but the last couple of years have been hard. Hard on me and, I'm guessing, hard on her too.'

'And the girls.'

'You've noticed?'

'I think Bethanne feels it most – she's that age, isn't she?'

Abi said. 'And she's so sensitive to everything around her. Rosie seems a little more robust and I think her age is protecting her a little.'

'Like it protected you, do you think?' Douglas said.

'What do you mean?'

'You and Ellen – there's the same difference in your ages as Bethanne and Rosie, isn't there?'

Abi's mouth dropped open at the realisation. 'I'd never thought of that.'

'Well, I'm just wondering, maybe your age protected you a little when your mother died. You've said you don't remember much about it?'

'Just bits and pieces.' Abi leaned back in her chair. 'Do you think that's what Ellen means when she says I'm the lucky one? That I didn't really understand what was going on with our mother?'

'I don't know,' Douglas said honestly. 'It could be.'

'I wish she'd talk to me.'

Douglas shook his head as if in despair. 'Do you think we should organise something?'

'What do you mean?'

'I don't know – an intervention or something?'

'Oh, Douglas! She'd *hate* that! She'd never forgive us!'

'But I really think it might do her good to talk to someone. Maybe with you.'

Abi mused this over for a moment. It did make sense and it might really help to have an outsider to talk to. Heaven only knew that Ellen hadn't been willing to talk to Abi over the years. But maybe a third party could break down that barrier and get Ellen to open up.

'I'm not sure,' Abi said.

'Well, we don't have to make a decision today. And just

remember, we're doing it – if we *do* do it, that is – because we love her.'

'I know.'

Douglas let out a long sigh and casually picked up the menu from its holder at the side of the table.

'Fancy a hot buttered teacake?' he asked.

Abi laughed at the sudden levity of his question and she nodded. 'Absolutely!'

By the time she got back to Winfield, Abi felt exhausted. Everything about Ellen seemed to take it out of Abi these days, even when she wasn't in her presence. Approaching her apartment, she fished for the key in her handbag and that's when she heard it. Barking.

She looked around the hallway, wondering where it was coming from, and it was then that the door to Tim's apartment opened and a little red dog shot out, sounding its displeasure in a volley of high-pitched barks.

'Pepi!' Tim cried, running out after the animal and catching hold of it a moment later, scooping it up in his arms and revealing the torn fabric of his shirt in the process.

'Hello Tim,' Abi called.

'Oh, Abi! I didn't see you there.'

'How are you?'

He gave a nervous smile, the lines on his forehead creasing dramatically.

'I've been doing a spot of dog-sitting. I hope that's okay?' he asked, realising he'd been caught red-handed.

'It is as long as it doesn't disturb anybody,' Abi pointed out.

'Of course,' Tim said, nodding vigorously. 'I'm not sure

what's the matter with this little one. He doesn't seem to like me.'

Abi looked at Tim's woebegone face and could see why an animal might not warm to him immediately. Tim did always seem a little sad around the edges. Abi didn't use the word *lugubrious* lightly, but that was often the one that sprang to mind whenever she saw Tim. And yet choosing him as her new tenant still felt like the right decision because she'd been drawn to his natural gentleness, which was evident now in the way he was cradling the dog in his arms like a little baby.

'How's the writing going?' Abi asked.

Tim shook his head. 'Not good. Well, I'm writing; it's just nobody's paying me. I've got a few proposals out in the world, but I seem to be playing an endless waiting game. Hence the dog-sitting.'

'Oh, I see.'

'And it gets me outside – out of my own head for a bit. That can only be a good thing, can't it?' He asked the question as if genuinely wanting an answer – as though he didn't quite trust his own personal judgement.

'I think so,' Abi said honestly. 'Have you been walking up on the downs?'

'Yes. It's beautiful up there.'

'We're lucky to have so many footpaths from here.'

He nodded and then grimaced. 'Of course, I did lose Pepi for half an hour the other day.'

'Oh, no!'

'He legged it into a wood and I couldn't find you, could I?' he said to the little dog in his arms. 'I was terrified he'd got himself stuck down a rabbit hole.'

Abi took a step closer to the little red terrier now that it had stopped barking, and reached a hand out to tickle its ears.

'He's a cute little thing.'

'When he isn't eating my socks, perhaps!'

'You sound like you're having quite a battle with him!'

'Yes. I thought dog-sitting would be easy compared to writing. Now I'm not so sure.' He sighed and flicked his hair back. Abi noticed the grey streaks through the dark and, once again, she was reminded of Beatrix Potter. He had that animal-like cuteness about him that seemed to bring out the maternal instinct in Abi, even though he was much older than her.

'Well, let me know if I can help with anything,' she said, genuinely wanting to help although unsure how she could as she couldn't write books and she didn't really fancy helping out with runaway dogs.

'Thank you,' he said, smiling in such a way that his cheeks bulged like an autumn squirrel's.

Abi watched as Tim took the little dog back into his apartment, talking to it gently. She smiled and then opened her door. It felt good to be back even though she'd wanted to see Douglas. She could feel the beginnings of a headache pulsing behind her eyes. She had thought about cycling over to Ronnie's. His company and his garden were so very welcome in times of turmoil or just anytime really, and she knew he'd have some sage advice for her situation with her sister. Wasn't it funny that she'd only known him for the last couple of years, and yet he was a very dear friend to her and she couldn't now imagine her life without him? She'd just naturally connected with him – without fuss, without toil and without preconceptions. Friends – good friends – really could feel like family, Abi thought.

And that thought brought her mind back round to Ellen. Unlike Ronnie, things usually felt so difficult with Ellen, as if Abi had to make a gargantuan effort not to upset or disappoint her. It was a source of constant pain to Abi that she didn't have the closeness to her sister that she so craved. Interactions, especially lately, were so stressful and Abi felt at a loss as to what to do, hence her thinking about a visit to Ronnie. A cup of tea under the apple tree never failed to make her feel better. But her tiredness prevailed and she found herself sinking onto her sofa. Anyway, hadn't she been meaning to invite Ronnie over to Winfield? She longed to show him her progress in the garden as well as to see if he had any tips for her, but it would have to wait.

Since the accident, Edward had tried to put his brother Oscar out of his mind, which wasn't easy because he texted and called Edward frequently, making requests for money. Edward was furious. As far as he was concerned, Oscar's three year driving ban and fine weren't anywhere near enough. If Edward had been judge and jury, Oscar would have got a lifetime ban from driving and a spell in prison to consider exactly what he'd done. But whenever Edward tried to express his feelings, Oscar retaliated.

'You don't get it, do you? We were having *fun!*' he'd said the last time he'd rung. 'Accidents happen and nobody got killed, did they? What's all the fuss about?'

Edward had no words. It was a sad fact, but Oscar would never acknowledge his own recklessness. It had always been the same, Edward thought. Why he should expect his brother to change now, he didn't know. He had hoped that dating somebody like Abigail would have made Oscar think twice about pulling a stunt like dangerous driving, but no – it had made no difference at all.

Just that morning, Edward had received six texts from Oscar asking for money. He'd ignored them, but then the seventh message arrived.

Dad said I can sell some of his stuff.

Edward cursed. He wasn't surprised that their father was willing to bail Oscar out, but Edward really couldn't think that there was anything of value at their father's home.

Then the eighth text arrived as Edward was at his desk answering emails from clients.

I'm trying to shift stuff. Need your car.

Edward closed his eyes. He could, of course, ignore the text, but he dreaded to think what Oscar might get up to if Edward didn't agree to assist him. He wouldn't be stupid enough to drive himself when he was banned, would he? Edward wasn't sure he wanted to find out. So he texted Oscar back.

When?

I'm at Dad's now.

Edward closed his laptop. It was clear he wasn't going to get any peace until he'd got this chore over and done with and, although every instinct told him not to get involved with whatever Oscar was doing and not to pay another trip to his father's home, he didn't really see a way out of it. Perhaps this would help Oscar get back on his feet anyway. Once he'd paid his debt to society, maybe he could start afresh, which might also mean leaving Edward alone.

He could only hope.

There were several bin bags in the hallway when Edward arrived at his father's house.

'What's in those?' he asked Oscar as he entered through the front door which had been left open.

'Just rubbish.'

'You've been tidying up?'

'Of course.'

Edward nodded, pleased to hear that his brother was occasionally useful to others and not just asking for favours and handouts.

As Edward moved into the living room, he saw his father sitting in an armchair, a can in his hand as he watched a chat show on the TV. He didn't turn around to acknowledge his elder son's arrival and Edward couldn't help wondering if he was inebriated already.

'What did you want my help with?' Edward asked his brother now, intent on getting this whole job over and done with as quickly as possible so he could return to Winfield.

'Upstairs. Furniture.'

'What furniture?'

Oscar led the way and entered the spare room, walking up to the little table by the window.

'You're selling the dressing table?' Edward said, aghast.

'Sure. Why not?'

'That was Mum's.'

'Yes, but it's just sitting here now, isn't it?' Oscar said in the tone of voice which clearly told Edward that this didn't need explaining. 'It should raise a bit. Practically an antique.'

Edward approached it and ran his hand over the wooden surface. It was horribly dusty, but the wood underneath was rich and dark. He couldn't believe Oscar couldn't see how special it was, and was treating it so callously. Honestly, he sometimes thought that the only thing he had in common with his brother and father was the time they'd shared.

'Do you remember her sitting here, brushing her hair in the evenings?' Edward asked.

'No,' Oscar said.

Edward wasn't surprised. It had been a house divided. Edward and their mother; Oscar and their father. Well, Edward remembered. He remembered how he'd loved watching her unpin her hair after a long day, watching its dark blonde waves cascading over her shoulders. She hadn't been an overtly beautiful woman – her long nose and short chin had always been a source of displeasure to her, but her hair had been glorious. Edward could almost see her reflection in the mottled glass of the mirror.

Oscar removed the mirror now and then nodded to the table. 'Come on – you get one end and I'll get the other.'

'Wait a minute,' Edward said, leaving the room.

'Where are you going?' Oscar called after him.

Edward went downstairs to the kitchen and came back with a duster, giving the wood the once-over and wondering if he should buy it from Oscar himself, but he really had no love of old, dark wood.

'Shall we move it, then?' Oscar prompted.

'Just one more thing.' Edward got his phone out.

'What are you doing?'

'I want a photo of it.'

'Why?'

'Because I want to remember it.'

Oscar shook his head at his brother's sentimentality. 'It's just a bit of old wood.'

Edward chose not to respond. Instead, he replaced the mirror and took a series of photos.

They then shifted the dressing table down the stairs and somehow managed to fit it into Edward's car.

'Why couldn't you get someone to collect it from the house?' Edward asked.

Oscar frowned. 'I hadn't thought of that.'

'Mind you, I wouldn't want anyone seeing inside.'

'Yes,' Oscar agreed. 'Might devalue the contents. There'd probably be a charge for collection too.'

There was a cardboard box in the living room full of bits and bobs and Oscar went back to get it. Edward saw that it was mainly china bowls and plates with a couple of silver candlesticks.

'Dad okay with you taking all that?'

'It was his idea. As long as I buy him a pint tonight.'

'I'm surprised he hasn't sold all this lot already to fund his drinking.'

'Me too,' Oscar said. 'I think he'd forgotten about most of it. I found it at the back of a kitchen cupboard in the box they're in now, but they were covered in a mouldy old tablecloth so maybe he overlooked them.'

'Well, we know he doesn't go into his kitchen cupboards often.'

'What do you mean?' Oscar sounded defensive.

'He doesn't eat properly, does he? He's never got any real provisions in. It's all beer and baked beans, isn't it?'

'I suppose.'

Edward drove them to an antiques centre on the edge of Lewes and the two of them took the table and the box of china inside. Edward then decided to wait in the car, hiding from the whole sordid business. It didn't take long. Oscar came out with a wad of notes just a few minutes later.

'What did you get?' Edward dared to ask.

'A hundred and sixty.'

'For the lot?' Edward said, shocked.

'Of course for the lot. I got her up from one fifty when I told her she had a smile like the rising sun.'

'Oh, for god's sake, Oscar!'

'What – it got me an extra tenner.'

'You wouldn't need any of this money if you were careful.'

'Don't start that again.'

Edward looked out of the car window, wondering if he should run into the shop to buy the dressing table back, but what would he do with it? It would look dark and awkward and decidedly feminine in his light, bright rooms at Winfield. He really didn't have a use for it, and yet it pained him to lose it. It was one of the last few vestiges of his mother. And now it was gone. He couldn't help wondering who would buy it and if they would give it the love and attention it truly deserved.

'How's Abi?' Oscar asked as they headed for home.

Edward almost choked. How did Oscar have the nerve to even mention her name?

'I think you've done enough damage for one day,' Edward told him.

'I'm just making a friendly enquiry. I still care about her, you know. Maybe I should call her myself and find out.'

'She's fine,' Edward intercepted. 'There's no need for you to call her.'

Oscar smirked. He'd got what he wanted. 'You seeing her, then?'

Edward felt his jaw tighten with tension.

'You are, aren't you?'

'No!'

'Oh.' Oscar tutted. 'But you'd like to – am I right? Still not made a move, though, huh?'

'I'm not talking about this.'

'What are you waiting for? I don't understand it. If you like her – and I can see that you do – you really should tell her before someone else like me comes along and snaps her up from under your nose. Hey, maybe I'll even try again.'

'Don't you bloody dare!' Edward cried, his anger rising in him so quickly that it scared him.

Oscar merely laughed. 'Don't worry, Bro. I'm not going near her again.'

They drove the rest of the way in silence with Oscar whistling an insanely irritating tune and Edward silently seething at the subject of Abi having been brought up.

When they pulled up outside their father's a few minutes later, Oscar turned to Edward.

'Coming in?'

'No.'

'There's beer in the fridge.'

'I'm driving. And working.'

Oscar shook his head. 'You never change, do you?' He got out of the car and slammed the door.

'And neither do you,' Edward said under his breath, watching as Oscar disappeared into the house.

CHAPTER SEVEN

Aura was updating the news section of her website. Thanks to Harry's help, she was much more media savvy these days, updating offers for regular clients, creating a monthly newsletter and using the social media platforms. As part of her Christmas present, Harry had hired a photographer to take a series of photos of Aura for publicity purposes and she now had one of her standing in front of the enormous amethyst angel wings which Harry's father Leonard had bought her as a thank you present. The photo was now on her website as well as on her social media pages. Aura hadn't recognised herself when she'd first seen the photos, and Harry had been delighted with them, choosing one to have framed for his apartment.

She loved how they had learned so much from each other – Harry teaching her how to present herself professionally on the internet, attracting more clients and keeping loyal ones happy, and her teaching him how to slow down, take care of himself and simply breathe. They were a good team, she thought, although the word 'team' seemed so unremarkable and hardly described the depth of feeling she had for him.

As Harry had a photo of her in his apartment, she had one of him in hers and she looked at it now. It was actually a selfie of them both taken high up on the downs above Winfield, the sun full on their faces and the wind blowing their hair back. Aura loved how spontaneous the photo was. It wasn't primped and posed – it was a spur of the moment, let's capture this feeling kind of photo. She touched its frame now and smiled.

Finishing her work for the day, she got up from her desk and stretched her arms above her head. As much as she knew the importance of keeping in touch with her clients, she still didn't enjoy the toll that computer work took on her. She could feel her eyes straining at the bright screen and her neck and shoulders stiffening. It wasn't natural to spend hours sitting in front of a PC and she was glad to finish her allocated time.

As a way of unwinding, Aura picked up a rough piece of pink tourmaline in quartz she'd recently bought. The striations in the stone caught the light, seeming to wink at her, and she found a deep comfort in their pink beauty. She had been working a lot with pink crystals and the tourmaline, in particular, had fast become a favourite. It seemed to have a slightly softer energy than the rose quartz she usually worked with in times of turmoil – when she needed to remember self-compassion and forgiveness. Just what she needed whenever she thought about her brother Johnny.

She'd been thinking about him a lot lately, even dreaming of him the night before. She hadn't heard from him since he'd left Winfield in a strop. Not long afterwards, both she and Abi had been burgled and Aura strongly suspected Johnny was the culprit. It hurt her that he could not only do such a thing, but that he could so easily walk out on her and not let her know where he was. He must know she worried about him. Her numerous letters to him during his prison sentences over the years were testament to that, but still he could disappear, not caring about those he left behind.

She gently put the crystal down and walked out into the walled garden. It was too perfect a day to be mired in the pain of the past. For one thing, it was the summer solstice – the longest day of the year. It was a time that Aura adored and one she looked forward to with the longer, lighter days, the warm glory of the sun, and flowers and foliage gifting the world their colour. And it marked a very special anniversary too. Aura smiled as she thought about the year before, high on the downs, sitting on the picnic rug with Harry. How shy and awkward he had seemed and how she'd adored that awkwardness.

Her fingers reached to touch her lips as she thought of the first kiss they'd shared. There'd been so many others since and so many yet to come, she hoped, and she loved that he'd planned a picnic for this evening to celebrate their special moment. Like last time, Harry had insisted on organising the food and drink and Aura hadn't protested. It was a lovely feeling to be looked after and to have someone who truly cherished her. She smiled as she thought of him, blessing the day that this special man had come into her life.

It had been agony to have to go to work that day, but it couldn't be helped. Harry sat at his desk, glancing at the time every few minutes, counting down the hours until he could be with Aura. He'd planned it all, buying a bottle of champagne to take with them on their picnic and making the food extra special. There was a part of him that wondered if the champagne might jinx things but, then again, they could drink it to celebrate the anniversary of their first kiss, whether she wanted to get married or not. If she said no, Harry was determined that it wouldn't change things between them. He knew plenty of couples who were perfectly happy not to be married. Indeed, he wasn't quite sure why he'd set his heart on it. Perhaps it was because his parents had set such a good example. In all the years they'd been together, he'd rarely known a cross word between them. Well, other than the usual marital spats about whose turn it was to take the rubbish out.

Harry grinned as he thought about his parents now, getting up to make everyone in the office a cup of tea. Leonard and Maria Freeman were so very different and yet they complemented each other perfectly. They were true partners, always there to support one another, guiding each other through the tough times and delighting in each other's successes. He also loved how they had changed in little ways over the years, learning from one another. Take the whole meditation thing for example. When Harry had introduced them to Aura, they'd both been sceptical about her beliefs, but his father had quickly come round to Aura's ideas, and his belief had led to his mother's belief. Harry loved that. They were happy to adapt, to evolve. That made life so exciting, he thought, and it reminded him of how he and Aura had learned so much from each other.

Finally, when it was time to pack up from work, Harry tidied his desk and said goodbye to his colleagues and left the office. He stopped off at a florists on the way to his car and spent far too long choosing a bunch of flowers, finally settling on a mixed bouquet of summer blooms which included red roses. Well, you couldn't not give your girl red roses when you were about to propose to her, he thought.

It felt strange arriving home at Winfield that evening. Different. Something had shifted and he knew what it was: him. There was no going back now. He'd imagined a future with him and Aura together and he couldn't now settle in his present. Entering the hallway, he wondered whether he should call and give her the flowers right away, but he felt a mess after a hot day in the office. He'd take a shower and get changed and call as he'd arranged later that evening.

Oh, how long the minutes stretched until that hour!

If there hadn't been a footnote in her diary, Abi probably wouldn't have known it was the summer solstice. Of course, Edward had knocked on her door the week before to tell her. She had to admit she was surprised that Edward knew about such things and she was even more surprised by his invitation. He'd called round one weekday morning when she'd been in the middle of a large painting she hadn't planned, but which she was enjoying immensely, so much so that she had streaks of paint on both her cheeks and in her hair. Edward had laughed when he'd seen her.

'You look a bit like a painting yourself,' he'd told her. Abi had felt her face flushing, adding yet more colour. 'Listen, Abi' he'd went on, 'I'd like to invite you to dinner – here in the walled garden.'

'What a lovely idea!' she'd said, doing her best to rub the paint from her left cheek, but just smudging it so that it looked like a big bruise.

'Would eight o'clock suit you? We could watch the solstice sunset.'

She'd nodded, wondering where this romantic version of Edward had suddenly come from. And was it indeed anything to do with romance? Or was he just being neighbourly and wanting to share the longest day of the year with his friend?

Either way, Abi had accepted and was looking forward to it immensely.

So, now that the day had arrived and the hour was approaching, Abi opened her wardrobe and peered inside. As always, she had heaps of clothes, but nothing to wear. What exactly did one wear to dinner in one's own walled garden? Was this classed as a formal occasion? What would Edward be wearing? Abi pulled a few hangers out, inspecting her collection of summer dresses. It was still warm outside and that would lend itself to something light and floaty so she chose an apple-green, full-length dress with tiny buttons down the front made of mother-of-pearl. It was one of her favourites and she was happy with her choice.

She fixed her long hair into a casual bun, securing it in place with an antique silver hair clip she'd found in a Brighton charity shop on a recent visit. Rifling through her jewellery box a moment later, she pulled out a pair of silver twist earrings which caught the light beautifully. She then slipped on a pair of strappy sandals and looked at her reflection in the bedroom mirror. She sighed, never wholly satisfied with her appearance. The summer weather had brought out even more freckles than usual, and her wily curls were already beginning to escape from her bun. But she'd have to do.

Abi couldn't help feeling awkward about going to Edward's empty-handed, but he'd insisted that he was taking care of everything this evening. Still, she couldn't resist nipping out into the garden and cutting a handful of creamy-pink sweet peas, popping them into a jam jar and tying a little blue ribbon around its rim.

She knocked on his door a moment later, smiling when he answered. He was wearing a crisp cream-coloured shirt and looked very handsome.

'Abi – you look lovely.'

'I do?' Her free hand automatically checked her messy bun, but then she remembered herself and handed him the flowers.

'Lovely,' he said, inhaling their scent. 'My mother's favourite.'

'Were they really?'

'Yes. She loved to have a vase on her dressing table and she particularly loved the pink ones,' he said and a sad look darkened his eyes for a brief moment.

'You must feel free to pick them whenever you want. There are plenty and they flower even more when they're picked.'

'Thank you. Come on through.' He gestured to her and she walked through his apartment towards the French doors which were open onto the walled garden beyond. Abi got her first glimpse of the table.

'Edward!' she cried. 'It's beautiful!'

'Is it okay?' he asked, sounding like an unsure schoolboy checking that he'd done his homework correctly. Indeed Abi watched as he rushed forward to straighten one of the candlesticks a millimetre.

'It's absolutely resplendent,' she told him sincerely, gazing at the simple cream tablecloth edged with lace which had been placed over the rustic picnic table. Three silver candlesticks marched down its centre and she watched as Edward placed her sweet peas among them.

'Have a seat,' he said and Abi suddenly felt awkward. It was all rather formal. Edward seemed to feel this too and shook his head.

'Sorry – that sounded very bossy and abrupt, didn't it?'

'No! Of course not.'

'I'm just – well – I'm not used to...' He took a seat opposite her, his sentence dangling unfinished.

'We usually eat out, don't we?' Abi said, trying to ease things a little.

'Yes. Maybe that's it.'

'Well, this is lovely, Edward. A real treat.'

He poured her some wine. 'Here's to the summer solstice.' They clinked glasses. Wine was good, she thought. Wine took the edges off things.

'How's your day been?' she asked.

'Okay actually. I got a new client via an existing one which is always gratifying.'

'Well done!'

'Thank you. And I've steered somebody away from making a really bad financial decision.'

'How amazing!'

'Well, it's kind of my job.'

'But that must be so satisfying – to know you're making a real difference to someone's life – to their financial future.'

'I suppose it is,' he said, 'but it's not the same as you. I mean, you *really* add value to people's lives.'

'You think so?'

'Of course. With your patterns and colours. You help people to see the beauty in the world, Abigail. That's a true gift. I just point out figures.'

'Edward Townsend! You do yourself a *huge* disservice! I bet your clients don't see it like that.'

'Well, I couldn't say.'

'I bet they value you greatly,' she said in all seriousness.

He smiled, but didn't seem completely convinced.

Edward then did the honours with the food – delicious summer fare, fresh and colourful, and for a while they chatted amiably about the garden and life at Winfield.

'Aren't Harry and Aura up on the downs this evening?' Abi asked as she thought about their tenants.

'Yes indeed.'

'I'm wondering if we'll hear some good news,' she said with a grin.

Edward's eyes widened. 'He told you?'

'Told me what?'

Edward quickly shook his head. 'Nothing.'

'Edward? Do you *know* something?'

'No, I...' he stopped, taking a sip of wine.

'You *do!*' Abi persisted. 'Come on – out with it! If you know something juicy, I want to know too!'

'Well,' Edward said at last, 'he didn't absolutely swear me to secrecy or anything so I guess it's all right to share it with you.'

'Please do!' Abi was on the edge of her seat now.

Edward cleared his throat. 'Harry's going to propose to Aura tonight.'

Abi squealed in delight, putting her wine glass down and clapping her hands. 'Oh, that's wonderful! I was hoping those two would get together – you know, officially.'

'He's nervous, though. He's not sure she'll say yes.'

'Really? But they're so in love.'

'I know, but marriage is well – it's a big step, isn't it?'

'Of course.'

'And I guess it's not for everyone.'

Abi picked up her glass again and saluted the hills with it. 'Well, cheers to them both and I hope we hear good news very soon.'

Edward raised his glass with her. 'Cheers to Harry and Aura.'

'That's so exciting. Winfield's first couple!'

'Yes.'

Abi noticed an expression fly across Edward's face. 'What is it?' she asked him.

'Nothing.' He shook his head and quickly poured more wine into Abi's glass even though she still had plenty.

'Are you worried about them?'

'Harry and Aura? No, not at all.'

'Then what is it?' Abi watched him closely. His awkwardness had returned and it made her uncomfortable to see him like that. 'Edward?'

'Abi.'

'Yes?'

'There's something I've been meaning to tell you. For ages now in fact.'

'Oh?'

He gave a smile, looking a little less uneasy now. 'I don't know why it's taken me so long. It really shouldn't have.' He paused and the pause seemed to be stretching longer and longer, making Abi more and more anxious.

'What is it, Edward?' she asked.

'It's just that... well, I've been feeling...'

It was then that they heard it. Abi put her wine glass down and turned around. 'Is that Samantha?'

At first, the noise was hard to pinpoint. It was a kind of whine, growing in intensity. Edward frowned and then winced as an ear-splitting sound of a microphone being tested filled the walled garden. They then heard laughter as music began.

'Is that a karaoke machine?' Abi asked, her eyes wide, half in horror, half in amusement.

Edward cursed.

'Don't let it spoil our evening,' Abi told him quickly. 'Edward!' She reached a hand across the table towards him. 'You were going to tell me something?'

He shook his head. 'It's nothing.'

'It didn't sound like nothing. It sounded pretty important.'

The music cranked up a notch.

'It'll keep,' Edward told her, standing up from the table.

Abi watched him as he began to clear the dishes. Was that it? Was their evening over? She stood and picked up a bowl.

'Leave that,' he said.

'Sorry,' she said quickly and then she heard him sigh.

'No, I'm sorry, Abi. It's this constant noise from Samantha. I'm finding it stressful.'

'I know. Why don't we go inside? It might not be as bad in there.'

Clearing the table together and moving inside, they soon discovered that the noise was just as bad.

'I'm so sorry, Abi.'

'It's okay.'

'How about we do this another time?'

Abi bit her lip. She was disappointed that the evening had come to an end so abruptly, but she was more frustrated that she wouldn't get to know what it was Edward had wanted to say to her. She'd seen a glimpse of tenderness in his eyes as he'd been about to speak, she was sure of it. But maybe it was nothing. Maybe he just wanted to say how much their friendship meant and to celebrate the good fortune they'd had in meeting one another and of being able to restore Winfield together.

'Okay,' she said reluctantly, knowing it was no good to push someone like Edward. The drawbridge was well and truly up now, she could see that. 'Thank you for this evening. It was lovely.' She crossed the space between them and leaned up to kiss his cheek.

And then she left.

High up on the downs, the only music that could be heard was a blackbird singing in a nearby hawthorn tree. The air was light and warm and Winfield seemed like a million miles away even though it was barely a quarter of one.

Aura was wearing a pearly-pink dress and her hair was loose apart from a single diamante clip twinkling above her left ear. Harry had the urge to kiss that ear and then let his lips travel down the soft skin of her neck but, instead, he cleared his throat. He had to concentrate this evening. He didn't want to get anything wrong.

'How about here?' he asked when they reached the top of a hill.

'Perfect,' Aura said with a sigh of contentment.

Harry laid the picnic rug out on the grass, choosing a patch free of stones and with a view into the valley below that was glorious. He scanned the landscape for possible distractions and was relieved when he found none.

'Are you okay?' Aura asked him as he opened the wicker hamper and began decanting the food.

'I'm fine,' he said. 'Why do you ask?'

'You just look – I don't know – strange,' Aura said as she helped to unwrap everything.

'How?'

She shrugged. 'I'm not sure. Just different.'

He laughed it off, focusing his attention on the picnic, but his eyes kept finding their way to Aura. She looked so beautiful this evening. But, then again, she always did. And it was more than her lovely face and pretty hair. She had a beauty of spirit that simply glowed. It was mesmeric and Harry could sometimes do nothing but stare at her.

'Harry! You're making me very self-conscious,' she said.

'Sorry!' He shook his head, mortified at being caught. 'It's just – well – you look...' he didn't get a chance to finish his sentence because she leaned across the picnic blanket towards him, kissing him fully on the mouth.

'Shall we eat?' she asked a moment later and he nodded, a huge smile on his face.

It was a wonderful picnic and they chatted easily, leaping from subject to subject, laughing and enjoying themselves. Then, once every single piece of food had been consumed, Harry started to get nervous. He'd managed to park his nerves for a few blissful moments while they'd been eating, but the real purpose of the evening was approaching and he knew he couldn't put it off any longer. Nor did he want to. The champagne bottle was still hidden in the hamper, wrapped in a scarf. He hoped they'd be cracking it open in a few minutes to celebrate.

'Aura?' he said softly, watching as she turned to face him. 'There's something I've been wanting to ask you. Something important.'

'What's that?'

'Well, when I say important, it makes it sound scary. Official. And it's not. I mean, it *is*, but I don't want you to be worried.'

'Harry – you *are* worrying me now.'

He took a deep breath. He could feel his heart pounding and didn't feel completely in control of himself. This wasn't going well. He knew what he wanted to say but, now that he was in the moment, he wasn't sure how to start.

'I have a question for you,' he began again, hating the way that sounded. It was like he was interviewing her or something. 'I want to ask you something.' He glanced up into the sky for a moment, as if he might find some kind of celestial guidance, but there was none to be had. 'Aura...'

'Yes, Harry?'

'Aura – it's you...' He paused, meaning to add something and not just let his sentence dangle so unattractively. He wanted to say something beautiful and simple and yet profound at the same time. Something she'd remember.

'Harry – are you trying to propose to me?'

He swallowed hard. 'I'm not sure – I mean, I am if you want me to, but not if you don't.' He ran a hand through his hair. 'I'm messing this up, aren't I?'

'No! No, you're not.'

'I'm not? Because I want to get this right. I want to make you happy, Aura.'

'But you do!'

'And I want you to be absolutely sure that what I want is what you want because – otherwise – it's not good at all, is it? And I know we should probably be really practical about all this and get to know each other better and talk about families and politics and all those kind of things, but I don't want to do that because I have this feeling when I'm with you that everything is all right. Does that make sense?' He gave a nervous laugh and Aura moved closer to him across the picnic rug, placing her hands in his. Instantly, he felt calmer, the touch of her warm skin on his, bringing him back to himself. He took a deep breath and began again.

'I have this really strong feeling that we're right together, you see. And I love being with you and, I think you know, I love you.' He paused, gazing into the softness of her face. 'Will you marry me, Aura?'

Thankfully, Harry didn't have to wait long for Aura's reply.

A big, wide smile broke across her face and she laughed before kissing him.

'Yes! Yes, I'll marry you!'

'You will?'

'Of course! Unless you're having second thoughts already?' she teased.

'Oh, no!' he said. 'Never.' He patted his pocket and brought out the little box, handing it to Aura. She opened it and gasped.

'Harry!'

'Do you like it?'

'I *love* it!'

'I thought the star was more you than a plain old solitaire.'

She kissed him again. 'Will you put it on for me?'

Harry nodded and took the ring out of its velvety home. His hands were shaking as Aura presented her left hand to him.

'Does it fit?' he asked a moment later.

'Harry, it's perfect!'

'Really?'

'Look?' She held her hand up and Harry saw the snug fit of the diamond ring which sparkled in the summer solstice sun. 'I love it! It's the most beautiful thing I've ever seen.'

'Not as beautiful as you,' Harry whispered.

They kissed again and then they lay back on the picnic rug, their arms tight around one another, their bodies held comfortably by the earth as they gazed up into a sky streaked with gold.

CHAPTER EIGHT

'It's very frustrating, Ronnie!' Abi said as the two of them sat down on the bench under the apple tree, its full leaves providing welcome shade on the hot June day as they sipped glasses of cool lime cordial.

'And you really thought he was going to tell you how he feels about you?'

'That's the kind of the vibe I was getting. What else could it have been? You don't make a big statement like that and then simply say that you value a friendship, do you?' Abi groaned. 'But what do I know? Edward's never really revealed very much so he might have been building up to a big statement about wallpaper for all I know.' Abi gave a hollow laugh. 'Maybe he wants my advice on decorating his rooms! Anyway, it was very disappointing. We were meant to be watching the solstice sun setting together.'

'I think I may have said this before,' Ronnie began, 'but you could say something to him, Abi. If you feel that's the right thing to do.'

'I know.'

'And?'

She looked out across the garden, enjoying the stillness of the summer day with its splendour of roses.

'The dinner was his idea. I couldn't hijack it and blurt out my feelings.'

'So you still like him?'

'Of course I do!' Abi turned to face Ronnie. 'He's the sweetest man, Ronnie, and I do have feelings for him. But I'm afraid of scaring him off if I say anything.'

'But it sounds to me like he can't get the words out himself. He might be relieved if you're the one to say something.'

Abi laughed. 'I hadn't thought of it like that.'

'Then give it a go. It seems very silly – if you don't mind me saying – that two young people are delaying a bit of happiness because they can't get the words out.'

'I know.'

'Then why not make dinner for him? Find out when this Susannah person–'

'Samantha.'

'*Samantha* – find out when she's going to be out so you've got some peace and quiet and no chance of interruptions.'

'I don't know, Ronnie. It makes me anxious just thinking about it.'

'Well, just kiss him and be done with it. No words needed!'

'Ronnie!' Abi was shocked by his boldness, but she was laughing too.

He gave a chuckle. 'And tell me how you get on. I want all the gossip.'

'I'll think about it, okay? But no promises! And I must introduce you to one another.'

'Yes, you must. I want to meet this hero of yours.'

'Hero – honestly, Ronnie!'

'What? We're the heroes and heroines of our own lives, aren't we?'

'I don't feel very heroine-like,' Abi said, glancing down at her dusty trainers and her summer dress which was covered not only in the usual paint splodges but also tomato stains from a little accident in the greenhouse earlier.

'But I believe you take responsibility for your own destiny,' Ronnie went on. 'It's so important to take action and not just let life pass us by, don't you think?'

Abi nodded, but she was only half-listening.

'I really should come and draw here. Would that be all right?'

Ronnie smiled and then yawned. 'It would be very all right.'

'I'm sorry, Ronnie. I'm tiring you out with all my angst, aren't I?' Abi said, standing up to go.

'No, no!' he protested with a wave of a gnarled hand. 'It's this weather. It's beating me, I'm afraid.'

'It's certainly a hot one today.' She gazed up into the cloudless sky. The garden was parched and begging for rain. Which reminded her, she had to check on her greenhouse again. On hot days like today, one watering wasn't enough. 'I'd better get back.'

'I'll walk you out.'

She shook her head. 'No need. You rest a while. I'll see you soon, okay?' She picked up their two glasses to take into the house. It was wonderfully cool inside and she stood for a moment, taking in the heady scent of the potted geraniums on the windowsills and dresser, and the piles of seed packets scattered anywhere there was a flat surface. It was such a wonderfully Ronnie room, she thought, popping through to the kitchen to wash the glasses.

It was only when she was half-way home that she thought

she should have offered to water Ronnie's greenhouse for him. No doubt he would be on top of it, but he'd looked so tired today and she felt a little guilty that she hadn't helped more.

Cycling through the country lanes, she thought about what Ronnie had said to her. Why shouldn't she tell Edward how she felt? She was a modern woman. She'd run her own company, for goodness' sake. Surely she could tell a man how she felt about him? And yet there was something that was holding her back – the thought of the embarrassment if Edward didn't feel the same way. The mortification she'd feel at having revealed her soul. But what if Edward was trying – and failing – to tell her exactly the same thing, only he'd been unable to because of the noise from Samantha's the other night and perhaps because of his shyness. What if they were destined never to get together?

As Abi reached the track to Winfield, she slowed down, feeling the softest of breezes from the downs. It helped to cool her although it did nothing to calm her anxiety when she thought about Edward. What was she going to do? Something? Nothing? Perhaps the summer would bring the answer if she gave it just a little bit more time.

Two people who weren't scared to confess their feelings to one another were Harry and Aura. They also couldn't wait to share their news with everyone and, just a couple of days after the summer solstice, Harry and Aura drove over to the Freeman's. Aura was both anxious and excited to break the news to Harry's parents. She really felt as if she'd been welcomed by his family. Still, so many questions had been swirling through her mind since Harry's proposal. Where would they live for one thing? Would they share one of their apartments? It would be rather odd to go on living separately. Or maybe they'd go somewhere else? Aura wasn't sure she liked the thought of leaving Winfield. Even though she was just renting her apartment, the place felt so much a part of her. And would she change her name? She had before. Anna Blake had never felt like her, but she did feel like Aurora Arden – Aura for short. But Aura Freeman sounded lovely too. Oh, dear! There was so much to think about.

As they pulled up to the Freeman's home, Harry reached across to squeeze Aura's hand.

'You know Mum's going to go crazy when we tell her? She's been waiting for this day for years and years.'

'But I haven't known you for years and years,' Aura said with a frown.

'Yes, but Mum's kind of been hoping I'd settle down for a while now. Only I hadn't met you, had I?'

They shared a kiss and then got out of the car.

'Just be ready for her to be a bit full-on, okay?' Harry warned as they rang the bell.

Leonard Freeman was the one to answer the door and embraced them both.

'How are you, Dad?'

'Good! Very good. I'm still doing all the practices, Aura.'

'That's brilliant,' Aura said.

'Still marching boys, Dad?'

'What?' he barked. 'Lord, no! I've swapped marching for meditating!' He coughed out a laugh. 'Come on in. Come on in!'

Aura noticed Leonard's bare feet and took off her own sandals in the hallway as did Harry. They then went through to the living room where Harry's mother met them.

'How well you both look,' Maria told them. 'How did the picnic go?'

'Good, Mum,' Harry said.

She looked from Harry to Aura. 'And?'

'And it was perfect weather,' Harry told her.

'Well, good,' his mother said patiently, while twisting her fingers into knots.

'And the sunset was glorious, wasn't it, Aura?'

'Oh, it was,' Aura said, going along with keeping the suspense up.

'Yes, I remember it was rather glorious,' Maria agreed.

'And...'

'And?' his mother said, her neck craning forward in anticipation.

'We have some news,' Harry said at last, obviously unable to keep it in a moment longer.

'Yes?'

Harry put his arm around Aura. 'I asked Aura to marry me and she said yes!'

Maria Freeman's scream reverberated around the open-plan barn conversion, piercing everybody's eardrums.

'Good heavens!' Leonard cried. 'You've deafened me, woman!'

Harry laughed and Aura felt tears prickling her eyes at Maria's obvious joy.

'Oh, my dears!' She moved forward, hugging them both at once.

'Well, I say!' Leonard joined them, pumping his son's hand up and down in a warm handshake and then giving Aura a resounding kiss on the cheek. 'This is cause for celebration! Do we have some half-decent wine around, Maria?'

'I think so, darling.'

Leonard rushed off and Maria turned her attention to Harry and Aura again.

'Show her the ring, Aura,' Harry said with a grin.

Aura had been hiding her ring finger until now, but Maria stepped forward to see it at Harry's insistence.

'Oh, let me have a look!'

Aura held her hand towards her future mother-in-law.

'Well, look at that beauty!'

'I chose it, Mum,' Harry said proudly.

'And look at it sparkling like a heavenly star! It's *so* Aura,' his mother said.

'That's just what I thought!' Harry agreed. 'I was delighted to find it.'

'It's perfect,' she told him.

'I'm so glad you like it,' Aura said.

'It's beautiful! And you two are going to have the most *beautiful* children!' Maria enthused.

'Mum!' Harry cried, obviously horrified.

'What? You *are* going to have children, aren't you?'

'Yes, of course we are, Mrs Freeman,' Aura said.

'Oh, Mrs Freeman, indeed! You have to call me Maria – I've told you before.'

'We haven't discussed children yet, Mum. We've only just got engaged!'

'Well, keep me informed,' Maria told him.

Wine was served after that, the sound of clinking glasses and excited voices carrying out of the great glass doors which had been opened into the garden. Maria then made a light lunch and they took it outside, eating at a table under a parasol while Leonard made sure their glasses were topped up. Harry didn't mind switching to juice as he was driving, but Aura felt as if she was getting positively merry. It was as if she was floating and, when the time came for them to leave, she was completely exhausted.

'I think they were pleased,' Harry told her as they got into the car and waved their goodbyes. 'You do know that she'll have the wedding all planned out before we see her again.'

'Well, I suppose we'd better talk about it – just to make sure we get our say.'

'Yes, I suppose we should,' Harry agreed.

'Something simple but beautiful.'

'Yes.'

'With music and lights and lots of flowers.'

'Sounds wonderful.'

They drove on.

'Harry?'

'Yes?'

'When were you thinking of?'

'For the wedding?'

Aura nodded.

'I don't know. What do you think?'

'Summer's too early, isn't it? Everything will be booked and people will be away.'

'Winfield won't be booked,' Harry said.

Aura gasped. 'Get married at Winfield?'

'Well, I don't think we'll be able to have the ceremony bit there, but we could definitely have the reception in the garden, couldn't we? It's beautiful and it's definitely big enough for whatever we want to do.'

'You know I have a very small family,' Aura said. 'I don't suppose we'll see Johnny and, even if I did know how to contact him, I don't think it's a good idea him coming back here after what he did. So it's just my mum as far as family is concerned.'

'My family's pretty small too, but we've both got plenty of friends to make numbers up.'

'Actually, I like the idea of a small wedding,' Aura confessed. 'But in the summer. It has to be summer!'

'Yes!' Harry agreed as they pulled into the driveway at Winfield.

'Shall I ask Abi what she thinks about letting us use the garden?'

'And I'll ask Edward.'

'Do you think we can pull this off for the end of the summer?'

'I'm sure we can.' Harry leaned across to kiss her. 'If it's what we want, we can make it happen!'

Aura was dreading seeing her mother, but she supposed she'd have to introduce Harry to her at some point before the wedding. It was only fair. After all, she knew Harry's parents pretty well whereas Aura's family still remained shrouded in mystery as far as Harry was concerned.

'I'm afraid we're not close,' Aura warned him as they drove, 'so don't expect a warm reception or anything. I'm not even sure if she'll come to be honest.'

'Not come to her daughter's wedding?' Harry sounded incredulous.

'I think she'd have skipped my birth if she could have.'

'Aura!' Harry reached out to touch her.

'It's okay. I've made my peace with all this a long time ago. We're different people with different lives, that's all.'

'And your father isn't on the scene, right?'

'No. He left when I was small.'

'And didn't keep in touch at all?'

'No. I think Johnny takes after him to be honest. He's good at disappearing too.'

'I'm so sorry, Aura.'

'It's okay. I know we can't all be blessed with parents like yours.'

'Well, I'm happy to share mine with you,' Harry told her and Aura beamed him a smile.

They parked outside the townhouse terrace a few minutes later.

'Is that the one?' Harry asked, nodding at a house with tatty net curtains.

'She's not really one for housekeeping,' Aura said, glancing at the old place.

They left the car and rang the bell a moment later. A dog barked from next door, its head pushing underneath the curtain to snarl at Harry and Aura.

'Charming!' Harry said.

'Yes, you're always guaranteed a warm wel–'

The sound of the door opening stopped Aura in mid-quip and her mother's frown greeted her.

Paula Blake had a strange face. It looked both pinched and punched – pinched around the mouth because she rarely smiled, and punched around the eyes because she never got enough sleep.

'How are you, Mum?' Aura asked, stepping towards her. Paula took a step back.

'Was I expecting you?'

'I texted you before. You did reply,' Aura reminded her.

Paula walked down the hallway without actually inviting them in, but Aura went in anyway.

'I can't be long. I'm off out with the girls later.'

Aura was used to that and she was glad that she wouldn't have to stay long anyway. Her mother had always preferred a night at the pub with her friends to spending any time with her children. Aura remembered the number of school nights when she'd been forced to make tea for her and Johnny and then attempted to help him with his homework while struggling with her own alone.

'Character building,' her mother had told her the one time Aura had dared to say anything. 'You need to grow up independent. You'll thank me in time!'

Somehow Aura didn't imagine Johnny would ever thank their mother for the guidance she'd given them.

'Mum? I want to introduce you to Harry.'

Paula turned around.

'Pleased to meet you, Mrs Blake.' Harry came forward, his hand outstretched in greeting. Paula took it uneasily.

'Shall I put the kettle on, Mum?' Aura asked, embarrassed that Paula hadn't offered yet and that she might not offer at all.

'If you want.'

They went through to the kitchen together and Aura got on with the business of making tea.

'I don't suppose you've heard from Johnny lately?' Aura asked.

'Why would he be in touch with me?' Paula snapped.

'I just thought he might have reached out, that's all.'

'Well, he hasn't.'

Aura glanced at Harry who was standing awkwardly in the doorway as if he wanted to make an escape.

'You still into those rocks?' Paula asked.

'Crystals, Mum.'

'Load of old nonsense. I don't know why you're throwing your life away on them.'

'It's not the only thing I do. I've told you. I teach yoga and meditation.' Aura stopped. She could see her mother wasn't listening. In fact, she was mumbling in that odd, angry way she often had. Aura turned back to the tea things and, a few minutes later, they were all sitting together, sipping tea in the living room. Aura was sitting next to Harry on the old sofa she'd grown up with and Paula was sitting in an armchair she'd bought as a shop-soiled second because of a child's dirty handprint deeply imbedded in the fabric. Aura could still see it peeping out from under her mother's left leg.

'Harry and I have something to tell you, Mum,' she said, putting her mug down on a table littered with an unfinished jigsaw puzzle. Her mother frowned by way of a response. 'We've just got engaged. We're going to get married!' Aura couldn't help smiling and Harry gave a little laugh, holding her hand. But Paula just continued to frown.

'When?' she asked at last.

Aura gave her the date at the end of the summer.

'I'll have to check at work,' Paula said, letting her daughter know that attending her wedding wasn't an automatic given. 'I wasn't expecting this. I've only just met this Henry.'

'It's Harry, Mum.'

Harry gave a nervous laugh. 'Yes, it's all been rather a whirlwind, Mrs Blake.'

She continued to stare at them without saying anything.

Aura stood up and took Harry's mug from him. He'd only had time to drink half his tea. 'We've got to get going.'

Paula didn't protest as Aura moved from living room to kitchen to hallway in swift succession, a perplexed Harry following in tow.

'Goodbye, Mum,' Aura called from the door a moment later.

'Goodbye, Mrs Blake,' Harry called.

Still nothing.

Aura got into the car and, when Harry started the engine and pulled away, she turned to face him.

'Harry – can it just be us?'

'At the wedding?' he asked, keeping his eye on the road.

Aura nodded.

Harry grimaced. 'I'm not sure my mum would forgive me.'

'Of course. We'll have your parents with us. And Abi and Edward.'

'And Uncle Arthur will have to come.'

'And Sylvie from the crystal shop and Bella – one of my best friends. But that's it. No fuss. No stress. I mean, I'll send Mum an invite, but I don't want to stress about it if she doesn't want to come.'

'Okay.'

Aura took a deep breath. 'Are you sure you're okay with that? It will only be...' she mentally counted, 'seven or eight guests. Did you have your heart set on a big wedding?'

Harry shook his head. 'Aura – all I want is to stand in front of you and tell you how much I love you. I don't need anyone else at all.'

'You have to have witnesses, though.'

'I know. Well, my parents can do that, can't they? They'll be thrilled to be a part of things.'

'And I'll send my mum a photo if she doesn't come. I think she'd prefer that anyway. Another photo of me to put in a drawer.'

Harry gave her a smile that was warm and so full of kindness and empathy that Aura thought that she might not have struck gold when it came to her family, but she'd found the very best man in the world to marry.

CHAPTER NINE

Edward was deleting a backlog of spam emails when there was a knock on his door. Glad of the chance to leave his screen for a moment, he was surprised to see Abi's tenant Tim standing in the hallway.

'I'm sorry to disturb you,' Tim began, 'only Abigail seems to be out and I wanted to – *needed* to – make sure that something *is* being done about Samantha. You see, the noise seems to be pretty constant. Day time, evening, night. I'm finding it hard to concentrate. I work from home – like you – and it's really winding me up. I came here because I thought it would be peaceful. I was *told* it would be peaceful.' He stopped, taking a deep breath. 'Sorry!'

'No need to apologise. It's me who should be apologising to you,' Edward said. 'She's my tenant and I'm more than aware of the noise issue. I've spoken to her about it and she makes promises that she'll keep the noise down in the future.'

'But she doesn't *keep* those promises, does she?' Tim said through gritted teeth. The colour had risen in his face and he looked as if he might be about to burst with frustration. 'I don't like to think badly of people. I don't like to cause trouble. But she's not a good tenant and she's certainly not a good neighbour.'

'I'm sorry you've been bothered by this, Tim. I am going to deal with it.'

'But when? I don't know how long I can put up with the noise.'

It was then that they heard a dog's bark. Edward frowned. 'Is that yours?'

'I'm dog-sitting.'

The dog continued to bark and that's when Samantha's door opened and she came charging out into the hallway.

'Here – is that your dog? I'm trying to sleep in there,' she cried.

'Sleep?' Tim said. 'If you slept at night and worked during the day like a normal person, it wouldn't bother you.'

'Don't you tell me how I should live!'

'You have the nerve to complain about a little barking when you keep us all awake in the middle of the night with your racket.'

'Tim?' Abi had just entered the hallway, a big bag of shopping in her arms. 'Is there a problem?'

'I'll say there is – this woman here is causing a nuisance and should be evicted.'

Samantha gasped in horror. '*You're* the one who should be evicted with your bloody noisy dogs!' She turned to Edward while pointing an angry manicured finger at Tim. 'He's got at least five in there!'

'Five! You're taking the mickey, aren't you? I've got one dog. *One dog*! And he's barking because he doesn't like the racket *you're* making now!'

'Please – let's talk about this rationally,' Edward interrupted, his hands raised in desperation.

'Yes, I'm sure we can sort this out calmly,' Abi agreed.

'So am I – by throwing her out!' Tim suggested. 'And the sooner, the better!' He turned around, charging back to his apartment and slamming the door behind him. Samantha did the same.

Abi and Edward were left standing in the hallway together, listening to the sound of barking and Samantha's radio.

'Oh, Edward! What are we going to do?'

'I'll try talking to her.'

'But you've done that already. Don't you think it's time to take action?'

'You mean give her her notice?'

Abi nodded and Edward ran a hand through his hair.

'This isn't exactly the Winfield we envisaged, is it?' Abi said.

'No,' he agreed. 'I have to say it's been a little spoiled.'

It was agreed that Abigail would have a little word with Tim to see just what the situation was with the dogs, and Edward would speak to Samantha again, impressing on her the imperative for peace and quiet at Winfield and mentioning that she was clearly in breach of her tenancy agreement. It was all very stressful and Edward was beginning to wonder why they'd decided to let apartments at all, but then he remembered the crippling bills he'd been faced with for the repairs to the hall. He also thought about Harry and Aura and how delightful they were as tenants. Well, he owed it to them as well as to himself and Abi to sort this mess out and so he strode across the hallway and knocked on Samantha's door.

But it wasn't Samantha who opened the door. A tall, butch guy with tattoos covering his bare arms glowered at Edward.

'Yeah?'

'I'd like to speak to Samantha please.'

'She's in bed.'

There was a radio blasting somewhere in the apartment and Edward found it hard to believe that somebody was really able to sleep with that noise. But then again, maybe the guy was telling the truth.

Edward took a deep breath. 'It's important.'

'So's sleep,' the big guy stated.

Edward was at a loss. He hated confrontation at the best of times and decided that now wasn't the time to get into one with a man who looked like an action movie heavy.

'Please tell her to call round at her earliest convenience.'

'Earliest convenience,' the guy mimicked before closing the door on Edward.

Edward closed his eyes for a moment, willing himself to be calm, but he was boiling with rage inside. Just who was this guy? Was he living there with Samantha? Come to think of it, Edward had seen a few people coming and going, but he'd assumed they were just visiting. Partying. But this raised questions now. This guy looked... comfortable. Edward had briefly caught a glimpse into the living room and it was a mess of pizza boxes, empty beer bottles and unwashed mugs. It was the sort of mess one person could possibly make as his own father certainly could, but it was more likely made by two.

Edward returned to his apartment and only hoped that Abi would get on better with Tim than he had with Samantha.

He'd just put the kettle on when his phone rang. Oscar's mobile number came up.

'What is it Oscar?' Edward was in no mood to speak to his younger brother. There was no reply. 'Oscar?'

He heard a sob.

'Oscar? What's going on?'

'Dad!'

That word struck icy fear into Edward's heart.

'What's happened?'

'He's in hospital. He collapsed at home. I found him on the floor.'

Well, there wasn't anything unusual in that, Edward thought, but it had never been serious.

'Where are you?' he asked.

'I'm at the hospital. Can you come?'

'I'm on my way.'

Edward grabbed his car keys and left the hall, driving as fast as was safe while his head spun with different scenarios. Oscar hadn't said how serious it was, but it didn't sound good. He thought about ringing his brother back to try and get more information, but he guessed he'd find out what was happening soon enough.

When he reached the hospital, he found Oscar in a crumpled heap in a hospital chair in a corridor. His face was ashen and his eyes were red. He stood up when he spotted Edward.

'He's gone, Ed. He's dead!'

Edward felt as if the world had stopped for a second. His sense of hearing seemed to be at fault and everything sounded as if it was underwater.

'What?'

'Dad – he died just after I called you.' Oscar wiped his eyes on an already sodden sleeve.

'Where is he?'

Oscar motioned to a door.

Edward swallowed hard. 'Have you seen him?'

Oscar nodded. 'I was with him. He just slipped away. He didn't wake up again.'

Edward hovered outside the door. He wasn't sure he wanted to see his father. The image of him alive was bad enough. He didn't think he wanted the image of his dead father haunting him too.

'Aren't you going in?' Oscar asked with a sniff.

'I don't know.'

'He looks... peaceful, but he's a mess. I tried to brush his hair.' Tears welled up in Oscar's eyes again and Edward couldn't help feeling sorry for him. For all his faults, Oscar had loved their father. Not that their father had deserved such devotion, but Oscar had given it all the same.

'What do you think it was – a heart attack?' Oscar asked.

'I'm putting my money on liver disease,' Edward said.

Oscar frowned. 'Really?'

'Oscar, he'd been self-destructing all his life.'

'What – the drink?'

'Yes, the drink!' Edward snapped and then felt bad. 'Sorry.'

Oscar nodded and gave a gargantuan sniff.

To be honest, Edward was surprised this hadn't happened sooner. Derek Townsend had destroyed his own body through years of drinking, smoking and an unhealthy diet. It was incredible that he'd lasted so long.

'Where was he when you found him?'

'On the living room floor. The TV was blaring as usual.'

Edward could easily picture the scene. 'Did a neighbour ring you?'

'No. I was going round with some beers.'

Edward sighed.

'I know what you're thinking, but it's what he loved. I was doing him a favour.'

'You were enabling him.'

Oscar cursed. 'Yeah? Well, it's what he wanted.'

There was no arguing with that.

'Listen, do you want a ride anywhere?' Edward asked, but Oscar shook his head.

'I'm going to stay with him a while.'

'I'll pop round to the house then,' Edward said. 'Clean it up.'

'It's a bloody mess,' Oscar warned.

'I'm used to that by now.'

Edward left the hospital. He drove straight to his father's home, letting himself in with his key. As Oscar had said, it was in a pretty bad state with all the usual cans, bottles and fast food boxes strewn across the place. Edward went straight through to the kitchen and pulled a bin bag out from the cupboard under the sink and started work. His mind was still reeling with the news. His father was gone. Dead. Finally, the old man had drunk himself into oblivion. And how did Edward feel about it? He wasn't sure. He felt numb, cold, angry and fearful. Yes, although he hated to admit it, he suddenly felt very scared because his father's passing marked the end of something – a barrier – a generation gone. Now, it was just him and Oscar left of their small Townsend family, and that was sad no matter which way you looked at it.

Edward continued to tidy, filling bag after bag of rubbish. He then set to work on the kitchen wiping down all the sticky surfaces and mopping the floor. Then he went upstairs with another bin bag, emptying the bathroom cabinet of old toiletries and flinging in the rock-hard towel and bath mat too. He'd leave the bedroom for another day. He wasn't sure he could face it. Perhaps Oscar could do it. He didn't suppose there was much in the way of clothes or possessions to sort out. His father was many things, but he wasn't a hoarder.

After disposing of the rubbish and washing his hands for a good five minutes, Edward left the house, sitting in his car to gather his thoughts before starting the engine. He almost jumped out of his skin when someone tapped on his window. It was one of his father's neighbours, Mr Howard. He'd occasionally rung about the noise, threatening to call the police.

'I saw an ambulance,' he said without preamble as soon as Edward had lowered his window down.

'Yes. My father died earlier today.'

Mr Howard harrumphed. 'Well, I'm sorry to hear that, but I won't miss the noise,' he told Edward. 'Or the mess.'

No, Edward thought to himself as he pulled away. *Neither will I.*

CHAPTER TEN

Aura was sitting by the French door, holding a labradorite crystal palm stone, turning it to catch the light and gazing into the flashes of blues, purples and pinks which the stone gave her. It was like holding a little light show in her hand and helped to calm her down after a particularly stressful session with a client who was going through a nasty divorce and had expected to find permanent inner calm and a solution to all her problems during her forty-minute session with Aura. Aura had done her best, of course, and the woman had finished her session with a smile on her face, so Aura hoped she'd helped to ease the woman's troubles if only in a small way, giving her a brief respite from her stress.

And now Aura was feeling stressed. Well, perhaps *stressed* was too strong a word. Anxious maybe. For she had a lunch date with Maria Freeman. It was silly really, but Aura couldn't help feeling a little nervous at meeting up with Maria in town. Perhaps it was because she'd be with her on her own. Harry wouldn't be there and neither would Leonard – both whom were firm champions of hers. Of course, Maria adored her too, but it hadn't always been the case and Aura sometimes worried that there might be an inkling of that feeling left in Harry's mother – that little niggle of disapproval at Harry's choice and the thought that he could have done better for himself with a truly accomplished career woman. But Aura put it to the back of her mind. After all, *she* was the one Harry wanted to spend the rest of his life with.

So she met up with Maria and, after lunch in a café in town, Aura and Maria hit the shops to look for a wedding dress.

'I don't want anything too fancy or fussy,' Aura declared, deciding to take charge early on just in case Harry's mother was one of those pushy women who liked nothing more than to micromanage every single detail of somebody else's wedding.

'Understood.'

'And nothing remotely meringue-like,' Aura added.

'Absolutely not!'

They began in a bridal shop, but it soon became obvious that everything was far too traditional and white. To say nothing of expensive. Aura was a little embarrassed as her budget was limited and, even though Harry had told her his parents wanted to contribute towards paying for the big day, she didn't want to spend a fortune. Aura left the shop feeling very disappointed.

'There's another one in town,' Maria told her and they had better luck there, with Aura trying on two dresses. One was a beautiful medieval style dress with long, tapered sleeves which she adored, and the other was a figure-hugging beauty with a sheen like moonlight. But they just felt too white.

'I'm not sure they're me,' she whispered to Maria as she came out of the changing room in her own rainbow-inspired dress.

Maria nodded. 'I know what you mean.'

'And I'm not sure they're really suitable for a registry office.'

'Aura – you can wear what you want. Just because you're not marrying in a church or a castle or somewhere like that, doesn't mean you have to wear a dull suit.'

'Oh, you'll never catch me in a dull suit,' Aura said, 'least of all on my wedding day.'

Maria smiled. 'What shall we do then?'

Aura thought for a moment. 'There's a vintage shop we could try.'

Maria blinked. 'Vintage – like *secondhand*?'

'Of course.' Aura saw Maria's look of disappointment and immediately realised that this was someone who'd never bought secondhand in her life. 'You'd be amazed at what you find in these places and I'll feel much more at home.'

Maria gave a guarded nod. 'Well, let's give it a go.'

It didn't take long to reach the shop Aura had in mind. It was one of her favourite places stuffed full of quirky hats, oversized belts, long bead necklaces and, of course, rail upon rail of vintage clothes.

'Well I never!' Maria exclaimed.

'Isn't it wonderful? I've found so many treasures here.' Aura watched as Maria walked slowly along the rails, her hands tentatively reaching out towards the clothes as if she was fearful of touching them. Aura was much less cautious, plunging in and pulling out. Velvets, cottons, satins and lace – nothing was written off or counted out at this stage. She wanted to see everything.

'Have you decided on a colour?' Maria asked.

'No. I thought that might be too restrictive. I'd rather wait and see what appeals. I'm hoping something will just leap out and be – well – right.'

Maria pulled out a velvet dress. 'Too red?'

'It's lovely. Very Pre-Raphaelite,' Aura said, 'but maybe a bit heavy for summer.'

'This?' Maria held out a creamy lace dress.'

'Isn't that a little too low cut?'

Maria looked again and blushed. 'Yes indeed! Maybe better for the honeymoon.'

It was Aura's turn to blush.

'Have you discussed a honeymoon yet?'

'No, we haven't,' Aura said. 'Where did you go?'

Maria smiled. 'Leonard surprised me with a trip to Italy. We stayed in a villa on the Amalfi coast, high above the sea. I can still smell the earth and those wonderful lemon groves.'

'Sounds magical.'

'It was and what was even more magical was that we simply drifted through it all. Now, I'm one for a timetable. I like to know what I'm doing and where I'm going, and holidays can often be stressful for someone like me because I want to make sure I don't miss anything. But that time we had in Amalfi, we walked and ate and slept and swam. We were just… together.'

Aura's eyes misted over at the beauty of her words. She'd never heard Maria speak that way before and it touched Aura that there was this poetry locked away inside her future mother-in-law.

'Maybe Harry and I should go there too,' Aura said suddenly.

Maria gasped. 'What a wonderful idea!'

'Or would that be odd?'

'You wouldn't have to stay in the same place as us,' Maria suggested.

'No,' Aura said. 'We could find somewhere else, I'm sure.'

They went back to searching for clothes. Aura soon amassed a heap of dresses that looked promising and took them to the changing room. The first – a simple cotton dress festooned with flowers – was, perhaps, a little too simple. It was more like something she'd wear to one of their picnics on the downs rather than a wedding dress. Still, she put it to one side because she wanted to buy it anyway. The second was a satiny fabric that clung to her body like a second skin. Aura decided that there was far too much of her on display in that dress and so put it back. There were a few others from her initial selection that she decided not to try on. One was too scratchy. One needed a few fiddly repairs and another was much too long. But the third dress she tried on was very promising indeed. It was full-length, sky-blue lace with long sleeves and a sweetheart neckline. The shade of blue was one of her favourites. It was the colour of summer, she thought, and it reminded her of the long days that the season gave them.

She drew back the curtain of the changing room.

'Maria! What do you think?'

Maria had been looking at a pie-crust collar blouse from the nineteen-eighties and turned around to look at Aura.

'Oh!' Her hands flew to her face. 'Aura! It's beautiful!'

'Yes?'

Maria nodded. 'It's like a piece of fallen sky!' She stepped forward, standing behind Aura as she looked in the mirror again. 'Harry will love it.'

'Do you think?'

'Have you any doubt?'

Aura shook her head. 'No. I think this is the one.'

The two women smiled at one another in the mirror.

'It's perfect for you.'

After that, Aura got changed and took the two dresses she'd found to the till. But she couldn't resist one last look around the shop, and reached a hand into a crowded rail and pulled out another dress.

'Maria – look at this!'

Maria turned to look at the floral dress. 'Nice.'

'It's cut on the bias so has a lovely swing – look!'

Maria, who'd turned away, looked again, her hand reaching out this time. 'It's a good fabric too.'

'And pretty colours – your colours, I'd say.' Aura held the dress up to Maria and the deep pink really did suit her colouring. 'You should try it on.'

'Oh, no!'

'Go on. I'd love to see you in it and it's only fair as I've tried so many on today.'

Maria seemed to consider this for a moment. 'Well, all right then. Just this one.' She took herself off to the changing room and came out a few minutes later.

Aura smiled. 'It really suits you.'

'Really?' Maria looked at herself in the mirror again and seemed genuinely surprised by what she saw.

'You should definitely get that.'

Maria didn't look so sure. 'But the deep pink's so different from your sky-blue.'

'Does that matter?'

'You don't think it does?'

'Not at all. I love all colours together all the time. I don't see why we should always be trying to match things and blend in. I think they'll look striking together – like one of those late summer night sky's that's both blue and pink at the same time.'

Maria nodded slowly, as if trying to imagine that very thing. 'Okay, I'll get it!'

'Good!'

A few minutes later, clothes bought and folded neatly into paper bags, they stood outside in the sunshine.

'Aura, my dear! You were right! Your dress is truly, *truly* you! And mine is so pretty too. I'm sure Leonard will be delighted with it. I'd never have thought to come here.'

'I was hoping you'd like it.'

'I do. It might just be my new favourite shop.'

'And you'll be the envy of all your friends when they ask you where you bought your dress because they won't be able to copy you.'

'That's right!'

'Secondhand and vintage really is special.'

They walked further down the street together and then Maria stopped.

'Aura?'

'Yes?'

'There's something that's been playing on my mind.'

Aura swallowed hard for there was still a part of her that was nervous around Maria, as if waiting for her to voice disapproval about her.

'What is it?' Aura dared to ask.

Maria took a deep breath, suddenly looking anxious. 'When I think of what I said and how I treated you – when Harry first brought you to meet us – I'm truly appalled and so embarrassed. Can you ever forgive me?'

Aura saw tears sparkling in Maria's eyes and so she did the only thing she could think to do and wrapped her arms around her.

'Oh, my dear!' Maria said.

'We're friends now. The very best of friends,' Aura told her as she took a step back.

Maria wiped her eyes and gave a polite little sniff. 'I've been thinking. There's something I'd like to do – my way of saying sorry, if you like.'

'Really, Maria – you don't need to do anything.'

'No, no! Hear me out. I want to book you your honeymoon – your Italian honeymoon. Will you let me do that?'

Aura's mouth dropped open. 'I couldn't. We couldn't! I mean, you're already contributing to the wedding.'

'Oh, but I've got my heart set on it now. Just think of it – sun, sea and lemon groves! And just you and Harry soaking it all up together!'

Aura smiled. It was hard not to when Maria painted such a picture.

'Say yes!' Maria persisted.

Aura bit her lip. 'Okay – yes!'

Maria gave a little squeal of excitement and the two women embraced, and Aura felt so lucky that she was being welcomed into such a wonderful new family.

CHAPTER ELEVEN

Edward's life was a blur of awfulness. Since his father's death, he'd had to make an endless stream of calls to sort things out. Luckily, his mother had made this whole process easier during her lifetime. She'd inherited money from her father and had been able to pay the mortgage off on the modest family home, and had arranged for wills to be drawn up for her and Derek. Knowing the character of her husband, their wills were pretty watertight – while he could live in the home they owned, he wasn't able to sell it. That might seem tough to some, but Derek Townsend had no ambitions in life to go anywhere or do anything and Linda was obviously aware that, if he held the power, he'd sell the house in a blink of an eye and drink the profits. She'd also appointed a family friend as executor for them both. Margaret Hunter was a no-nonsense sort of person and Edward felt he was in safe hands which, at least, took some of the stress away from the whole business.

As Oscar was a wretched heap of emotions, it fell to Edward and Margaret to liaise with the funeral home and organise things for the impending day. She suggested putting a notice in the local paper, but Edward didn't like the idea. He knew that Abi read it and had a feeling the name Townsend might leap out at her and lead to a slew of questions he wasn't ready to answer.

Abi. Edward sighed as he thought about her. As far as she was concerned, Derek Townsend was long dead already. Edward had really dug a hole for himself there, he thought, groaning at the unintentional pun. Actually, digging a hole for the old man was off the cards seeing as the will specified cremation. And thank goodness for that. Edward couldn't bear the thought of having to watch a coffin being lowered into the ground.

So many dark thoughts crowded his mind whenever he thought about his father's passing. The most pressing one was what a waste of life it had been. His father had led such a small, insular existence especially since retiring. His whole world had consisted of his living room and the local pub. He didn't go anywhere else, he didn't meet new people or show an interest in the world at large. The only things he knew about other people were from the blaring television programmes he watched.

Edward sometimes wondered what life might have been like. It was a ridiculous waste of time to speculate on such things, of course, but his mind often drifted in different directions, imagining other lives they all might have led if his father hadn't spent his life with his nose in a pint glass. What might it have been like to have a father who actually took an interest in what he did – asked his thoughts and opinions on things, debated with him, gave him advice? Edward would have welcomed that. But no. His father had never shown any interest in Edward. At least, not since he'd started to question his father's behaviour. That had been from around the age of eight, Edward thought, remembering a time he'd dared to mention the drinking issue during a Sunday meal. His father had practically filled the table with beer cans, crowding out the plates of food his mother had prepared for them, and belching loudly over the candles she'd lit.

'Why do you drink so much, Dad?' Edward had asked with the unencumbered clarity of a child. His father's face had heated up alarmingly.

'*What?*' he'd bellowed, thumping his fist on the table and making the redcurrant jelly jump in its little china dish. Edward could still see the scene now, still *feel* it. His mother had told him not to question his father, but Edward couldn't help it. He went on questioning him, year after year, amazed that his father never changed his ways when they were obviously so abhorrent to those around him. But it soon became apparent to the young Edward that his father's behaviour was ingrained. He was never going to change.

And he never did, Edward thought now, replying to an email from the funeral director, confirming a non-religious ceremony and booking their celebrant. So many decisions – big life decisions – had to be made quickly at the moment, and it had fallen to Edward as Oscar was pretty hopeless, dissolving into tears whenever Edward managed to get him to answer his phone.

'You do it,' Oscar would tell him.

Edward had tentatively asked if Oscar wanted to say a few words at the funeral, but he'd baulked at the idea.

'You do it,' he'd said again.

'And what the hell would I say?' Edward had asked. 'The old man hated me. Do you want me to stand in front of people and say that?'

'I guess not.'

'We'll leave this celebrant guy to do his thing, okay? I want to get in and out of there as quickly as possible.' He knew this confession made him sound heartless, but he was fast losing patience with Oscar.

His brother had texted him earlier today.

What do we do with the house?

Edward had replied. *Get a clearance company and then get it deep cleaned by professionals.*

That wasn't what Oscar had meant so he'd rung Edward.

'I want to live there.'

'Well, I don't see why you can't for the time being,' Edward acquiesced. 'It'll be better to have someone there for security. But I guess we'll have to sell it. The will leaves it to both of us.'

'But you've got Winfield.'

Edward closed his eyes now. Of course, Oscar thought he had the right to inherit a whole house because Edward already owned one. The fact that Oscar hadn't had a full month's employment in his whole life, hadn't saved any money, had got himself into debt and hadn't planned for his future didn't count. As far as he was concerned, the family home belonged to him. Edward hung up on him in the end. The will was clear. He'd let the executor and solicitor sort things out.

He was just about to make himself a strong coffee when there was a knock at his door.

It was Abi. She looked pretty in a pale pink summer dress, a fabric belt tied at its waist. Her fair hair was loose and looked slightly flyaway today. What a vision she was to his addled brain.

'Oh,' she said, looking closely at him. 'Is this a bad time?'

'No.'

'Only you look – I don't know – sad.'

'Do I?'

'Or confused. Or tired, perhaps.'

'Tick yes to all three.'

'Oh, Edward! What's going on?'

'Just – you know – business,' he said, skating over the fact that it was family business.

'Well, I was thinking,' she began, 'we've not had a swim for a while, have we?'

'No, we haven't.'

'And it's summer and the sun is shining and – well, time's precious, isn't it? Especially at this time of year.'

'You're right,' he agreed, swallowing hard at the thought of all he was keeping from her. 'When were you thinking of going?'

Abi peered behind him, her gaze venturing right out through his windows to the sky beyond.

'Why not now?'

Edward laughed almost as a reflex. He was not a spontaneous person. He liked to plan things, to write them in his diary and have time to think about them. But then he thought about the way he'd been feeling all day and how he'd been unable to shake that melancholy until he'd seen Abi in her pink dress. Sure, he could hang around his apartment for the rest of the day doing his best to get some work done while thinking about the impending funeral. Or he could go swimming with Abi.

'Give me five minutes,' he told her.

Abi grinned. 'I'll give you two! See you outside.'

Abi had spent the morning pacing up and down her living room. She'd been restless ever since Ronnie had suggested that she should be the one to tell Edward how she felt. She'd seen it as a non-starter at first, shunning the idea completely in case she embarrassed herself but, the more she thought about it, the more sense it made. She felt sure – well, as sure as she could be – that Edward had been trying to express his feelings towards her that evening in the walled garden, but had been rudely interrupted by the noise from Samantha's. And Abi wondered just how long it was that he'd been building up the courage to say something. Well, it was time to find out, one way or another, if he did have feelings for her. Not that Abi was going to ask him outright. She wasn't going to prise a confession out of him. That wasn't what this was about at all. But she did want to tell him how she felt. It was time. No more skirting over the surface of things, she told herself. Whichever way it went, however it turned out, she would speak the true feelings of her heart.

Abi drove for a change and Edward appreciated the chance to let his mind wander. It had been a ghastly day following a week of ghastly days and he couldn't see an end of them until at least the funeral was over and done with. No doubt the solicitor and probate would take an age to get through and the threat of Oscar staking a claim on the family home would be stressful. Perhaps Edward shouldn't have given him permission to stay there. Well, he wasn't going to think about that now. Abi was telling him about her plans for some jewellery designs and he was fascinated to hear about her new venture.

'I got introduced to a jeweller recently and she looked me up and loved my work and wondered if we could work on something together.'

'That's really exciting.'

'It is, isn't it? Don't you just love how life can surprise you?'

Edward nearly choked, thinking that not all surprises were good, alas.

They drove through the Sussex countryside, the sun bright and high. Edward was surprised when, a few minutes later, they parked in the lane by the footpath that led to his favourite stretch of river.

'When you suggested a swim, I thought you'd head to the coast,' he confessed now.

'Too busy. Too crowded.'

Edward nodded. He favoured the solitude of the river too.

'And this was where we had our first swim together, wasn't it?' Abi said. 'It'll always be special because of that.' She smiled at him and he found himself smiling back, remembering Abi's hesitancy at getting in the water that day.

There was no such hesitancy today, however. The sunshine bathed the river in light and made it far easier to get in. Abi took the lead, slipping herself down the bank onto a small sandy shore and walking into the river with only the tiniest of squeals as the water embraced her bare limbs. Edward followed, taking deep breaths to relax himself and acclimatise. He hadn't realised how much he'd needed this release today. If Abi hadn't called, he'd have continued to tie himself up in emotional knots and probably given himself a headache into the bargain. He was glad Abi had broken that cycle. He watched her now as she swam out into the centre of the river, her strokes gentle but strong, her face full of sunlight and joy as she took in the beauty of her surroundings. Life at river level, the trees towering above them, casting their shade across the water and dappling their bare limbs.

They swam in silence for a few blissful moments. There was no need for words. The river did the talking for them with a moorhen scuttling across the water with a harsh cry, and swifts screeching overhead. It was nice not to talk, Edward thought. So many of his recent days were a jumble of words that only seemed to get him into trouble. Words, sometimes, could be a hindrance. That's what he thought anyway – that's where his mind was at. And so he took in the calm, blue beauty of the river and the sky without the need to describe them. He simply imbibed them. Then, when it was time to climb back out onto the river bank, he smiled at Abi and she smiled back, and they sat in companionable silence, watching the river flow by them on its journey to the sea.

It was Abi who spoke first.

'Feeling better?'

Edward nodded. 'You've no idea how...' he stopped. He was giving too much away or was in danger of doing so.

'How what?' Abi asked him gently.

He shook his head. 'Just how much this means. Coming here now. It's just what I needed.'

'You know you can tell me anything,' she said gently.

'I know.'

'Something's wrong, isn't it? Is it Oscar?'

'It involves him.'

Abi sighed. 'I hope he's not in trouble again, is he?'

'No. It's just... family stuff. Don't worry about it.'

Abi leaned back, tilting her head to the sky. Edward watched her, envying her clear gaze which seemed so content with life, so unclouded by the misery he was having to wade through at the moment. And, as he watched, her gaze moved from the sky to his face and she smiled that bewitchingly beautiful smile of hers and, almost imperceptibly, she moved towards him as if getting closer to him was the most natural thing in the world to do.

And then she kissed him. Fully, warmly, passionately.

Edward didn't feel the surprise he perhaps should have. Maybe it was because this kiss was so longed for that anything resembling surprise or protest had no place there. So he wrapped his arms around Abi and pulled her closer and their bare limbs, cooled by the river and warmed by the sun, entwined, and it felt so good.

'Abi!' Edward exclaimed when they finally broke apart.

She laughed, holding his gaze so confidently. Her face was the blush of a perfect pink rose and he reached a hand up to stroke her hair which had dried into fantastic corkscrew curls after their swim.

'I wanted to tell you how I feel about you, but it seemed better to show you instead,' she told him.

'I've been wanting to kiss you for a long time,' he confessed at last.

'I did wonder,' she said, her smile one of brightness and amusement.

'And I don't know why I haven't. I've tried to tell you too.'

Abi nodded, as if she knew.

'I've tried to tell you how I feel,' he went on. 'How much you mean to me.'

'And you to me,' Abi said.

'I love you, Abi!'

'Oh, Edward – I love you too – so much!'

They kissed again. It was gentler this time – a kiss full of the promises of a future full of *I love yous*.

'I can't believe you beat me to it,' Edward said a moment later.

'It doesn't matter who made the first move – not to me,' Abi said.

'Yes. But I wish I'd said something – so long ago.'

Abi shook her head. 'We're here *now*, aren't we?'

They lay back in the grass, their fingers laced together. Abi rested her head on his chest and it felt oh so right. He didn't want to move – ever. He wondered how long they could stay there on the river bank, snuggled next to one another. Nobody knew they were there. Nothing could touch them. They were safe, happy and together.

'Edward?' Abi said after several blissful minutes of just cuddling and kissing.

'Yes?'

'I hope what happened with me and Oscar doesn't make you feel, well, uncomfortable.'

He shook his head. 'It's all in the past.'

'Yes. Absolutely.' Abi sat up a little, resting on her elbows so she could see Edward's face as she spoke to him. 'And, just so you know – we were never... close.'

Edward leaned up to kiss her cheek. 'You know, I wanted to tell you – I was *trying* to tell you – before Oscar came onto the scene. But he, well, he's got more...' He paused, as if searching for the right word.

'Confidence? Cheek? Chutzpah?'

Edward grinned. 'Yes! *All* of those! Anyway, he charmed you before I had a chance.'

'But you can only get so far on charm, can't you? It doesn't last, does it?'

'I don't think Oscar's kind does, no.' Edward sighed. Even here on their sacred river bank, it was impossible to get away from Oscar.

They both sat up, shoulder to shoulder now, gazing ahead at the river.

'It's sad. The tension between you and Oscar,' Abi said.

'It is what it is,' Edward said with a shrug. 'Nobody's life is perfect, I guess.'

'I know. Well, you know how tricky things are with my sister, don't you? Families can be difficult, can't they? I think that's why it's especially important to make our lives as beautiful as possible, and to grab days like this with both hands – to be in charge, or at least to feel in charge, even if it's just for a few hours.' She laughed. She was looking at him directly now, her eyes full of emotion and sincerity. 'I'm so glad I found you. And Winfield.'

'I'm pretty glad too. More than you'll ever know.'

'Thank goodness for that auction!' Abi joked.

'Yes! And for Winfield being the wreck it was and for me losing my job. They seemed like devastating setbacks at the time, but they were leading me to you.'

They kissed again, hugging each other closer together, their bare skin soft and warm.

'We're still wearing our swimming costumes,' Edward said at last.

'I know,' Abi said, giving him a look that was all invitation.

'Abi...?'

She nodded. 'Nobody will see us here.'

CHAPTER TWELVE

Being in love was wonderful at any time of the year, but being in love in the summer – and an English summer where the sun blesses you with warmth and light each and every day – that was a magical experience.

Abi was sitting in the walled garden, sketching her beloved sunflowers. It was the day after the swim in the river and the memory of it curved her lips into a smile. The swim, the confession, the kisses – it had all been perfect. Edward had been so sweet and tender, so loving and giving, and Abi felt a deep peace within her that they'd shared that moment together and knew how they felt about one another. She'd always been happy in Edward's presence, but there'd been a kind of anxiety too in that she'd never been sure what he'd been feeling and she'd worried about crossing a line with him – trespassing into the place beyond friendship where he might not want her to be. Well, he'd obviously felt the same about Abi and so they'd been tiptoeing around one another for months. How silly that was, Abi thought now, watching as a butterfly landed on the open face of a dazzlingly white cosmos flower. People made things so complicated sometimes, denying themselves joy, hiding themselves away for fear of hurting someone or being hurt. Love could be a complicated business.

But no more. Abi and Edward were good. She'd opened her heart to him on the river bank, and he'd told her how he felt about her. There was still so much to learn about him though. She already knew a little bit about his family. Well, Oscar. It was a shame she'd never know his parents because he'd lost them years ago, but that couldn't be helped. Maybe he'd tell her more about them one day. She'd like to know. He knew about her upbringing with Aunt Claire. It would be nice if he shared more about his childhood.

'But not today,' she told the sunflowers, her pencil gliding over the page as she sketched. There was no rush to know more about the past. What was important was the present. They were good in the present.

And they were going to be together today – they'd made sure of that. Edward had told her he'd have to do a bit of fancy footwork with work, but that he could be ready for eleven that morning. So, at eleven sharp, they met at the front of Winfield. Abi was wearing a light summer dress in yellow and was carrying a denim jacket. Edward looked summery too in light trousers and a white shirt.

'So, are you going to tell me where we're going?' he asked, getting into her car.

'No. It's a surprise.'

He grinned. 'Okay. I'm not used to surprises. Nice ones, I mean.'

Abi's heart ached, glad that she'd organised this day for him. 'Well, I want to share somewhere special with you like you shared your river with me.'

'I'm looking forward to it.'

'Gosh, I hope you like it,' Abi said, suddenly nervous that her surprise might be rejected in some way. Wouldn't that be awful? To build up to something and present it as a kind of gift only for it to turn out to be something the recipient didn't like at all. She glanced at Edward. No, he'd like it. She felt pretty sure of that.

'Okay,' she said, positivity flowing through her once more. 'Let's go.'

It was just over an hour's drive from Winfield. Abi took the main roads for speed, but there were still some beautiful places and the countryside of the High Weald to enjoy as they journeyed across East Sussex.

'I still have no idea where you're taking me,' Edward said once they'd turned onto the smaller country lanes.

'You're about to find out,' she told him, pulling into their destination a few minutes later. The car park had sweeping views over the surrounding countryside and the ancient outbuildings and massive compost heap gave it all a rural feel, rather like that of a farmyard. It felt friendly and welcoming.

'Welcome to Great Dixter,' Abi said.

Edward smiled, but he looked a little nonplussed.

'You've never heard of it?'

'Erm, no.'

'Well, it's a very special garden created by Christopher Lloyd. He died a few years ago, but this garden was his life. It's quite famous.'

'You've been here before?'

'No. But I've wanted to come for years,' Abi confessed. 'I've read everything about him. He's one of life's visionaries – a creative soul with a real sense of purpose and passion. I love that. I find it so inspirational, don't you?'

As they got out of the car, Abi noticed Edward looking at his phone.

'No signal,' he said.

'Oh, dear. Is that a problem?' Abi asked.

He turned to look at her, a big smile on his face. 'No. It's a huge relief.'

Abi sighed happily. 'Good!'

They bought their tickets and entered the garden, leaving the cares of the outside world behind them and losing themselves among the flowers and foliage. As Abi had found from reading and researching, it was a garden of rooms, each with their own distinct personality. There were huge, formal borders billowing with colour, and looser areas where long grasses waved, flouting their featheriness. It was a place to wallow in – body and soul – to wander and wend – to *feel* one's way around.

Abi took endless photos and notes in a little book she was carrying with her, promising herself that the garden at Winfield would be filled with even more colour the next summer. She was inspired by the multi-coloured majesty of the snapdragons and the blowsy beauty of the poppies. It was impossible not to smile and it was even more impossible not to feel totally at peace as they walked, hand in hand, together through this paradise.

After having lunch in the grounds, they explored some more, taking their time and stopping to pause for photos and just to soak it all in. They walked through a meadow where a neatly mown path wove its way through the yellow and white flowers towards a rustic gate at the end of the garden. They leaned against it together, gazing into the fields beyond. It was a moment of peace away from the crowds in the rest of the garden and they took advantage of the brief solitude with a kiss.

'Thank you for bringing me here,' Edward said.

'Thank you for trusting me.'

They kissed again and, like the day before on the river bank, Abi wanted to stop time and linger. But another couple was approaching through the meadow, hand in hand. It was their turn to enjoy the solitude of the place, Abi thought, so she and Edward continued their walk.

Approaching the house, they discovered some shallow steps covered in tiny pink daisy-like flowers. How pretty they looked, scrambling up the steps and wall. They must grow them at Winfield, Abi thought. That was the joy of gardening. You never finished – there was always something new and exciting to discover.

'Let's sit!' she declared, sitting down on the steps. Edward joined her, picking up her hand and kissing it, then clasping it in both of his.

'You think of the loveliest things to do,' he told her.

'You think so?'

'I'd never have thought to visit a garden or to sit down on some steps.'

'Simple pleasures.'

'Yes.'

'Has it helped?' she asked.

'Helped?'

'You looked stressed before – when we were in the car.'

'Did I?'

She nodded, not wanting to pry or remind him of the outside world, but concerned for his well-being.

Edward took a deep breath. 'It's just been one of those weeks.'

'Do you want to talk about it?' she asked gently.

'No,' he said, blurting the word out so quickly that it shocked her.

She bit her lip, wishing she hadn't brought the subject up. 'Sorry,' she told him.

'No, I'm sorry, Abi. I just don't want to spoil this moment. This day. It's all so perfect – being here with you. I feel like I've run away for a few hours.'

'We should do this every day.'

'What – come here? It's a bit of a trek, isn't it?'

'No! I mean run away,' Abi said. 'Even if it's just into the walled garden at Winfield. We should make time to get away from everything and just sit and, well, not do anything.'

Edward chuckled. 'Some days don't let you escape from them, I'm afraid.'

'But you shouldn't let them rule you like that. *You* should be in charge.'

Edward squeezed her hand. 'Oh, to have that power.'

They sat for a little while longer, listening to the sound of the bees in the flowers, the sun warm on their skin.

'Why did we take so long to find each other?' Edward whispered, leaning his head towards Abi. 'I mean, this feels so good, so right, doesn't it?'

Abi smiled. 'Do you believe in fate?'

'No.'

She laughed at his bluntness. 'I'm not sure if I do or not. Sometimes, it's hard to when – well, you know what happened to me in London. But other times, it's really easy to believe that things happen because they're meant to be. Like us both falling in love with Winfield.'

'But what if *you'd* made the winning bid that day? We might never have met,' he pointed out.

'But we might have. I might have decided to do what you did when all that extra damage reared its ugly head.'

'You think we would have found our way to each other, then?' Edward asked.

'I like to think so.'

He smiled. 'So do I.'

They kissed, closing their eyes against the sun in a moment of bliss.

'I just want you to know how special you are to me,' Edward said. 'And I know I can sometimes seem a little... distant.'

'Thoughtful,' Abi corrected.

'Is that how you see me?'

'Yes. You're one of life's thinkers.'

'Well, that's a nice way of putting it. There are those that see it as inaction or procrastination.'

'You mean Oscar?'

'Yes, Oscar. And my friend Stephen. They can never understand how I take so long to weigh things up.'

'Did you weigh me up?' Abi asked, a teasing grin on her face.

'You know I did.'

'I know you did before you offered to sell half of Winfield to me, but I meant did you weigh me up before deciding you were going to tell me how you felt about me?'

He took a moment before answering. 'If I'm absolutely honest, I think I was weighing myself up more than you – you know – asking myself what it was I wanted and how my life might change – all those dull sorts of questions that prevent you from going after life spontaneously.'

'That sounds sensible to me.'

'Ah, but sensible can often stop you in your tracks.'

'But you were the one who made the winning bid on Winfield. You went after what you truly wanted then.'

He laughed. 'I think that was the single bravest moment of my life! Perhaps I was only able to do it because I had no idea of what lay ahead.'

'I guess, sometimes, you just have to leap. A bit like wild swimming.'

'Exactly.'

'You know,' Abi began, 'I think you may have a little of the introvert about you, that's all.'

'You think so?'

'Don't you?'

'I've never thought of it like that before. That word, I mean. It sounds so specific. Limiting perhaps.'

'But it's a spectrum thing, isn't it?'

'I guess.' He stared out into the garden.

'I'm one too, you know?'

'You are?'

'Most artists are, I think.'

'But I'm not an artist.'

'Maybe you're more of an artist than you think,' Abi told him. 'After all, you saw the beauty in Winfield and have restored it so perfectly.'

He leaned towards her, kissing her cheek. 'Thank you.'

'You don't need to thank me.'

'Oh, but I do! You've given me so much, Abi.'

Abi felt stunned by his praise and wasn't sure how to respond and so she kissed him, cupping his face in her hands as if she never meant to let him go.

They walked around the rest of the garden after that and then browsed around the nursery where Abi couldn't resist buying a couple of plants for Winfield. And then it was time to go.

They chatted easily and amiably as they left Great Dixter, swapping stories about their lives prior to Winfield and agreeing how lucky they felt that they not only got to call Winfield their home, but that they were able to work there too.

It was as they hit the main road that Edward's phone beeped.

'I'm afraid the signal's back,' he said.

'Anything urgent?' She glanced quickly at him, seeing a dark look cross his face as he looked down at his phone.

'Nothing that won't keep,' he said, immediately switching it off and putting it in his pocket.

It was almost with sadness that Abi pulled into the driveway of Winfield, parking outside the hall as the sun disappeared over the flank of the down. They sat for a moment without getting out of the car, as if prolonging their day for as long as they could.

'We should go in, I suppose,' Abi said at last.

Edward sighed. 'It's been a wonderful day, Abi. I don't want it to end, but...' He motioned to his phone in his lap.

'The real world strikes again.'

'Yes. Unfortunately, it does tend to follow you around,' he said.

They got out of the car and walked into the hall, Abi carrying her plants. They stopped at the foot of the stairs with Abi about to turn right and Edward left, and there they kissed.

A dog barking from Tim's apartment broke the spell and then the sound of music from Samantha's blared into the hallway.

'The real world,' Abi groaned. 'Let's run away again as soon as possible!'

Edward smiled and nodded. 'Absolutely!'

As soon as Edward was in the privacy of his apartment, he switched his phone back on. There were texts. Lots of texts. Voicemails too. All were from Oscar and, when Edward read them and listened to them, he could hear the panic in his brother's voice. The fear too.

Where was their father's body? Should they see him? Where was the funeral going to be? What should he wear because he didn't have anything. Could he borrow something?

Edward took a deep breath and answered Oscar with a single text.

Don't worry. I've arranged everything.

CHAPTER THIRTEEN

Abi sometimes resented the real world. After their trip to Great Dixter, she and Edward hadn't spent anything close to a whole day together. They'd grabbed little bits of days whenever they could – a swim here, a walk there, lunch at Edward's, supper at Abi's. It was frustrating, but Edward seemed to have a lot on. Abi had asked if there was anything she could do to help as he was always busy, but he'd simply shake his head and change the subject. It was clear he didn't want to talk about work when he was with her. Abi felt sad that she couldn't help, but maybe just being with him was help enough. She often watched him physically unfold before her eyes. He would sink into a chair and his shoulders would fall and his eyes would close for a minute or two. She'd make him a drink and try not to ask how his day was going, and he'd ask her to tell him what she'd been up to. He liked hearing about her art and looking at her projects and she loved sharing them with him.

Abi wished Edward would share more of himself with her. She couldn't help feeling that there were things he wasn't telling her. Maybe it was just work stuff, but surely that wouldn't cause Edward to look so emotionally drained all the time. He'd often talked about the joy of being self-employed and how he could choose his clients more carefully these days and coordinate his timetable. More or less. Of course, he needed to make sure he was earning enough to pay the bills and Winfield wasn't a cheap place to maintain, so that put a certain pressure on a person. But Edward was clearly overworking. Or something else was going on, Abi reasoned. Still, she didn't question him too much, hoping he'd share anything important with her.

It wasn't just Edward who concerned Abi, though. Ellen was still as tricky as ever. Abi had an appointment to see her later that day, and Ellen had actually used the word 'appointment' to book her sister in.

'It's chaos here,' she'd said, sighing dramatically down the phone. 'Douglas is away – *again* – and I've been left to cope with the builders.'

'What are they doing?'

'Tearing the bathroom apart and doing it very noisily.'

'Well, I expect that kind of thing necessitates a bit of noise,' Abi said.

'They've got a radio blaring too. They left the house the other day to get some tool or other and left the bloody thing on. It was driving me crazy for over an hour before I realised they weren't even here!'

Abi had had to stifle her laugh.

When she arrived at her sister's, Ellen was making dinner for the girls and Abi made herself a cup of tea. She offered to make Ellen one, but she shook her head. Abi watched as she buzzed around the kitchen. There was something distinctly uneasy about the way she was moving. She looked... Abi paused, trying to think of the right word for her sister. Vague. That was it –

there was something a little bit vague about Ellen. Her forehead was creased as if she was constantly trying to remember something and her movements were jerky, giving the impression that she kept changing her mind about what she was doing.

'Is there anything I can do?' Abi offered.

'No.'

'You can help me with my maths homework,' Rosie suggested, tomato sauce dripping down her chin.

'You should have finished that before dinner,' Ellen told her.

Rosie pouted. 'It's too hard.'

'Then you should have got Bethanne to help you.'

Bethanne glared at her mother. 'I had my own homework to do.'

'I'll help – after dinner,' Abi chimed in, doing her best to prevent the scene that was threatening to build.

Pugly whimpered in his corner of the kitchen.

'Don't you start!' Ellen chided.

'I'll let him out,' Abi said, opening the kitchen door into the garden. Pugly trotted out and Abi followed to keep an eye on him. A minute later, Ellen followed her into the garden, a tea towel flung over her shoulder.

'You okay?' Abi asked.

Ellen didn't answer.

'Ellen?'

'What?'

'Are you okay?'

She shrugged. 'I'm tired.'

Abi watched her carefully. 'I think it's a little more than that.'

'What do you mean?'

'Are you taking care of yourself?'

'What?'

'You know – all the things we're meant to do to stay well? Eating properly, getting enough sleep, taking time off.'

Ellen made a scoffing sound and Abi stretched a hand out towards her, squeezing her shoulder.

'I think you need to slow down. You're putting too much pressure on yourself.' Abi paused, waiting for a sharp-tongued quip from her sister – maybe some snip about Abi not knowing what real pressure was. But Ellen didn't say anything which, in some respects, felt more worrying than a put-down. Instead, Abi watched as her sister called to Pugly and went back into the house.

Abi stayed with them a little while longer, helping Rosie with the ghastly maths homework and then looking in on Bethanne in her bedroom. She was reading a book about Vincent Van Gogh.

'I'm hiding it from Mum,' she confessed to Abi. 'She thinks I'm reading about Marie Curie.'

Abi couldn't hide her smile. 'And do you like his work?'

'I love the colours and the texture of his paintings. But is it true he never sold anything in his lifetime?'

'Yes, I think that's true.'

'And he died poor?'

'Yes.'

'That's so sad.'

'It is. His work sells for millions of pounds now.'

'That's so unfair.'

'I know,' Abi said. 'Life can often be unfair, I'm afraid.'

Bethanne seemed to take this in with a small nod of her head. 'I would have bought one from him. One of his sunflower paintings.'

'And a very wise decision that would have been. One of those sold for nearly twenty-five million pounds.'

'But I wouldn't have bought it because I thought it would be worth something one day. I'd have bought it because I love it.'

'And that's exactly how art should be bought,' Abi said, bending to kiss her cheek.

'Did you start drawing sunflowers because of Van Gogh?' Bethanne asked.

'No. I drew them because they make me happy.'

'And that's how art should be,' Bethanne said, echoing Abi's own words. They exchanged a smile as if sharing a great secret.

Ellen was in the kitchen when Abi went downstairs to say goodbye. She was standing by the sink staring out into the garden, the tea towel still hanging over her shoulder.

'Ellen?' Abi approached her. 'Hey?'

Ellen jumped and turned to face her. 'You startled me.'

'You looked miles away.'

Ellen gave a wan kind of smile.

'Why don't you sit down and let me make you a cup of tea?' Abi suggested. 'We could have a chat.'

'What about?' Ellen looked concerned.

'I don't know. Something? Nothing. *Anything.*'

'I'm tired, Abi. I think I'll just tidy round for a bit.'

Abi watched as Ellen filled the washing up bowl with soapy water. As she picked up a mug from the kitchen counter, Abi noticed that her hands were shaking. It was very slight, but noticeable all the same. She watched as her sister washed the mug, placing it on a draining board a moment later, her hand still shaking. She then turned to pick up a plate.

'Let me do that,' Abi suggested. 'Ellen?'

'Just go, Abi!' Ellen cried, flinging the cloth she'd been

holding into the sink, but then she closed her eyes and sighed. 'Sorry. I'm just a bit–'

'Tired – I know,' Abi said. 'And I want to help.'

'It would help me if you go.'

They locked eyes for a moment in a kind of stalemate. Ellen looked away first, her gaze turning towards the window and the garden beyond.

Abi's mouth opened to say something, but the words dried up. The truth was, she didn't know what to say to Ellen anymore, and she was beginning to think that Douglas's suggestion for getting help for her might actually be a good one.

The end of the summer couldn't come quickly enough for Harry. He knew Aura would chide him for wishing his life away and projecting into the future when it was the present he should be making the most of, but he just couldn't help it. He couldn't wait to be married to Aura. Aura's husband. He grinned as he sat at his desk at work.

I'm going to be married, he thought to himself. *I'm going to have a wife.*

It was a very grown-up thing to do, wasn't it? And he hadn't imagined it ever really happening to him although his mother had dropped enough hints over the years. But then he'd met Aura and it seemed impossible to imagine life without her now.

They'd chatted late into the night about their plans for the wedding. Aura had recently been shopping for a dress which she refused to show to Harry even though he'd begged to see it.

'It's unlucky!' she'd protested and he'd respected her superstition. He still had to buy his outfit, and then they had to decide where to live. They knew that Winfield would remain their home, but they were still deliberating over whose apartment they'd choose. Harry adored Aura's apartment with the French doors leading out into the great expanse of walled garden. It definitely had the advantage over his with the slim bit of garden available to him. But Harry's had the all-important second bedroom. Aura was aware of that although nothing had been said about the need for extra space in the years to come. Harry had thought about it, though. He couldn't resist dreaming of filling that room with little Auras and Harrys. They'd not talked about children together – not in so many words. There'd been vague references to their future together. Family life. But it was quite enough to think about just the two of them at the present time.

Harry sent his last email of the day and switched his computer off before saying goodbye to his work colleagues and leaving the office. He then ran a few errands in town before driving out to his parents'. His mother was out, but he left a bunch of flowers he'd bought for her in the sink, running fresh, cool water over them to keep them happy.

'That you, Harry?' Leonard called through from the living room.

'Yes, Dad!'

'Good. I'd hate to have to deal with a burglar at the moment. I'm all relaxed after meditating.'

'You've been meditating?'

'Of course,' Leonard said matter-of-factly.

Harry grinned as he sat down opposite his father. 'I think I could do with a session. I've spent all day on the computer and my back's killing me.'

'Aura sent me a link to her new YouTube channel. Have you seen it?'

'I have. It's good, isn't it?'

'She has a very calming presence even when you're not in the same room as her.'

'Yes, we're hoping the channel will really take off. She's planning all sorts for it. Guided meditations as well as yoga practices, crystal therapy – even nature walks.'

'The world is lucky to have her,' Leonard said and Harry nodded, loving his father's sincerity and generosity. 'So, how are the wedding plans going? Need me to write a speech or anything?'

'Oh, no! Really – nothing like that please, Dad. We're good. It'll be a simple ceremony with the registrar and then back to Winfield for a small party with food in the garden.'

'I think your mother's taken charge of the food, hasn't she?'

'She and Aura are planning everything together, yes, but it sounds like Aura's going to do something magical in the garden.'

'And they're getting on?'

'I believe so. Aura told me the shopping trip went well.'

'Aura got your mother to buy a secondhand dress!' Leonard said, barking out a laugh.

'Erm, *vintage*, Dad! Don't let her hear you call it secondhand or she'll be billing you for a brand new one.'

'Good point, son!' They shared a knowing smile and then Leonard sighed. 'She's changed us all, hasn't she?'

'Mum?'

'No – *Aura!*'

Harry nodded. 'She really has.'

'You're a lucky man.'

'Oh, I know – believe me.'

'And your mother and I couldn't be happier to welcome her into our family – small though it is.'

A quiet moment passed between them.

'Dad?' Harry said at length. 'Did you and Mum only ever want a single child?'

His father looked surprised by the question, but then his face clouded over. 'We – erm – that is, your mother, she found it difficult to...' he stopped, puffing out his cheeks. 'She found it difficult to carry full-term. She – that is we – lost two before having you.'

Harry swallowed hard. 'I didn't know.'

'She doesn't like talking about it.'

'No. Of course not.' Harry could see how moved his father was and how difficult it was, even after all these years, for him to talk about it. 'I'm so sorry, Dad.'

Leonard nodded and then cleared his throat. 'But then we had *you*, didn't we? Mustn't complain, *eh?* All worked out?'

'I hope so!' Harry said, sniffing away the emotion that had risen. He watched as his father heaved himself out of his chair.

'Tea, I think, eh? And a nice normal tea bag while your mother's not here flinging herbs about.'

'Great,' Harry said, listening to the familiar sounds from the kitchen as Leonard made the drinks. Harry stared out of the window, but he wasn't looking at the view. He was thinking about the life that his parents had led – a life before him, with so much sadness that he hadn't even known about. Harry might have had a couple of siblings. Or maybe not. Maybe his mother would have stopped at one or two had they lived and Harry might never have been born. But Harry didn't want to ask his dad that. As Leonard had said, it had all worked out.

But it did make Harry wonder if those early losses were the reason why his mother was so fixated on Harry getting married and having children. Or maybe it was just her way. He'd met women who simply went crazy as soon as grandchildren were on the scene and, if he and Aura could give that gift to his mother, it would be wonderful.

'Here you go, son,' his father said, handing him a mug of tea which was twice as strong as Harry liked it. 'All right?'

Harry grinned. 'It's perfect, Dad.'

CHAPTER FOURTEEN

July came round so much faster than Edward had imagined it would and, suddenly, he was waking up on the morning of his father's funeral. He wasn't sure if the brilliant sunshine was a blessing or a mockery. Either way, it didn't make him feel better. The service was in the afternoon at quarter past two. A strange, in-between time, he thought. The crematorium was obviously a busy place to give such a precise time using the quarter hour. Edward has pushed for an earlier slot, but there hadn't been one available and so he had the agony of a morning to get through.

He took a shower, shaved and put on a pair of jogging pants and a T-shirt, eyeing up the clean shirt and suit he'd be wearing later. He'd dropped a suit round to Oscar the week before, telling him he'd want it back, just in case Oscar thought about trying to sell it on eBay. Oscar had taken it from him and Edward had stepped briefly into the old family home. It had felt odd to be there. The curtains were drawn tight against the summer sun which seemed a shame, but it was a lot tidier than when their father had been alive. Oscar had clearly made an effort.

Edward couldn't manage much of a lunch before the funeral and so he just had a couple of slices of toast and a cup of tea. Luckily, he hadn't changed into his suit when there was a knock on his door. It was Abi, and he was relieved not to be dressed head to toe in black. It would have necessitated another lie and he really didn't want to lie to her any more than he had to.

'Hi Edward!' she sang, her face full of enthusiasm for the summer day that was leaving Edward feeling nothing but cold.

'Hi Abi. Come in.'

She entered his apartment and they kissed, taking a moment to enjoy the physical sensation of each other.

'I thought we could go out somewhere. A walk maybe? Or, well, I was actually thinking of going to Sissinghurst. We enjoyed Great Dixter so much, didn't we? I thought we might explore a few more of the great gardens together. What do you think?'

'Oh, Abi – I'd love to, but I can't.'

'Don't tell me you're working – not on a gorgeous day like today?'

'No, I'm not working.' He sighed. 'I've got somewhere I have to be.'

'You can't get out of it?'

'Not really.' He thought of the funeral and the dark hours that lay ahead of him, and then he thought about Abi and how wonderful it would be to go walking in the sunshine with her. They'd find some shady nook and sit down together and he'd kiss her underneath the deep green leaves of the summer trees, and the rest of the world would vanish.

'That's a shame.' She glanced out of his window. 'Although it is probably a bit late for Sissinghurst now. We should really spend the whole day there.'

Edward nodded.

'Will I see you this evening?' she asked.

'I'm not sure,' he told her, thinking he'd probably be in no fit state to talk to anybody. He'd just want to come home, shut the door and close his eyes against the whole world. Even Abi. He wouldn't want her to see him like that and he wouldn't want to taint her with his misery. 'How about later in the week?'

She reached out and hugged him. 'Okay. Don't work too hard now, will you? You look as if you have been.'

He nodded and kissed her and watched as she left his apartment. As he closed the door, he couldn't help feeling that all the sunshine of the day had vanished with her. He felt awful for lying to her like that, but what could he do? Tell her that he was about to go to his father's funeral? The father Abi already thought was long dead. God, what a mess he'd got himself into. Well, he'd simply have to get through this and hope she never found out. At least his father really was dead now. Abi wouldn't know that he'd died only recently rather than years ago. Oscar wasn't likely to come round and let that particular secret out, was he? Edward just had to get through today.

There were a surprising number of people in the crematorium's chapel when Edward and Oscar arrived. Edward didn't recognise many of them, but a few had nodded at Oscar. Drinking buddies, no doubt. He and his brother made their way to the front, sitting next to one another. Oscar's right leg was jigging nervously. Edward's instinct was to reach out and place his hand on it to stop it, but that would have felt intrusive and they didn't have the closeness that would have allowed such a gesture. Still, it pained Edward to see his younger brother in such obvious distress.

The funeral was all a bit of a blur. The coffin was brought in, the celebrant said some words, some music was played – music that Edward had asked Oscar to choose, but that he didn't recognise. Were they pieces his father had loved? He didn't know. There was so much about his father that he didn't know and never would now. And so much about Edward that his father hadn't wanted to know. Father and son. It should be one of the closest relationships and yet there'd been nothing but a great chasm between them.

He was glad when the celebrant said the final words and the curtain was drawn across the coffin. Oscar sniffed loudly and wiped his nose on the back of his jacket sleeve. Or rather Edward's jacket sleeve as it wasn't actually Oscar's.

Some people hung around afterwards. There was some handshaking and some utterances. They hadn't arranged a wake and people soon drifted off.

Oscar, who looked red-eyed and pale-faced, turned to Edward. 'I need a drink,' he said, his voice a croak. 'Coming? Some of us are heading down the pub.'

So, that was in lieu of a wake, Edward thought

'No. I'm going to head home.'

'Don't be a stiff,' Oscar said and then laughed.

Edward glared at him. 'For god's sake, Oscar!'

'Sorry. Unintentional pun.'

Edward shook his head and left, eager to get as far away from the ugliness of the day as possible.

When he got home, he took his suit off and showered for the second time that day. The water felt heavenly on his body and he wondered whether to go for a swim, but it didn't seem right to go without Abi and he wasn't in the mood for her company.

So he opened the doors out into the garden and sat in his chair until it was a decent enough time to crack open a bottle of wine he'd been saving for a special occasion. He had hoped it would be shared with Abi after one of their beautiful days together, but he really felt in need of it now. He'd buy another for them some time. But, right now, his need was great and, although he hadn't the capacity for alcohol that his brother and father had shared, he was pretty intent on drinking enough to at least take the edges off the day.

The July sun was warm and the clear blue sky was dotted with clouds of the purest white. The downs were dimpled and dappled with shade. It was a beautiful day to be out among it all and Abi couldn't wait to see Ronnie and his garden. It seemed like an age since she'd last visited and she felt bad about that, but she'd been so caught up in her new romance with Edward and the inspiration she'd found for her jewellery designs. Wouldn't Ronnie be delighted when he heard her news? After all, it had been Ronnie who'd encouraged her to tell Edward how she felt, and his gift of his late wife's brooch had helped to inspire Abi in her jewellery designs. She had an awful lot to thank him for.

She took her bike today, delighting in the feel of the wind through her hair as she rode down the lanes and up the hills, crossing the downs to Ronnie's village. The sound of a lawn mower came from a garden in the village and Abi inhaled the delicious scent of the cut grass. As before, she dismounted from her bike to avoid riding into the potholes in the unmetalled road and she took a moment to take her helmet off and place it in her basket, glad to free her hair and feel the full effect of the breeze on her face.

There was a car in the lane outside Ronnie's cottage that she didn't recognise and it suddenly struck her that she knew very little about his life. He'd told her a bit about his late wife, Emma, and Abi knew he had a nephew, but was there any other family? And how about friends? Then again, Ronnie hadn't met any of Abi's friends or family. That never seemed to matter when they were together. They were enough. Although she did hope she could introduce him to Edward soon.

She opened the little wooden gate into the garden, leaned her bike against the wall of the cottage and walked down the path lined with hollyhocks, their yellow heads like glorious suns, and the scent of sweet peas drifting from deeper within the garden. She couldn't see Ronnie anywhere so knocked politely on the front door, which was open, and stepped into the hallway.

'Hello?' she called, not wanting to intrude. 'Ronnie?'

There was no reply, but she could hear the sound of footsteps on the floorboards in the front room and a man in his late-fifties appeared at the doorway a moment later.

'Can I help you?'

'Hi. I'm here to see Ronnie. I'm Abi. I live in the village across the downs.'

'You're a friend of my uncle's?'

'Yes.'

There was a pause before he said, 'I'm Kenneth. Come and have a seat.'

Abi took a seat at the table by the window. She noticed that the seed packets that usually lay scattered around the room had all been tidied away into cardboard boxes.

'I see you're having a tidy up in here,' she said with a smile.

Kenneth nodded, but didn't smile back. 'Yes.'

Abi felt a sudden chill. 'Where's Ronnie? Is he okay?' She waited as Kenneth pulled out a chair opposite her and sat down.

'I'm very sorry to have to tell you this, but my uncle died a week ago.'

Abi's mouth dropped open, but no words came out. Instead, a few painfully silent seconds passed as she closed her eyes against the world.

'Are you okay?'

She blinked and focused on Kenneth sitting opposite her. 'Are you sure?' she asked after a moment and then shook her head. 'Sorry. Of course you must be. I'm sorry.'

'It's okay. I can see it's come as a shock to you.'

'Yes. I've been meaning to call, you see. I hadn't seen him for a little while.' She could feel the sting of tears in her eyes now at the thought that she'd never see her friend again. She'd left it too late. The days had passed and Ronnie had passed with them. 'Wh-what happened?'

'He died peacefully in his sleep,' Kenneth said. 'A neighbour alerted me when she hadn't seen him. She noticed some of his plants wilting in the greenhouse and knew something must be wrong.'

Abi gave a tiny, sad smile.

'I'd spoken to him a couple of times recently and he'd seemed tired – more so than usual.'

'Yes,' Abi said, remembering the last time she'd seen Ronnie and how she'd blamed the heat of the day for his tiredness. If only she'd known. She could have done more for him – so much more.

'Did you know him well?' Kenneth asked gently.

'Well, I didn't know him very long.'

'That's not what I asked you,' he said with a little smile.

'No, it's not.' Abi took a deep breath.

'And I know my Uncle Ronnie had a knack for making friends.'

Abi nodded. 'He always made me feel so welcome here. Whenever I visited, we'd just talk and talk.'

'Ah, yes. Uncle Ronnie was good at that.'

'He really was. We used to sit in the garden together – under the apple tree. I love this garden so much. Ronnie – your uncle – taught me so much.'

'You're a gardener?'

'Well, I'm not sure I'm allowed to call myself a gardener yet, but I do love it!' She gave a nervous little laugh and then her throat felt thick with emotion.

Kenneth glanced at the boxes between them. 'Would you like these seeds? I'm not sure what to do with them all and it seems a shame to throw them out.'

'Oh, don't throw them out!' Abi cried, suddenly feeling distressed at the thought. Ronnie's seeds were his life. It would be like throwing a part of him away.

'It's okay – they're yours.'

Abi's eyes misted over. 'I'm sorry!'

'No, no – it's all right. You're all right. Here, can I get you a drink? A water or something?'

'Thank you.' Abi watched as he left and she felt the emptiness of the room, her heart breaking in the knowledge that she'd never see Ronnie in it again. They'd never sit at this table talking about seeds. Idly, her hand reached out to one of the boxes Kenneth had packed and she pulled out a packet of bright pink cosmos.

'It's a single,' Abi whispered, recognising the open flower that Ronnie favoured. 'For the bees.' Tears misted her eyes again and she glanced out of the window. What would become of the place now without Ronnie to tend it? Was Kenneth going to sell it? Would new owners love it the same way? Would they serve tea and cordial to the walkers who stopped by? Would they make jams and chutneys?

Kenneth returned with a glass of water and Abi sipped gratefully.

'I mustn't keep you,' she said.

'Really, you don't have to rush off. Take your time. I'm here all day.'

'Do you live nearby?'

'No. Cambridge. I've just come down for a few days to sort things out.'

Abi so desperately wanted to ask more. What were his plans? Would he vet new buyers if he was going to sell and make sure they'd love the place – *really* love it as Ronnie had and not rip the heart of it out and modernise it and whitewash it and tarmac the garden for their multiple cars. Abi took a deep breath. She was getting herself all worked up about something she wasn't in control of and it certainly wasn't her place to question Kenneth about his plans – if, indeed, plans were his to make.

'Did you come by car today?' he asked her.

'No. Bike.'

He glanced down at the boxes of seeds.

'I can take a few in my basket,' she told him, fearful that he wasn't going to let her take the seeds with her.

'Okay. And do you want me to keep the rest for you? Maybe I could put them in the greenhouse and you could come back for them?'

Abi nodded, wincing inwardly at the thought of seeds in a hot summer greenhouse. Ronnie would be hollering from the beyond if he knew.

'I'll pick them up as soon as I can,' she assured him.

'Good. I'm glad they're not going to waste. Uncle Ronnie would be pleased.'

Abi could feel the tears vibrating again and quickly busied herself, choosing some of the more recent packets Ronnie had obviously bought. There was the beautiful rainbow chard she'd seen growing in one of the beds and the cavolo nero, as well as his favourite tomatoes and bell peppers that had been wilting in the greenhouse and alerted the neighbour that something was wrong. Then there were the flowers – oh so many. Abi made a silent promise to each and every packet that she would grow them all, giving them their time in the light.

'Would you like me to let you know when the funeral is?'

Abi flinched. Of course there'd be a funeral. She hadn't thought. Hadn't had time to think. 'Yes – very much,' she told Kenneth.

They swapped phone numbers and then Abi left Ronnie's with a small box full of seeds which she placed in the basket of her bike. It was as she was wheeling it out into the lane that she stopped, her heart beating so fast that she thought she was about to faint. Leaning her bike against the low garden wall, she turned and ran back into the house.

'The brooches!' she cried.

Kenneth spun around from where he was standing at the dresser. 'Pardon?'

'There was a little wooden box of brooches in the dressing table upstairs. Did you find it?'

He frowned. 'Oh, yes. It went to an antiques place. It wasn't worth much. No big diamonds or anything, and they have a little jewellery counter where they sell bits like that.'

'Oh.'

'They were Aunt Emma's, but I'm afraid I've no use for them.'

'No, of course,' Abi said, feeling sad that the little collection of brooches had flown out into the world and would all probably part company.

'Were you interested in them?'

'I didn't mean to sound...' Abi stopped, feeling awkward. 'It's just that Ronnie showed them to me once. He gave me one, actually. I love it. And they were all so beautiful.'

Kenneth smiled. 'You could try the antiques centre. I'm sure they won't have sold them all yet.' He told her the name of the place and Abi instantly recognised it.

'Thank you and – well – I'm so sorry for your loss. Ronnie was a very special person and I know he's going to be missed by a lot of people.'

Kenneth came forward and shook her hand. 'Thank you. That means a lot.'

Abi left, putting her helmet on and got on her bike for the ride back to Winfield but, instead of being full of joy and lime cordial after a couple of hours with Ronnie, she felt weary and depleted.

She wasn't quite sure how she got herself back that afternoon, but she was glad to reach home, putting her bike away and carrying the precious seeds into her apartment. Her hands were shaking, she noticed, and she felt tired and numb. Her greenhouse would need watering, no doubt, and she should check on the bird bath too. She also had a couple of emails to reply to, but it would all have to wait.

Abi went upstairs to her bedroom, cool from having the curtains drawn against the summer sun, and she fell onto the bed. And then the tears came.

CHAPTER FIFTEEN

Abi returned to Ronnie's cottage the next day, picking up the seeds his nephew had left for her in the greenhouse and putting them in the boot of her car. It felt a comfort to have them – like taking Ronnie's dreams forward in time with her, giving them a life that he would never see. After shutting the boot, she paused, glancing back at the garden. The greenhouse door had been left open and it was obvious that somebody was looking after it. The little lawn had been cut too, but the tables and chairs for walkers were no longer there and the produce Ronnie had had for sale by the garden wall had been removed.

Abi looked up at the cottage, its windows unnaturally closed on this summer day, and it made her sad that she'd no longer wander through the gardens, listening to Ronnie's happy commentary on all that was growing there. And she wouldn't get to enter the cottage and inhale the wonderful smell of geraniums while Ronnie made them drinks. She glanced back at the downstairs windowsill and noticed that the plants were missing. Maybe Kenneth had taken them home or given them to neighbours. Abi hoped that they would be loved.

She got in her car, sitting for a moment, dreading pulling away for the last time, but determining that she would still cycle and walk across the downs to visit the cottage every now and then, keeping an eye on it and allowing herself the time to honour Ronnie's memory in that way.

And then she left.

The antiques centre was on the outskirts of town. Abi parked her car nearby and walked in, suddenly feeling anxious, but she knew that Ronnie would want her to have the brooches. Abi only hoped she wasn't too late.

She approached a woman behind the counter.

'Can I help you?' the woman asked, putting down a cranberry-coloured piece of glass and giving Abi her full attention.

'I hope so,' Abi said. 'I believe you bought a box of brooches recently. They were in a little wooden box.'

The woman nodded and then bent down, retrieving something from out of sight.

'I think you mean this?' the woman said.

Abi recognised the box immediately and was spun back in time to when she'd seen it at Ronnie's. He'd held it oh so gently, so beloved were the contents.

'Yes – that's it. May I look?'

'Of course,' the antique dealer said, handing the box to Abi. 'I haven't had time to put the brooches on display yet. Pretty, though, aren't they? Is there one that you have in mind?'

'Yes,' Abi said. 'I mean, all of them.'

The woman looked surprised. 'Well I haven't priced them yet.'

'What do you want for them – the box too?' Abi handed the box back and the woman started poking around, pulling out brooches and holding them up to the light.

'That's paste. And that. This one's garnet, though.'

Abi nodded.

'This is silver set with a single amethyst. And this one's pewter.'

'So, any idea how much?' Abi prompted, knowing that she was doing herself no favours by sounding so keen. The woman gave her a figure after a couple of minutes of calculating and Abi handed her debit card over. 'Did you purchase anything else from the man who sold you the brooches?'

'There was a dressing table. Nice piece from the thirties,' the woman said as she processed Abi's card.

Abi's heart leapt. 'I'd like to take a look at that please.' She glanced around the shop, hoping to see it.

'I'm afraid that's gone already. I had a client looking for one and she snapped it up as soon as I sent a photo through.'

'Oh.'

'But I do have a similar one over there with a lovely old mirror.'

Abi shook her head. She didn't want just any old dressing table – she'd wanted Emma's. Still, she took a look at it as she made her way to the door, running her fingers over the rich, dark wood and noting her pale reflection in the mottled mirror. It was a little bit bulky, but it did have a charm about it. She stood back and then she placed the box of brooches on the dressing table, marvelling how at home the box looked. Glancing at the price tag, she made her decision.

Edward had been meaning to call on Abi, he really had, but he'd been feeling exhausted since his father's funeral and had laid low, burying himself in work for a few days and making his excuses via text message. Abi had seemed placated by his apologies, telling him not to worry, but he was worried now because he hadn't seen her for a while. He usually caught sight of her in the garden, pottering about among her plants or sketching in the sunshine. He'd been so wrapped up in his own thoughts and feelings that he had, essentially, shut Abi out and now he wondered if something might be going on with her.

Without further delay, he closed his laptop and left his apartment, crossing the hall and knocking on Abi's door.

'Abi? Are you in?' he called. 'Abi? It's Edward.'

A moment later, the door opened and Abi greeted him. 'Edward? I thought you were working.'

'I have been, yes. I'm sorry I've not seen you.' He bent to kiss her. 'It's been a bit hectic.'

She nodded and he entered her apartment.

'I've not seen you in the garden as much,' he told her.

'No. I've been going out at dusk when it's cooler,' she said, 'and darker.' She rubbed her eyes and he noticed that they looked red and sore.

'Abi – what's wrong?' He reached out and touched her face and her eyes immediately filled with tears. 'Sweetheart! What is it?'

'Ronnie.'

'Your friend?'

'He died.'

'Oh, Abi! I'm so sorry.'

She gave a big sniff and quickly mopped her eyes with a tissue from her pocket. 'I miss him so much!'

'What happened?'

'I went over there a few days ago and his nephew was there. He told me Ronnie had passed in his sleep.'

'Well, at least he didn't suffer. And isn't that how we'd all like to go?' Edward said in a soft voice.

'Yes, of course, but it's just so unexpected. I know he was old and I know he was getting tired, but he had so much life in him! And he was such a good friend – not just to me, but to so many people. And I'm so mad at myself that he didn't get to meet you. I kept meaning to bring him over here so he could see the garden and you two could meet and now that will never happen. I was always putting it off. I thought we had all the time in the world, but we didn't, and now he'll never see it.' Abi let out a long sigh as if she'd been holding all these emotions in for a long time.

'But you talked to him about Winfield, didn't you?'

'Yes of course – all the time. I'd tell him what I was growing here and the progress we've made and all the plans I had.'

Edward moved closer and placed his hands on her shoulders. 'Then he saw it, Abi. He saw it in you.'

'But he'd been gone a week, Edward! How could I not have known? How could I not have *felt* that?'

'You're being much too hard on yourself. If we all lived like that – worrying about everyone else, we wouldn't take care of ourselves, would we?'

'It seems so wrong, though.'

'I know. But you can't be everything to everybody all the time, can you? You have to live your own life.'

'I just feel like I've been a really bad friend.'

Edward wrapped his arms around her, pulling her close. 'You could never be that – not to anyone. You're too damned caring.' He held her as she cried, stroking her hair and kissing her forehead. He felt so awful for locking himself away from her, shutting her out in his own misery, and having no idea what she was going through.

'Why didn't you tell me sooner?' he asked at last.

Abi leaned back a little and looked up at him. 'Because you've been so busy. I didn't want to bother you.'

'But what's my purpose if it isn't to be bothered by you when you need me most?' He put his head to one side, eliciting a smile from her. 'I can't bear the thought of you over here crying your eyes out on your own.'

'I've been okay.'

'Have you?'

She gave a sniff again. 'No! Not really. I miss him so much and I think I'm going to miss him forever. Does that sound strange?'

'Not at all.'

'I know I didn't know him for long, but he was one of the sweetest souls I've ever met. He just had this way of understanding me. I sometimes wouldn't even need to say anything – he'd just know how I was feeling.'

'He sounds like a very special man.'

'He was.' Abi sighed. '*Was*. I hate using that word! People like Ronnie should be allowed to live forever, shouldn't they? It's so unfair that he's gone. He should have had another decade at least, and now I'm worrying about his house and garden and what'll become of it.'

'Did you talk to his nephew about that?'

'No. I didn't think it was my place.'

'Well, perhaps a lovely young couple will buy it and love it just like Ronnie and his wife did. And they'll have children who will get up to all sorts of adventures in that garden.'

'Yes, perhaps.'

Edward kissed her again. 'Have you been out at all?'

'Not really. I drove over there to pick up Ronnie's seeds and then I went to this antiques place. His nephew had sold some bits and pieces. Remember the brooch Ronnie gave me? The one that you found in the garden after it was stolen?'

'Yes. It's a lovely piece.'

'Well, there were more and I was frantic when I heard Kenneth had sold them.'

'So you got them?'

'Yes. Let me show you. They're upstairs.'

Abi and Edward went up to her bedroom.

'Here!' Abi said, striding into the room and picking up the little wooden box from the dressing table. She opened it up and Edward saw the contents, sparkling prettily in the light of the room.

'They're beautiful. I'm so glad you found them.'

'I know it's a foolish thought, but I couldn't bear to think of them all being parted from one another. They're a collection, you see, brought together over years with love.' Abi picked one of the brooches out. It was made of a silver metal and set with a large blue stone that was cut in such a way that it seemed to wink at them both.

'It's lovely,' he said, watching as Abi returned it to the box. 'Abi?'

'Yes?'

'That dressing table...' he began, crossing the room and reaching out to touch the dark wood. 'Where did you get it?'

'The same antiques centre where I got the brooches.'

'On the outskirts of town?'

'Yes. Why?'

Edward turned to look at her. 'It was my mother's.'

'What?'

'This belonged to my mother.'

'You're kidding!'

'No. It's the same one with the same mottled mirror.'

'You're telling me that I bought your mother's dressing table? How has that happened? Didn't you lose your parents some time ago? Do you know what happened to the furniture? Was there a house clearance perhaps?'

Edward suddenly felt awkward and unsure of how to answer and so he kept quiet.

'I was actually looking for Ronnie's wife's dressing table, but it had been sold and the woman in the shop pointed this one out and I loved it. I think it looks absolutely perfect here, doesn't it?'

'Yes,' Edward agreed. 'I didn't think it would.'

'What do you mean?'

Edward cleared his throat. 'I mean, I wouldn't have thought to put a dark antique piece in these light rooms. But you're right – it looks very much at home.'

'I can't believe it was your mother's. Isn't that the weirdest thing?' Abi approached him and put her hand up to his shoulder. 'Would you like it?'

'What?'

'Would you like it in your apartment?'

'Oh, Abi – no!'

'Because I feel odd about having it now.'

He shook his head. 'No – you mustn't feel odd. I *love* that you have it and that it found its way to you.'

'Are you sure?'

'It was obviously meant to be.' She put her arms around him and he smelt the sweet scent of her hair under his chin.

'Edward?'

'Yes?'

'Will you come with me to Ronnie's funeral?'

'Of course I will.'

'Thank you.'

He kissed her again and they embraced.

'And don't ever think you have to hide your emotions from me, okay? If you're going through something, I want to know!' As he chided her gently, he was all too aware of the hypocrisy of his words and how he was hiding so much from Abi.

'I promise. No more hiding. We'll be absolutely open and honest with each other.'

'Yes,' he said. 'We will.'

Edward left Abi's apartment feeling rotten to his core at the truth he'd kept from her and the promise he'd made. Seeing his mother's dressing table had shaken him a little, but he genuinely loved the fact that Abi had been drawn to it. It somehow seemed to bring them closer to one another, adding a special layer to their relationship, uniting his mother with Abi as if she was somehow giving Abi her blessing from the great beyond. How he wished he could confide in Abi. But it was too late for that. It would do too much damage. She wouldn't understand why he'd lied to her in the past. She'd accuse him of being dishonest and mistrustful, and rightly so. As far as Edward was concerned, it was best to keep moving forward.

But the pain she was in. Edward hated seeing her torn up like that and yet he almost envied Abi her grief because it showed her great love and that had been the vital thing that had been missing from his relationship with his father. Abi was able to feel so much grief for someone who'd only been in her life for a short time, while Edward felt nothing but a void for someone he'd known his whole life.

No, he thought, not quite a void. It felt more like a weight that he was carrying – something deeply unpleasant which was lodged within him and going nowhere.

～

Grief was the strangest of emotions, Abi soon realised. Just when she thought she was over the worst, when she believed she'd cried as much as she possibly could, another wave would hit her. She felt exhausted by it all.

It was a couple of days after Abi had told Edward about Ronnie and she was sitting in her living room because she didn't have the energy or the heart to do anything else. She watched the sunlight on the floorboards, she listened to a skylark. Even her sunflowers were unable to bring her comfort.

It was mid-afternoon when she finally managed to shake herself into doing something and she left Winfield, heading across the downs in the hope that a walk might jolt some sort of life into her. But this wasn't one of her carefree, loose-limbed walks. Her body felt heavy and unyielding, and so she sought out the shade of a tree and lay underneath it, her limbs moulding to the hard ground, and she gazed up into its depths, believing that it had grown over the decades simply to provide her with this moment of green peace, as if it had known that it could provide that little sanctuary for somebody one day.

After a while, she sat up, gazing out across the wide landscape.

This view right here, right now, is mine and nobody else's, Abi told herself. *And I claim it.*

She took a deep breath as if to internalise it all so that the view became a part of her forever and she could draw on its beauty and its strength whenever she needed to. And, although she could see its beauty, it pained her because she knew that somebody she had loved would never see all this again.

Death was so final. There was no arguing with it.

She got up and continued her walk, thinking of Ronnie. There was so much about him she didn't know. She had so many questions she wanted to ask him now, but couldn't. Why had she spent so much of their precious time talking about herself? She should have been asking him things like... like – had he ever been to Sissinghurst? What was his favourite dessert? What were all the jobs he'd done? How did he like to eat his potatoes best? She'd never know the answers now. But did any of it matter? She couldn't tell anymore and she felt as if she was becoming obsessive, trying to remember details about their friendship. What had they talked about? What was the last thing he'd said to her?

By the time she got back to Winfield, she felt completely depleted. So much for the green therapy idea. There was no easy cure for what she was feeling. Time, perhaps. That was the old cliché, but that didn't help very much when you were stuck in the present.

CHAPTER SIXTEEN

There was a definite shadow hanging over the summer, Edward couldn't help thinking as he stepped out into the walled garden early one morning and looked up into the great weight of blue above him. The sky was clear, promising a perfect day, and yet his heart felt distinctly heavy. Abi must be feeling the same, he guessed. She'd felt the loss of her friend so deeply and it pained Edward to see her so sad. He wished there was something he could do to help.

And then he thought of something that might just be perfect. He recalled their recent visit to Great Dixter and how he'd managed to lose himself for a few blissful hours. Well, he mostly had. It was virtually impossible to shut out the real world, though. But he wanted to give that gift to Abi now. She'd mentioned Sissinghurst, hadn't she? Perhaps he could take her there for the day. He nipped back inside, opened his laptop and looked it up on line. Then again, would a trip to a garden remind her too much of Ronnie? He didn't want to take that chance.

Where else could he take her? They could go wild

swimming again, but he wanted something different – something fun, silly, all-consuming. And that's when he thought of it.

Without stopping to think or plan it out in detail as was his usual way, he left his apartment and went straight across the hallway to Abi's and, when she answered the door, he spoke before she had the chance to.

'I think you could use a day out.'

Her face, which had looked sad at first and then puzzled to see him quite so early, broke into a beautiful smile.

'I think you're right,' she replied.

Half an hour later, he was driving them away from Winfield, away from the confines of their homes and, hopefully, the confines of their heads. He was searching for that place – the one he found while swimming. That place beyond thought where you're transported to somewhere outside of yourself, and that didn't mean you had to be in nature or anywhere that was peaceful. It just had to be a place that took you away for a little while.

'Where are we going?' Abi asked him.

Edward grinned. 'It's a surprise.'

And it really was. As they approached Brighton, he could feel Abi's eyes on him.

'Brighton?'

'Yep!'

'Really?'

'Why not?'

Abi laughed. 'Why not indeed? I – well – I wouldn't have guessed. I thought you had something more... or something less... I don't know. But not Brighton!'

'Want to give it a go?' he asked, just to be sure.

'Yes! Absolutely!'

'Good.'

After parking, they visited the pier, walking under a cloud of seagulls hoping to be thrown some tasty treats by the tourists. It was a popular venue and Edward liked the smart black and white railings and the grand Victorian feel of it all. It was a bit like stepping back in time or at least it would have been if it hadn't been for all the vending machines. But that's what made it fun, and fun was exactly what he'd been hoping to find that day, although the fairground rides at the end of the pier looked like a little too much fun. Abi shook her head when he offered to take her on one.

'I'm not too keen on the whole feet leaving the ground phenomenon,' Abi confessed.

He nodded. 'Let's keep walking then.'

They strolled along the seafront eating hot, vinegary chips from a paper cone. They scrunched across the pebbly beach and skimmed stones into the waves. They went into an arcade that was loud and bright and everything they both hated – and they had a fabulous time. Edward even won a soft toy. They weren't quite sure what it was. It looked part gorilla, part teddy and it was a lurid shade of yellow.

'Sorry I didn't win you something slightly prettier,' Edward apologised, handing it to Abi. 'Maybe one of your nieces will like it?'

'You're kidding! I'm going to keep this – this – whatever it is!' She laughed and squeezed the toy tightly to her.

They walked around a few of the shops after that, browsing through things they didn't need and swapping stories and laughing. It was good to hear Abi laughing again, Edward thought.

On the way home, they stopped the car and walked up a hill overlooking the sea which was clear and bright below them. They sat on the grass and Edward drew Abi close to him.

'Thanks for today,' she whispered. 'You were right. I needed to get out.'

'Sometimes, you just have to eat chips by the sea,' he said. 'It makes everything better.'

They sat watching the sun slowly slipping towards the horizon, the colours of the sky deepening from blues to pinks and oranges. It would be easy to slip into melancholy at such a sight, Edward couldn't help thinking, making the moment mean more than it did – the end of another day, time passing, life slipping away, a scene of great beauty unseen by loved ones who had passed. Edward was all too aware that Abi was still and silent next to him and he glanced at her now. Her expression was serene and sad and he hugged her close to him.

'You okay?' he asked.

'A little cold.'

'Yes. The breeze has definitely picked up.' He stood up and offered his hand to Abi who took it, and they walked to the car together.

When they got back to Winfield, Abi invited Edward into her apartment and placed the yellow toy on her sofa.

'Cup of tea?' she asked.

'Please.'

Edward followed her into the kitchen and the two of them moved around one another quietly and happily, as if they'd been doing exactly that all their lives. It was a comfortable feeling and one which Edward knew he could quickly get used to.

Tea made, they sat on the sofa together, a small lamp on to chase away the darkening evening. The Abi of the pier and the beach and the arcade seemed to have slipped away, left behind on the cliff watching the sunset, Edward thought, and he wasn't surprised when she started to cry.

'I'm sorry,' she said. 'I don't want to spoil a lovely day.'

'It's okay, it's okay.' He put his arms around her and let her cry. He lost track of the time, but he didn't want to be anywhere else but by Abi's side.

'Edward?' she said at last.

'Yes?'

'Will you stay?'

He kissed her. 'Yes. I can do that.'

It was a sultry July morning. Abi was sitting at the table in the living room. In front of her was Emma's wooden jewellery box and, very carefully, Abi opened it, taking out each of the brooches and laying them on the table in the full light of the sun. There were fifteen in all, including the one Ronnie had given her. How very precious they were to her. She felt so lucky to have found them and to be able to give them the love and attention they deserved. She was going to sketch them all, learning about the different styles and how stones were matched to metals. Abi had always been drawn to things from the past and she hoped the brooches would inspire more designs for her modern pieces.

She picked up one shaped like a crescent moon, set with paste stones. Its pin fastener suggested that it was quite old and Abi couldn't help wondering how Emma would have worn it. There was a simple bar brooch set with a small trio of purple stones, and there were a couple of enamel flower designs that were breathtakingly beautiful. Each was so different, but Abi's favourite remained the one Ronnie had chosen for her – the gold filigree set with coloured flowers that reminded her of the downs in late spring. She was going to wear it today, pinning it to her dark dress so that she had a little piece of Ronnie close to her.

She closed the box and glanced at the clock. She'd given herself this special moment of calm and connection, but she knew it couldn't last. It was time to leave.

Edward drove them both to the village church set deep in the downs. It dated back to the thirteenth-century and sat on a small hill looking down over the village. The churchyard had been left to grow wild and was full of ox-eye daisies which made a sea of white and yellow around the gravestones. Ronnie would have loved it, Abi thought, as she gazed around in wonder.

As they walked into the cool, white-washed interior of the church, she recognised a few faces from the village – people she'd nodded to as she'd cycled to and from Ronnie's. By the number of people there, it was easy to see just how loved he had been. And there was Kenneth, Ronnie's nephew, sat in the pew at the front of the church with a woman next to him and two grown-up girls. Again, Abi felt the loss of a life that she had known so little about. Ronnie hadn't talked much about his family and Abi wondered if the two girls were his great-nieces. Had they been close? Had they visited their Great Uncle Ronnie?

Abi wasn't sure how she got through the service. There was a mix of eulogies and singing and the vicar spoke of Ronnie as a true friend – someone who would be missed by the whole community. It was all so moving. And, throughout the entire service, Edward sat next to her, holding her left hand so that her right was free in case she needed to mop her eyes or blow her nose. Which she did at frequent intervals.

It was such a comfort to have him there, his quiet presence

beside her. He hadn't even met Ronnie and yet he hadn't hesitated in being here today – for her.

As the final hymn was sung and the final words were spoken, Abi noticed the light shining through one of the stained glass windows, casting pools of red, blue and green on the floor of the aisle. It was a moment of beauty among the bleakness.

And then it was over.

It felt good to be back outside, the warmth of the sun on their faces. They walked the short distance to the village pub where the wake had been arranged, but they didn't stay long. Instead, after chatting to a few people, Abi and Edward walked the short distance to Ronnie's cottage.

'I wanted you to see it,' she told him, stopping at the garden gate which was now resolutely closed to her.

'It's lovely.'

'It's missing Ronnie. Those flowers need staking – look.' Abi felt the urge to open the gate and wander in, tidy some of the beds and check that the greenhouse and various pots were being kept watered, but she knew it wasn't her place. Not anymore.

Edward put his arm around her and squeezed her shoulder. She turned to face him.

'Thank you for coming with me today.'

He nodded and gave a small smile. It was then that Abi noticed how emotional Edward looked.

'Hey – are you okay?'

He sighed. 'I don't know. I guess it's brought back some memories for me.'

'You mean of your parents?'

He nodded. 'That eulogy the nephew gave.'

'Yes, it was moving, wasn't it?'

He took a deep breath. 'Yes.'

Abi observed the sadness in his eyes. 'Oh, Edward, I'm so sorry. Was it very long ago – the loss of your parents, I mean?'

'Not so long ago, no.'

'These things take time to process, I guess.'

'Yes.'

She turned to leave and Edward broke away from her for a moment, releasing her hand from his.

'Abi?'

'Yes?'

'It was this month.'

'What was?'

'My father's funeral.'

Abi frowned, quite sure she must have misheard him. 'What do you mean?'

Edward's eyes scanned the ground and he idly kicked at a stone. 'My mother died years ago, but my father...' His voice disappeared and Abi watched as he looked from the ground into the sky. 'My father died in June. His funeral was earlier this month.'

Abi stared at Edward in disbelief. 'But you told me–'

'I know.'

'You told me he'd died years ago.'

'Not exactly. Not specifically.'

'What do you mean, not specifically?' Abi could feel her confusion now morphing into anger.

'I didn't go into detail. I guess you filled in the gaps.'

'Edward, I don't understand.'

'I'm sorry, Abi. I didn't know how to tell you.'

'You're saying your father just died and you went to his funeral *this* month and you didn't tell me?'

'Yes.'

'Why? *Why* didn't you tell me?'

She saw Edward flinch at her words, stunned, perhaps, at her fury.

'My family... they're not easy to talk about.'

'Oh, is this about you and Oscar again?'

'No.'

'Because you lied to me about him too, didn't you? You told me you were all alone in the world – that you had no family at all. And then he turns up at Winfield.'

'I know.'

'And now you're telling me that your father was alive and well until last month and you didn't think to mention him to me?'

'I didn't have a good relationship with him.'

'But shouldn't you have at least told me the truth about him?' Abi couldn't believe that Edward wasn't understanding how she felt about all this. 'And then he dies. Your father *dies* and you don't tell me about it! You go to his funeral and I know nothing about it? How could you shut me out from something like that? I thought we were friends – *more* than friends!'

'We are, Abi!'

'I thought we were close. But you went through all this without telling me.' She stared at him. 'Was this when you were busy all the time? Oh, god, Edward – you told me it was work and I believed you. And all that time you were, well, what were you doing? Organising the funeral? I don't know because you didn't trust me enough to tell me!'

'It has nothing to do with me not trusting you.'

'You shut me out.'

'I know. I'm sorry. I'm really sorry.'

'Who's going to suddenly pop up next? Your mother?'

'No.'

'Any more brothers? Or perhaps there are a couple of sisters you haven't yet told me about or a child or two!'

'Abi – please!'

'Why didn't you tell me?' she cried.

'I'm telling you now.'

Abi shook her head. 'I told you everything about me – *everything!* And it wasn't easy! But I did it because I love you and I believe in honesty and not hiding things that are important.'

'I know. I do too.'

'How can you say that? You lied to me, Edward – over and over again – and about something so vital as family.'

Edward made a scoffing sound. 'I'm not sure I'd use the word vital to describe my family.'

'What does that mean?'

'It means that not everybody has a great relationship with their family and I don't find it easy to talk about.'

'I know that,' she told him. 'And you *know* I understand that. I've told you about my Aunt Claire, haven't I? And you know my father left when I was young. And, well, you know how tricky my sister can be.' She stopped, giving him a moment to respond, but he didn't. 'Edward – I'm really trying to understand you.'

He shrugged his shoulders in a gesture that was all awkwardness. 'I don't know what to say.'

Abi stared at him in disbelief. She couldn't help feeling deeply disappointed with him. He'd lied to her and, perhaps worse than that, he seemed to be refusing to tell her why he'd lied in the first place. She felt at a loss as how to respond to that. Standing before her was a man she no longer seemed to recognise. And so she turned away from him and started to walk up the lane.

'Let's go home, Abi. You're exhausted and emotional.'

'Don't tell me how I feel.'

'I think we should get back.' He held his hand out towards her, but she didn't take it.

'I think I'll walk.'

'Abi!'

'I need to clear my head.'

'I'm not letting you walk. You're not dressed properly. You'll break an ankle in those shoes.'

Abi glanced down at her attire and silently cursed. He was right. She'd do herself a terrible mischief if she attempted to cross the downs back to Winfield wearing what she was. So they walked back to Edward's car and she reluctantly got in.

They drove home in silence, Abi blinking back the tears, not at all sure now if she was crying over the loss of Ronnie or Edward's betrayal.

'I'm sorry, Abi. I don't know what more I can say.' Edward said as he parked a moment later.

Abi wanted to shout at him that he could tell her the truth and he could explain exactly why he'd thought it necessary to hide so much from her, but she didn't have the energy.

'I'm tired.'

He nodded. 'I know.'

'And I'm not sure I can be with someone who doesn't trust me enough to tell me the truth.'

'But I *do* trust you – that's not the issue here.'

Abi got out of the car and then turned to face him. 'Yes, but can I trust you anymore?'

'Abi – please! This isn't easy for me,' he called as she charged into the hall, going straight to her apartment. Edward was still calling her name, but she ignored him, closing her door between them. She couldn't talk to him. It was obvious they weren't able to communicate. He said he trusted her, but how could that be true? Abi had never felt so hurt.

She went upstairs to her bathroom and washed her face with cold water. Her skin was hot and her eyes stung with emotion. She looked at her reflection and winced. She looked awful which wasn't surprising really.

Abi had had some pretty tough days over the last few years, but this one was right up there with the worst of them.

CHAPTER SEVENTEEN

Aura loved working with her online clients and one of her favourites was Heather Close.

'How's the candle business going?' Aura asked her after they'd finished a meditation together.

'Really well!' Heather told her with a smile. 'I'm going to send you my 'Relax and Unwind' candle. It's lavender and jasmine essential oils. I think you'll like it.'

'It sounds heavenly,' Aura told her, looking forward to lighting it one evening, perhaps when Harry was round.

They said their goodbyes and Aura switched her laptop off. She was about to make herself a lemon and hibiscus tea when there was a gentle knock on her door.

'Abi. How lovely to see you,' she said as she opened it and saw her neighbour and landlady standing there. It felt like an age since they'd spoken properly. 'Come in. Is everything okay?'

'Everything's fine,' Abi said. 'I mean. Well...'

Aura noticed Abi's pale face and her expression which looked lost and confused at the same time.

'Come and sit down. I was just going to make some herbal tea. Would you like some?'

Abi looked as if she'd been handed a lifeline and nodded. 'Yes, that sounds wonderful.'

Aura made the tea and, a moment later, the two of them were sitting together in the living room, a warm breeze coming in from the garden.

'How are you?' Aura asked, noticing that Abi's eyes looked sore.

Abi drew in a deep breath and sighed it back out. 'Tired. I've not been sleeping properly for some time now.'

'Do you know what's causing it?'

'I have a pretty good idea.' Abi then told Aura about losing her friend Ronnie and touched briefly on the recent upset with Edward. 'I think we've broken up,' she finished.

'Oh, Abi!'

'And we'd only just got together. It took us *such* a long time to come together and yet such a short time to lose it all.'

'Are you sure it's as final as that?' Aura dared to ask.

Abi gave her a pained look which told her she didn't want to talk about it.

Then something occurred to Aura. 'Is it going to be awkward for you both with the wedding party here?'

'No! Not at all!'

'Because we can arrange something else if it is.'

'You mustn't do that! I'm really looking forward to it.'

'Oh, good,' Aura said, relieved.

'It'll be the best thing this summer.'

'Thank you for letting us use Winfield.'

'I was so thrilled when you told me it was top of your list for your wedding.'

'I can't think of anywhere nicer,' Aura said.

'And have you thought about where you'll live – after you're married?'

'We're still discussing that,' Aura admitted. 'You know how much I love my apartment, but we think it might be more practical for me to move into Harry's. Harry's asked Edward if that's okay and he's happy about it. But I'm not sure. We don't want to leave Winfield – at least not immediately, but the space has to be right for us and, well, our future.'

'You mean children?' Abi asked with a smile.

Aura beamed a smile back at her and nodded. 'We love this place, though. It's hard to imagine living anywhere else now.'

'I feel the same way,' Abi confessed and her expression changed from joy to sadness so quickly that Aura gasped.

'Are you all right?'

Abi gave a sniff and Aura could tell that she was doing her best to hold the tears back.

'I'm just thinking how awkward it's going to be with me and Edward. I think that's one of the reasons we took so long to share our feelings. We were both so aware of the implications if it didn't work out.'

'But it'll be all right, won't it? Surely you'll sort things out?'

'I don't know,' Abi told her. 'It doesn't feel very hopeful at the moment.'

'Well, I remember thinking that it wasn't going to work out for me and Harry. His mum made it very clear that she didn't think I was good enough for him and I hated coming between him and his parents like that. But cut to this summer and I'm planning the wedding with her and we're even going clothes shopping together and talking about honeymoons!'

'I'm so happy for you, Aura!'

'But that can happen for you too, Abi! I mean you don't have to get married,' Aura said, blushing, 'but things change.

Situations change. Don't write you and Edward off just yet. You're both way too good together.'

Abi gave a weak smile, but it was clear she was feeling uncomfortable.

'This is such a lovely peaceful room, Aura. I love how you've made it so relaxing. I almost don't want to leave.' She got up.

'You don't have to,' Aura told her, standing up too. 'Not yet at least. We could do a little meditation together if you like. Maybe it'll relax you and help you sleep better.'

'Really?'

'Yes. I'm just in the mood for one. It'll prepare me for my class I'm taking this afternoon.'

'Well, if you're sure it's no bother.'

'No bother at all. Where would you be most comfortable?'

Abi glanced down at the soft cushioned sofa she'd been sitting on. 'Is here okay?'

'Perfect. Why don't you lie down and pop one of those cushions under your head?'

Abi didn't need to be asked twice and Aura smiled as she watched her kicking off her sandals and making herself comfortable on the sofa.

Aura then sat opposite Abi and guided her through a series of easy breaths, slowly deepening them to induce total relaxation. She felt the breeze tickling her face and dancing through her hair as she led the session and she could smell the sweet scent of newly mown grass from the walled garden. It all helped to create a moment of serenity.

Finally, Aura took one last deep breath.

'And, when you're ready, slowly blink your eyes open and come back into the room,' she told Abi, smiling across and noticing that Abi's eyes were still closed. 'Just blink your eyes open when you're ready,' Aura repeated. But Abi's eyes remained shut. 'Abi?'

Aura stood up and tiptoed towards the sofa and smiled as she gazed down at her exhausted friend.

She was fast asleep.

'So, they *were* together, but now they're not?' Harry asked Aura as they spooned heaps of spaghetti onto their plates in Harry's kitchen.

'That's what Abi told me.'

'When did all this happen?'

'Recently.'

'I had no idea,' Harry said. 'Mind you, I've been caught up with you and the wedding.'

'Yes, weddings do kind of blinker a person.'

They paused what they were doing and shared a kiss over the spaghetti pan.

'Poor Edward,' Harry said when they parted.

'Poor Abi. She was really sad and exhausted. She's just lost a friend as well. She's really going through it. She fell asleep on my sofa during a meditation.'

'What did you do?'

'I let her sleep.'

Harry smiled as he ladled the tomato sauce out. 'Sounds like she needed it.'

'She did but she wouldn't stop apologising when she woke up. She was really embarrassed, but I told her that meditations often give you exactly what you need. Sometimes that's tears, other times it's tapping into that quiet little corner of yourself that the world often hides from us, and other times it's just a nap.'

'Here's to naps!'

'Exactly! I gave her a blue lace agate too.'

'Blue lace agate,' Harry repeated. 'Let me see – for calming?'

'Yes! I'm hoping it might help her sleep better.'

'Nice.'

They took their plates into the next room and sat down at the table.

'This sauce is great, Harry!' Aura said after a few mouthfuls.

'Thanks. Slightly more chilli than usual.'

'I love it.'

They finished their spaghetti and Harry cleared their plates away before bringing out two slices of cherry tart.

'Homemade. All vegan,' he said proudly.

'You're totally spoiling me! I won't be able to get into my wedding dress if you keep feeding me like this!'

'So you've got your dress?' He waggled his eyebrows.

'You know I have. I bought it with your mother, remember?'

'Yeah, I know. Just trying to prise more information out of you.'

'Yes, well, you won't!'

'She said she loved shopping with you, by the way.'

'She can be a lot of fun.'

'When she lets her guard down a bit,' Harry said with a laugh. 'Have you heard from your mum recently?'

Aura sighed. 'I texted her the date for the wedding so she has it in front of her, but she didn't text back so I'm not sure if she's coming or not.'

Harry sighed, obviously baffled by such behaviour from a parent. 'I'm sorry, Aura.'

'It's fine,' she replied with a half-smile. 'I'm kind of hoping she won't come. Is it awful to say that?'

'Not if it's how you feel.'

'I just think she wouldn't enjoy it, so why turn up and spoil things for everyone else?'

'Exactly. No point in that.'

Finishing dessert and clearing their things away, they sat on Harry's sofa together, arms around each other in a snuggly cuddle.

'Spaghetti, cherry tart and you,' Harry said. 'I can't think of a better evening.'

Aura giggled, but then her mind turned back to what they'd been discussing earlier. 'Is there anything we can do?'

'About?'

'Abi and Edward.'

'Like what exactly?'

'I don't know.'

'Got any magical love crystals that will bring them back together?' Harry asked.

'Well, a bit of rose quartz never did anyone any harm.'

'I think we'd better leave them to it.'

'It's going to be awkward for them, though – at our wedding party here.'

Harry shook his head. 'The walled garden's big enough. They'll find a space of their own.'

'But it'll be so sad.'

'They'll probably be back together again long before that,' Harry mused. 'If it's meant to be, that is. It might not be, you know.'

Aura gasped. 'Harry – they're *so* meant to be together!'

'Then they'll find a way back to each other, won't they?' He stroked her hair gently and kissed the tip of her nose. 'You're worrying too much. They're grown adults. I'm sure they've been through worse and they can sort out whatever it is that's come between them.'

'You didn't see the look on Abi's face. I'm worried about them. And Winfield.'

'Why are you worried about Winfield?'

'Because what if one of them feels so awkward being here that they decide to leave or even sell?'

'I don't think that's likely,' Harry said, but Aura could see the look of uncertainty in his eyes and it made her feel even worse about everything.

Edward hadn't spoken to Abi since his confession after Ronnie's funeral. They'd only crossed paths once – a horribly awkward moment when they'd both been leaving their apartments at the same time. Their eyes had met across the hallway and Edward had watched in dismay as Abi had done an about turn and disappeared back inside. That, he thought, was exactly the reason he'd taken so long to tell Abi how he felt about her. The fear of rejection or of finding themselves in the place they were now had been so great.

He'd sent her several texts, left voicemails and had even handwritten a couple of notes which he'd popped under her door, but she hadn't replied to any of them. But his messages all felt so inadequate because he knew he couldn't give Abi what she wanted – a full explanation as to why he'd lied about his father. He just couldn't face it. It was a part of his history that he didn't want to revisit and it had been pretty well hidden up until now. But he'd wrecked what he'd had with Abi and he could see what a terrible mistake he'd made. And he hated that she'd shut him out at a time when she was still mourning her friend. He wanted so desperately to be there for her, but that wasn't possible. Would Abi ever trust him again? Would they ever make it back to that sweet place they'd shared for such a brief time?

He'd never felt more wretched in his life. There was a part of him that wished he'd never set eyes on Winfield. He should have stayed in London or bought a property somewhere else. Anywhere else.

He picked up his to-do list. It had been his saviour over the last few days as he'd thrown himself into his work, shutting his doors and windows against the summer, hiding away from the world. He hadn't even gone swimming recently. He couldn't bear to – not without Abi. Of course, that had meant upping his medication to deal with the pain in his leg, which was frustrating but necessary.

He glanced out of the window now, briefly noting the blue sky above the downs and imagining the sweet air up there, and then he turned his attention back to the bright screen of his laptop and his never-ending to-do list.

CHAPTER EIGHTEEN

Abi didn't mean to walk to Ronnie's village, but her feet somehow found their way there. She'd been walking a lot recently. She'd have loved to have gone swimming and to feel that cold embrace of the water which washed away every single dark emotion, but that little adventure was so much wrapped up with Edward that it wouldn't be the same going alone. So she walked.

Arriving at Ronnie's, she stopped by the gate. It was open today and Abi peered into the garden. There was a part of her that wondered, for a split second, if she might see Ronnie walking out from the green depths, waving cheerfully and ushering her inside where he'd make them some lime cordial. She wished with all her heart that his death had been part of some terrible nightmare, but that she'd woken up now. But it wasn't Ronnie who emerged from the garden – it was a woman. She looked to be in her seventies and she smiled kindly when she saw her.

'Abi, isn't it?'

'Yes. Ronnie's gardening friend.'

She nodded. 'He used to tell me about you. I'm Dora. Come in, dear.'

Abi entered the garden, feeling instantly embraced.

'I've been keeping an eye on the place. Ronnie's nephew – what's his name?'

'Kenneth.'

'That's right! He asked me to keep things watered. I can't do any of the heavy work, mind, and I told him that, but Ronnie's garden's always been a little on the wild side, hasn't it?'

Abi smiled. 'Yes. I love that. He allowed things to breathe, didn't he?'

She followed Dora into the garden, noticing how well the tomatoes and peppers were looking in the greenhouse.

'It's so sad that he won't get to enjoy all the things he was growing,' Dora said. 'But perhaps you'd like to take some home? There are plenty of tomatoes.'

'Thank you,' Abi said. Although she was growing her own, she'd love to have some of Ronnie's.

Dora gestured Abi inside the greenhouse and Abi inhaled that wonderful warm smell of things growing. She picked a handful of tomatoes, popping them in one of the little punnets that Ronnie kept stacked for the purpose.

'Well, I'd better get back to my own plot,' Dora said when Abi rejoined her.

'Do you know what's happening to the house?'

'Kenneth tells me it'll be going up for sale as soon as probate is sorted.'

Abi looked back at it. 'I wonder who'll buy it.'

'I don't suppose you want it?' Dora said.

'Me? Oh, but I've got a home. Winfield Hall. Well, half of it.'

'Oh, of course. That's right.' Dora sighed. 'What a shame. You'd fit right in here.'

Abi smiled, and a part of her quickly created an alternative life for herself where she'd buy Ronnie's cottage. The small rooms were warm and welcoming and the garden wasn't as grand as the walled one at Winfield, but it was charming and quintessentially English. It would be such a different experience from living in a grand Georgian manor, but Abi could truly imagine herself living there. She just needed two lives in which to do it.

And then a thought crossed her mind. 'Dora – would you mind if I took some photos?' Abi got her phone out of her pocket. 'I have an idea about someone who might just be interested in buying it.'

When Abi got back to Winfield, she looked through the photos she'd taken of Ronnie's cottage. During her walk back, she hadn't been able to think of anything else but the beautiful country home, and she was delighted to see Aura and Harry in the walled garden.

She opened her French doors and waved across to them.

'Hi Abi!' Aura waved back.

'I'm so glad I caught you two,' she said as she approached them. They were sitting on the grass together and Abi joined them.

'How are you?' Aura asked, her face full of concern.

'I'm good, thank you. I've just had a walk across the downs. Actually, I went to Ronnie's cottage. I took some photos of it.' She showed them the photos on her phone.

'Wow!' Harry said. 'It's lovely.'

'It is, isn't it?'

'And look at the garden,' Aura said. 'I bet you could find fairies living in it!'

Harry and Abi laughed at the notion.

'It's coming up for sale,' Abi told them, watching their faces for their response.

'I wonder who the new owner will be,' Harry said. 'They'll be lucky, that's for sure.'

Abi nodded. 'I was wondering if it might be you.'

Harry looked at her and frowned. 'Me?'

'You and Aura.'

Aura glanced at Harry and then took another look at the photos on Abi's phone. 'We couldn't afford it, surely?'

Harry nodded. 'Yeah, those kinds of properties here in Sussex always go for a premium, don't they?'

'I'm not so sure,' Abi said. 'It needs modernisation. I think Ronnie and his wife were there for decades so it is a bit...' she paused, looking for the right word, 'tired.'

'Still,' Harry said, 'I don't think we're in the market for somewhere like that.'

Abi took her phone back and did a quick search for local property. 'Look, this one's similar. It's about the same size with a garden.' She turned the phone round to show them.

Harry whistled. 'Look at the price!'

'I don't think we could afford that,' Aura said with a sigh. 'And we're really happy here. I know we're just renting, but it works for us at the moment, doesn't it?'

'It does,' Harry agreed.

'Of course,' Abi said.

'I'm so sorry, Abi. It was so kind of you to think of us and I know you're anxious about the cottage.'

It was true. Abi had really put her own needs before Harry

and Aura's. She'd been so desperate to find someone she'd thought suitable for the place she loved so much rather than leaving things to the whims of fate, but it now became clear that it wasn't at all suitable for the budget of a young couple starting out.

'It's okay,' she said. 'I hope I didn't build your hopes up.'

'Not at all,' Harry assured her.

'You've given us something to dream about,' Aura said.

Abi smiled, glad to give them that at least.

Later that night, once Harry and Aura had said their goodnights, Harry found himself wide awake, staring up at the ceiling of his bedroom. He couldn't help but feel frustrated. Abi had well and truly planted a seed and he hadn't been able to think about anything but the cottage she'd shown them earlier that day. But, no matter which way he looked at it, he simply couldn't afford a mortgage on a place like that. Not yet at least. He might have been able to do it on the salary from his last job, but the fledging company he was working for now wasn't paying him enough to cover the monthly fees, and he really didn't have enough in savings for a deposit yet and he was sure Aura didn't either.

Abi's idea of buying Ronnie's cottage had been a good one and she'd meant well suggesting it to them. But all it had done was to make Harry feel insecure about how far they had to go if they wanted to be homeowners one day. And it was very easy to imagine their future selves in such a place. Harry could easily see him and Aura there.

And the children.

He smiled as he pictured a future together, somewhere like

Ronnie's cottage, with children running barefoot around the garden. The details were sketchy – like the exact number of children, but there would be a fair few, he imagined – enough to fill a garden like the one he'd seen in Abi's photos. There'd be little Harrys climbing the apple tree and scuffing their knees, and little Auras having tea parties among the flowers. It was all so easy to envisage.

Funnily enough, Aura hadn't mentioned the place again which surprised Harry. She was practical, far more than he often gave her credit for. But he couldn't help dreaming. A place of their own, a place that was truly theirs. It was a heady thought. But Winfield was wonderful too and they would be happy in his apartment. That much had been decided.

He couldn't wait to start their new life together. They'd agreed that, as much as they hated being apart, they wouldn't move in together until after the wedding. Harry liked that old-fashioned approach. But Aura had slowly been moving a few things into Harry's apartment and he'd been making room for her. They'd even been shopping for a few things together to make the place more *theirs* than simply *his*. And Aura had given her notice to Abi. Abi had teased her saying that Edward had stolen her favourite tenant, but she'd wished them both well and was glad that Winfield wouldn't lose them altogether.

Unable to sleep, Harry got up and walked through his apartment. There was a blue and silver throw on the back of his sofa now, and there was a bowl of crystals on his coffee table. They were going to need some specialised equipment to move the enormous pair of amethyst geode angel wings his father had bought Aura, but he loved the idea of being surrounded by the gentle energy of the crystals. And the gentle energy of Aura herself. How had he got so lucky? He often asked himself that. Mind you, it had taken quite a few years and a fair few disastrous relationships before he'd met the person who was right for him. But one thing was certain: he was never going to take it for granted. He'd spent so many years alone and the funny thing was that he'd honestly believed he was happy. Well, he knew the truth now. He'd never been more content – in his relationship with Aura, his home at Winfield and his work.

But Abi's photos of Ronnie's cottage had made him realise something. That, no matter how content you were in life, there was always room for improvement.

It was the next day and Abi was feeling listless. Her plan for Harry and Aura to buy Ronnie's cottage wasn't going to happen and it had left her feeling hugely disappointed. Taking herself off into the hills with her sketchbook, she idled away an hour or two, sketching butterflies and wild flowers. Nature had a wonderful way of easing one's woes because, if you really immersed yourself in it, your mind had little room left for anything else.

However, as soon as she got back to Winfield and switched her phone on, she saw she'd had three missed calls from Douglas. Panicking, she rang him immediately.

'Douglas? It's Abi.'

'Abi, thank god!'

'What is it?'

'Ellen. It's Ellen.'

'What's happened?'

'It's bad, Abi. I've never seen her like this before. She was just sitting on the sofa staring at nothing. It was really scary. She wouldn't talk to me or anything. And now she's locked herself in the bathroom. Can you come?'

'Yes, of course.'

'Right now?'

'I'm on my way.'

There was nothing quite like somebody else's problems to make you forget your own, Abi thought as she pulled up to her sister's home a little later. The front door was unlocked and she went straight in.

Douglas, who'd obviously been pacing as he'd waited for her, greeted her in the hallway, his face ashen.

'Abi – thank god you're here.'

'Where are the girls?' Abi asked immediately.

'With our neighbour.'

'Good. And Ellen?'

'She's still in the bathroom.'

'Has she said anything?'

'No. She won't talk to me at all.'

'I'll go up right away.'

Douglas nodded. 'I'll give you some space, okay? Call me if you need me.'

Abi raced upstairs to the bathroom. The door was locked as Douglas had told her and Abi knocked lightly on it.

'Ellen? It's Abi.' She paused. 'Are you okay in there?' She gave her sister a moment to answer, but she didn't. 'We're all really worried about you. We need to know you're all right. Can you say something to me? Just a word or two.' Abi waited again. This wasn't going to be easy. She looked around the upstairs landing as if there might be something there to help her, but there wasn't. She knocked on the door again. 'You can hear me, right? Let me know you can. Please!'

Abi sat down on the floor outside the door. 'Douglas is worried about you. He loves you so much.' She paused, hoping Ellen was listening and that the words were finding her. 'And I do too. We don't say it very often, do we? But I do love you. Very much! And your girls. They're round a friend's, aren't they? But I'm sure they'd be here with me now, telling you exactly the same thing if they knew you were alone and locked in the bathroom. They'd be just as afraid as I am now and they'd want to know you were okay.' She paused. 'Are you okay, Ellen?'

Abi sighed. She could hear her heart hammering in her ears, counting the seconds, the minutes, each with no response. Who would have thought that a simple bathroom door could be so very sinister?

'Remember when we were little?' Abi began, suddenly recalling another time when a door had played a major role in their lives. 'When we'd hide together in the airing cupboard? I can't remember why now. Had we been watching something scary on the TV?' She let the question hang a moment, but Ellen didn't answer it. 'But what I remember was how snug we were. There wasn't much space and it was pretty dark with just the landing light piercing the cracks in the wood, but you'd put your arms around me and tell me it was okay. Everything was going to be okay. And I believed you. Well, I want to tell you that now, Ellen. Whatever you're going through, we can get through it, okay? But I wish you'd let me help you. I really want to give you a hug – just like you used to hug me all those years ago.'

Abi closed her eyes, reliving the memories she had of those airing cupboard moments with her big sister. And that's when she heard it. The lock. A second later, the door opened a crack.

Abi scrambled up from her home on the floor.

'Ellen!' Her sister, pale-faced, was standing in front of her. Abi embraced her, hugging her close. 'We've been so worried about you.' Abi leaned back and brushed Ellen's fair hair out of her face. It was damp, stuck to her skin with the tears she'd been crying. 'Come and sit down.'

Abi led the way through to the main bedroom and they sat down on the bed together. Almost immediately, Douglas appeared in the doorway.

'Ellen! Are you okay?'

'She's all right, Douglas,' Abi told him quickly. 'I've got this.'

Douglas nodded, his eyes glued to his wife. But he backed away, giving them the space they needed.

Abi looked at Ellen's face. She'd never seen her sister looking so ill. It was as if she'd sunk deep inside herself and Abi was afraid that she'd never surface again.

'Can I get you anything?' Abi asked, placing a hand on hers. 'A tea or a glass of water?'

Ellen shook her head. 'I'm okay.'

Abi was relieved to hear her sister's voice at last.

'You scared us, you know.'

Ellen's mouth twitched slightly, but it was impossible to tell if she was attempting to smile or grimace.

'It's not like you,' Abi said.

'Why?' Ellen asked in a small, fragile voice.

'Why what?'

'Why isn't it like me?'

Abi was surprised by her question. 'Because you – you know – you cope.'

Ellen shook her head. 'I don't. And I haven't been.'

Abi took her sister's hands, holding them in hers and noting how cold they felt. 'We know you've been struggling recently. We've seen that. And we should have helped more. I have tried to, but you always push me away.'

Ellen seemed to take this in. 'It's hard for me. To accept help.'

'I know. Maybe it's because you're the elder child. Perhaps there's something in you that wants to be in charge.'

Ellen swallowed hard. 'But I don't want to be. Not all the time. It's too much. Why do I always have to be the strong one? The one who holds everybody and everything together?'

'You don't.'

'But I feel as if I do. I always have. Ever since we were little. Ever since Mum...' Her voice petered out.

'Ever since Mum... what?' Abi dared to prompt. 'Ellen?' She squeezed her sister's hands. 'If something's upsetting you, it might help to talk about it. And I need to know. You know that, don't you? You know I'd like to understand what happened when we were young.'

Ellen nodded. 'I know you would. But – well – it's not easy to talk about.'

'Of course not.'

They sat for a little while longer. Ellen's hands felt warmer in Abi's now, the heat from her own having passed to them, and she released them as Ellen reached for a tissue from her pocket, dabbing her eyes which looked red and sore. Abi had never seen her sister looking so helpless and vulnerable and it cut her deeply knowing that she'd been suffering on her own.

'What do you remember about Mum?' Ellen asked at last.

Abi sighed. 'Just bits and pieces. Piggybacks round the living room. A trip to the theatre. Bags of sweets on Sundays.'

'You were so young.'

'Yes.'

'What do you think she died of?'

'Well, she was ill, wasn't she?' Abi said. She'd never been told exactly what was wrong with their mother. She wasn't totally sure Ellen even knew, and Aunt Claire certainly hadn't ever talked about it.

Ellen nodded. 'In a way.'

'What do you mean?'

'She was ill. She had problems and couldn't cope so she turned to pills. Lots of pills.'

Abi frowned. 'Are you saying she overdosed?'

Ellen was staring down at her pale hands in her lap and nodded. 'That night you remember – you know the one you dream about?'

'Yes?'

'It happened.'

Abi felt tears stinging her eyes as she took this in. So it hadn't been just some random dream. It had been a real memory that had haunted her and hounded her through the years.

'Is that the night she died?' Abi dared to ask, dreading the answer, but needing to know it all the same.

'No. But she attempted to overdose that night.'

'Attempted? You mean her death was deliberate?'

Ellen nodded. 'I think so.'

'What happened?'

'The night you remember, Aunt Claire was coming over. It makes me wonder if it was a cry for help that time, but I really don't know. But Aunt Claire was the one who called the ambulance.'

Abi nodded, remembering the lights, the strangers and the stretcher. 'Maybe it was an accident. Maybe she took more pills than she realised.'

'Maybe. But it happened again, didn't it? I think she must have wanted to die.'

Abi flinched. It was too awful to imagine.

'And I'm so scared, Abi!' Ellen went on.

'What about?'

'What if I'm like Mum? What if I have her fragility and can't cope with life?'

'But you *do* cope, Ellen! You always cope with everything life throws at you. You just worry too much, that's all.'

'I sometimes have these feelings inside me, telling me I'm not enough. And I'm terrified of leaving my girls like Mum left us. They're not much older than we were when Mum died.'

Abi nodded. She'd had the same thought about the girls' ages recently, and vague memories of her and Ellen being packed up and sent to Aunt Claire's house and not understanding what was going on. They'd been so young, so desperate to be loved.

'Listen. I've got an idea, but you're not going to like it,' Abi said, sounding far more confident than she felt.

'What is it?'

'We have to talk to Aunt Claire.'

'Why?'

'Because she'll have answers and she owes us the truth.'

'What truth?'

'What exactly was going on with Mum? Had she always been like that? There's so much about her that we don't know and I really want to know, don't you?'

Ellen shook her head vehemently. 'I don't think that's a good idea.'

Abi had had a feeling Ellen would respond like that. 'We'll go together,' she assured her. 'We need to do this, Ellen. I really think we need to know more.'

'But what is there to know? Our mother killed herself, Abi! She didn't want to be around anymore. We weren't enough to keep her alive!' Ellen's voice was high and sounded out of control. She was crying again now and Abi held her.

'It's not that we weren't enough,' Abi whispered. 'It's just that the world was too much for her. Perhaps. I don't know. Maybe there's more to it than that. That's why we need to talk to Aunt Claire. She's the only one who might be able to help us.'

'She's never talked about it before,' Ellen said through her sobs.

'But we've never asked her – not directly. And imagine how painful it must be for her. Mum was her sister.'

'Like you and me.'

'Yes. And Bethanne and Rosie,' Abi added. 'It's a special bond, isn't it?'

Ellen nodded. 'Yes.'

Abi waited a moment. 'So we'll go?'

Ellen dabbed her eyes and gave a sniff. 'Okay. We'll go. *Together*.'

CHAPTER NINETEEN

Abi was exhausted the next day. Her time with Ellen had left her utterly drained and she slept in late, which was most unlike her. Once she was up, she made a cup of tea, opened the French doors and settled herself at her table where she'd arranged all of her recent jewellery sketches. Emma's box of brooches had pride of place and Abi had immersed herself in the world of gemstones, finding a beautiful brooch at another antiques centre. It was set with spring-bright peridots that never failed to make her smile when she looked at them. She'd also bought a job lot from an online auction and had spent many happy hours looking through the contents, admiring their myriad colours and taking inspiration from their shapes.

Abi's instinct was to share her excitement about her jewellery project with Edward but she couldn't. They still hadn't spoken since Ronnie's funeral and Abi couldn't easily see a way of making things better between them. Maybe time would ease the pain and the awkwardness. Maybe they'd be able to find their way to some sort of civility if not friendship.

But what was quite clear in Abi's mind was that she couldn't imagine them ever returning to that loving place they'd found together earlier in the summer.

She turned her attention back to the sketches she'd been making, picking up one of the filigree brooches that had belonged to Emma. Bethanne and Rosie would love looking at the pieces when they next visited, she thought with pleasure. They would sift through the box of auction brooches with as much joy as Abi had and it would be fun to introduce them to the whole concept of brooches. Abi wasn't sure if they were still considered to be rather old-fashioned by younger generations – the sort of thing pinned to an old lady's cardigan. Natalia, the jeweller she was working with, had dismissed that whole notion, declaring them an essential item for anyone who cared about beauty and individuality. Abi liked that about brooches. There were so many different designs – you could always find just the right one to suit your mood and outfit.

She sketched some new ideas for an hour or so, making a second cup of tea and nibbling on a croissant as she worked. She'd already sent some of her early ideas to Natalia who had loved them. It was fun to be working with somebody again. Abi had missed bouncing ideas off another person and getting feedback and encouragement. It all helped her creativity. And so she gave herself the rest of the morning to dream and create.

But Abi knew that she could only distract herself for so long. Immersing yourself in art was a very good way of helping to distance yourself from anything unpleasant or worrisome. But the real world couldn't be avoided forever and it was with reluctance and some misgivings that she pushed her work to one side and picked up her phone. She'd told Ellen she'd make the call to Aunt Claire today. Delaying things would help nobody. Still, looking at the screen of her phone now, she wondered if what she was about to do was a good idea. All too clearly, she remembered the last trip to pick up her mother's sewing machine which Ellen had been keen to have. Her aunt had let her into the house, but no words of kindness had been exchanged. Aunt Claire had remained as distant as ever and Abi had been glad to get away. Was she really going to persuade her aunt to open up now?

What choice do I have?

The little voice inside her told her all she needed to know. Aunt Claire was the only link with their mother that Ellen and Abi had. If they wanted to know anything, she was the one they needed to talk to. So Abi rang the number.

'Yes?' Aunt Claire's voice was sharp and unwelcoming and Abi wondered if her name had come up on her aunt's phone or if she answered to everybody in the same abrupt way.

'Aunt Claire? It's Abigail.'

'Yes.'

'Ellen and I would like to come over.'

'What for? There aren't any more sewing machines.'

'It's not to do with sewing machines,' Abi said, frustrated that her aunt seemed resentful about their last encounter. 'We'd just like to talk.' Abi hoped that she wouldn't spook her aunt and make her hang up, which she didn't put past her. 'Aunt Claire?'

'What do you want to talk about?'

Abi swallowed hard. 'We just have some questions. About the past.'

There was a long, deep pause.

'Aunt Claire? Ellen's not been well. She needs to – well, we *both* need to talk to you.' Abi waited again. '*Please.* It's important.'

'I can't see you this week.'

'Okay.'

'It'll have to be the week after,' Aunt Claire said, as if begrudging them any time at all.

'That would be great.'

Aunt Claire gave a day and time and Abi agreed to it on the spot and then her aunt hung up without so much as a goodbye. Abi sighed. She'd got what she'd asked for. At least for now.

It wasn't every day that Harry witnessed his father climbing over a stile. The sight was odd to say the least. Leonard Freeman was a big man and his exercise over the last few years had been somewhat confined. But his doctor had told him that he should up his activity and so he'd taken to the hills, slowly at first, but with great determination, building his strength and stamina. Harry's mother would often go with him and she'd agreed to come with them now as all four of them enjoyed a day out. Harry grinned at her pristine white trainers, her neat floral blouse and her immaculate trousers. It was clear that his mother was never going to invest in big ugly walking boots or anything resembling a pair of jogging pants. Although she was now happily wearing chic yoga pants in a paisley print for her sessions with Aura.

Harry watched as Aura climbed over the stile with the grace of a fairy princess, practically flying over it, her long red hair falling forward and hiding her face for a moment. He held a hand out to her – not because she needed his help, but because he wanted to hold hers.

'Your father seems to be enjoying himself,' she told Harry.

'Yes. He's adapting well to this walking business.'

'He's got real colour in his cheeks.'

'So have you!' Harry said, kissing her quickly while his parents' attention was diverted to a distant view of a church spire.

'I like walking with your parents,' she said.

'Me too. I can't remember the last time we went out on a walk together. Must have been years ago.'

'It's a lovely thing to do.'

'So, Harry lad – where are we having this picnic?' Leonard asked, stopping for a moment, hands on hips, to survey his son.

'Oh, Aura's in charge of picking the spot.'

'And what say you to this view of the valley?' Leonard asked.

'I'd say it was about perfect,' Aura said.

The four of them set to work with the picnic rug and food which Harry and his father had been carrying in backpacks between them and, soon, they were all sitting enjoying a simple al fresco lunch of salad sandwiches, cheese and onion quiche, crudités and lemon sponge made that morning by Maria. There was also a bottle of elderflower cordial which was going down very well after the effort of the walk.

'This is the life!' Harry said, laying back on the picnic rug after finishing his lunch, gazing up at the blue sky above.

He heard his father chuckle and his mother sigh in contentment.

'Everything coming together for the reception?' Maria asked.

'Very well,' Aura told her. 'Thank you for booking the caterer. I've heard such good things about her.'

'Yes,' Maria said. 'She sources everything locally and it's all seasonal food too.'

'Sounds perfect,' Harry said.

'We've chosen a cake,' Aura told her. 'And we're working with a florist who's going to liaise with Abi and use some of the flowers from the walled garden to make my bouquet and the displays.'

'How lovely!' Maria enthused.

'Need any help with anything?' Leonard offered.

'I think we're nearly there, Dad. Mum and Aura are pretty good with organising everything.'

'And it's only a small gathering,' Aura reminded them.

Maria nodded. 'I think that's very wise.'

Harry smiled as he sat back up. 'I never thought you'd agree to it, Mum.'

'Why not?'

Harry shrugged. 'Thought you'd be all for inviting everyone from your clubs and the WI.'

'Well, it would be nice to include everyone,' Maria admitted, 'but it isn't my day, is it? It's yours and Aura's.'

'You're not disappointed, are you?' Aura said, suddenly sounding anxious.

'Not at all!' Maria assured her. 'I like the idea of it being select. *Exclusive!* Makes it all the more special, don't you think?'

Aura smiled in relief.

'And you've got a photographer?' Leonard asked. 'Want to make sure we've got pictures!'

'Yes. The brother of a chap from work is doing that,' Harry said. 'He's just started his own business. Thought it would be nice to give him the work.'

Maria frowned. 'He *can* take photos, can't he? Proper photos and not those things with filters and nonsense?'

'Yes, Mum. He can take proper photos. I'll send you a link

to his website and you can take a look. He recently covered the wedding of Lord Landon's daughter.'

'Oh, well that's all right then,' Maria consented, sounding much relieved.

Harry and Aura exchanged amused glances. His mother, Harry had to admit, could still exhibit traits of extreme snobbishness.

'It sounds like it's going to be a wonderful day,' Leonard said, reaching for a second slice of lemon sponge. Maria stopped him with a quick slap to his hand. 'Ouch!'

'I'm just watching your heart, darling.'

Leonard grimaced, looking very woebegone.

'Here, have this if you're still hungry,' Maria said, passing her husband a carrot stick.

He took it with a heavy sigh, crunching it in resignation.

Harry laughed and picked up a carrot stick for himself in an attempt to show support.

It was the day of the meeting with Aunt Claire. Abi had slept badly the night before as she'd tortured herself with the different unpleasant scenarios which might unfold the next day. As soon as she got up, she texted Ellen to make sure she was okay. Her reply came through in seconds.

Didn't sleep a wink.

Me neither, Abi texted back. *I'll pick you up at 10 x.*

Abi did nothing but glance at her artwork on the table that morning. There wasn't time nor did she have the motivation with their upcoming appointment. And it really did feel like an appointment too – there was no joy in the thought of visiting their nearest relation. They were being slotted in to Aunt Claire's busy timetable and Abi knew that she'd begrudge her nieces her time.

Ellen barely said a word when Abi called round and the drive to their aunt's home was made in silence.

When they finally arrived in the London suburb, parking outside number seventy-three, Abi and Ellen sat in the car for a moment, neither wanting to make the first move.

'I'm not sure I can go in,' Ellen said.

'You don't have to. But I think we should.'

'What if I can't do this? What if I can't ask her anything or listen to the answers?' Ellen looked at Abi, and Abi could see the fear in her eyes.

'Then you can leave,' Abi told her. 'Any time you're feeling overwhelmed, let me know and we can leave.'

'You promise?'

'Of course.' Abi was shocked to hear how insecure her sister sounded. Mind you, she wasn't feeling especially courageous herself. Aunt Claire didn't exactly inspire warmth or confidence. But they were here now. This was what they'd pushed for and it had taken years to get to this point. If they didn't do this now, they never would. So they got out of the car and, a moment later, knocked on the door.

'This place doesn't change, does it?' Ellen said, noting the regimentally neat pots either side of the front door with their identical evergreen plants.

'No, it doesn't,' Abi said, remembering that it was years since Ellen had last visited while Abi had been there more recently to pick up the sewing machine.

As they mused on this, the door opened and Aunt Claire appeared. Their aunt's face had been beautiful a lifetime ago. It wasn't that she was old; it was simply that she hadn't smiled in decades and that took its toll on a face, Abi couldn't help thinking as she let them in. Abi remembered the photo she'd seen in the dim light of the room at the back. It had been of Aunt Claire and their mother. They'd both been smiling. Indeed, it had been hard to tell them apart. Two beautiful young women, full of the joys of life.

They followed Aunt Claire into the sitting room. She hadn't said anything yet and the three of them stood awkwardly.

'Shall I make us some tea?' Abi offered, doing her best to keep things light and affable.

'If you want,' Aunt Claire said.

Abi went through to the kitchen and found mugs, tea, milk and sugar. The kitchen hadn't changed since she and Ellen had lived there. The grouting in the tiled countertops was grey and broken and the wooden doors of the cupboards stuck. It was a joyless room.

Tea made, Abi returned to the living room, placing the tray with the tea things onto the table in the centre. Aunt Claire was sitting in a chair and Ellen was on the sofa opposite. Abi handed the mugs out and then took a seat next to Ellen.

'How are you, Aunt Claire?' Abi asked.

Aunt Claire gave her what could only be described as a grimace. 'I think we'd better get this over and done with, don't you?'

Abi cleared her throat. 'Yes. Of course.'

'What do you want?'

'We want to know about our mother,' Abi replied quickly.

Aunt Claire nodded. 'I thought as much.'

'You've never talked to us about her before,' Abi went on, undeterred by her aunt's abrupt manner. 'And we'd like to try to understand what happened.'

'You mean the night she died?' Aunt Claire asked, eyes narrowed.

'Well, yes, but more than that. We want to know all about *her*,' Abi said. 'I've only got a handful of memories and Ellen – well Ellen needs to know things too.'

'Like what?' Aunt Claire still looked horribly guarded and Abi feared she wasn't going to tell them anything at all.

'Like if they share common traits.'

Aunt Claire glared across at Ellen and Abi reached her hand out to take her sister's. For what seemed an age, Aunt Claire remained silent and the ticking of the clock on the mantelpiece was the only thing that could be heard. Abi glanced at it now. She'd always hated that clock. It was the ugliest she'd ever seen – a big bulky wooden thing with a dull grey face and big bold hands that seemed to be ridiculing her – telling her that she was wasting her time trying to talk to Aunt Claire.

'Please, Aunt Claire,' Ellen whispered.

Aunt Claire took a sip of her tea and Abi could feel her heart hammering, fearful of what her aunt was going to tell them, but even more anxious that she might tell them nothing at all.

'Your mother,' she began, her voice low and measured, her fingers tight around her mug. 'Kristen.'

Abi swallowed hard. It was so odd to hear her mother's name. *Kristen*. It was beautiful.

'She was always the happy one,' Aunt Claire said, her words slow and measured. 'Until she wasn't. I'm not sure when it first surfaced – the change. Maybe it was always there. When you're growing up, you're more concerned with your own moods, I suppose. It became apparent something was wrong when she was about fifteen. Our parents thought it was just teenage angst.

Hormones. But it was more than that. I could tell. But these sorts of things weren't really talked about back then. Not like they are today. People understand more now about mental health. But there was still a stigma then. You were just meant to be able to cope and people weren't always tolerant if you couldn't.'

Abi glanced at Ellen while Aunt Claire took a sip of her tea. Ellen's eyes were fixed on their aunt, desperate to hear more.

'The dark moods increased in her early twenties. They seemed to last longer too and she found them harder to shake. I'm guessing you might have noticed the mood swings,' Aunt Claire said, addressing the question to Ellen who nodded. 'One minute, she'd be happy. No, not just *happy*. She'd be practically bouncing like Tigger from *Winnie the Pooh*!' Aunt Claire smiled at her own reference. It was the first time Abi had seen her smiling in years. 'We called her that for a while. Tigger!' She gave a laugh and Abi saw Ellen jolt in surprise. 'And then the clouds would descend and all that happiness would just slip away. I didn't understand it.'

'Did she get help?' Ellen asked.

'Not until her mid-twenties. She saw several people and was prescribed various things, but she hated taking pills. Well, at first. Then they put her on something. I can't remember the name of it. But she was taking a lot of them, often with alcohol. I'd tell her to slow down, but she'd tell me she had everything under control. But I could see she was still struggling.' Aunt Claire glanced up at the ceiling and Abi thought she could see tears in her eyes. 'This isn't easy for me to talk about.'

'We know,' Abi said gently.

Aunt Claire closed her eyes for a moment and Abi wondered what she was thinking and feeling. And then she began again.

'I tried to help her. You should know that. *So* many times, but it became difficult. She had you girls, and family life and work meant we didn't see each other as often as we might have. But she'd call me. Sometimes it was in the middle of the night when she couldn't sleep. She'd blame the pills and would be self-medicating with alcohol, trying to knock herself out so she could sleep. It was a vicious cycle of depression and addiction and nobody seemed able to reach her.'

'Oh, god!' Ellen cried. Abi squeezed Ellen's hand.

'I don't know what else I can tell you,' Aunt Claire said.

'What about the night Mum died?' Ellen asked.

'I think you know what happened now. She overdosed.' Aunt Claire's stark words hung in the air between them. Abi felt hollow and horrified at the same time. It was so... unsatisfactory somehow. How could something so small as a pill, no matter how many of them there might have been, take their beautiful mother away from them? It didn't seem possible.

'Was it an accident?' Ellen dared to ask.

Aunt Claire sighed, closing her eyes again briefly. 'I don't think so. She was in so much pain. I think she needed to go.'

Abi's throat felt thick with emotion and she closed her eyes in an attempt to stop the tears from coming. Ellen wasn't doing as well and was crying beside her. And then something strange happened. Abi heard sobs coming from across the room. Aunt Claire was crying.

Abi leaned in a little closer.

'Are you okay?'

Aunt Claire, who'd been bent forward, now looked up. There were tears running down her face.

Abi was beside her in an instance, wrapping her arms around her.

'It's okay! It's okay.'

'No it's not! She's gone! She's gone! My *beautiful* sister!'

Abi felt her heart stabbing with pain, not just for the loss of her mother, but for her aunt's distress. Abi had never seen her like this before. She wasn't an emotional person. Or, at least, she'd never shown this sort of emotion before.

'It's okay,' Abi said again, not knowing what else to say, but wanting her aunt to know she was there. Abi glanced up at Ellen who was pale-faced and sitting stiffly on the sofa, tears streaming down her face.

'For years, I blamed you girls,' Aunt Claire said at last, wiping her eyes with a tissue and looking up at them both. 'You were too much for her, I thought. She couldn't cope with herself let alone two little ones. The pressure was too much.'

Abi let the words settle in her mind, not trusting herself to respond, but Ellen got in ahead of her anyway.

'Is that why you treated us the way you did?'

'What do you mean?' Aunt Claire was immediately on the defensive.

'Well, you didn't exactly make us feel loved,' Ellen said. Abi's eyes widened at the anger in her sister's voice. 'If anything, we thought you hated us!'

'I never hated you!' Aunt Claire cried. 'How could I? You were my sister's girls!'

'But you never spoke to us except to tell us what to do! You didn't spend any sort of time with us. You didn't *know* us!'

Abi couldn't believe the fury she could hear behind Ellen's words. It seemed that Aunt Claire couldn't either.

'I gave you a home.'

'But it never felt like one,' Ellen countered. 'It was just a house to us. I didn't even want to come in today. I hate this place.'

'Ellen!' Abi warned. It was all getting too raw, too personal.

'No, Abi – she should hear this. You feel the same way, don't you? You were never happy here! God! We couldn't get away fast enough, could we? And you couldn't wait to see the back of us.'

'That's not true!' Aunt Claire said.

'Oh, really!' Ellen retorted, her voice full of sarcasm.

'I just didn't know how to – how to – *be* around you.'

'You never got the hang of it – after *all* those years, watching us grow up without our mother? You never thought we might need a bit of love and it might be a good idea to *try?*'

'Ellen!'

Ellen flashed Abi a look that was so full of pain and anger that it startled Abi into silence.

'I think we should go,' Ellen said, standing up.

Abi stood up too. She'd promised her sister they could leave whenever she needed to and it seemed like that time had come.

'Aunt Claire...' Abi began, but Ellen grabbed her arm and marched her into the hallway.

'Girls – wait!' Aunt Claire called, following them.

Ellen was at the door, but Abi hung back.

'Ellen, wait a minute.'

Ellen frowned, but then glanced back at her aunt and Abi saw a look pass across Ellen's face: it was the smallest glimmer of compassion. Abi turned to face her aunt and saw a woman she barely recognised. She looked frail and helpless, as if all the fight had drained right out of her, and something cracked in Abi.

'I'm sorry,' Aunt Claire whispered. 'I'm so sorry.'

Abi felt Ellen's hand slip into hers.

'Let's go, Abi.'

'No!' Abi cried.

There was a strange sort of stand-off where the three women stood in the dark hallway not quite knowing what to do.

'I'm sorry,' Aunt Claire said again, her voice a feeble croak.

Abi nodded because she had no words to offer. And then she thought of something.

'Aunt Claire?'

'Yes?'

'Can I show Ellen the photo of you and Mum in the back room?'

Aunt Claire looked surprised by this request, but then nodded.

'Ellen? Come and see.'

Ellen didn't look happy at the idea of spending more time there, but followed Abi into the room at the back of the house. Abi wondered if Aunt Claire would join them, but she chose not to, giving the girls their space as she returned to the living room.

'Here,' Abi said, nodding to the photo on the sideboard.

Ellen gasped, picking up the frame and staring at the image inside it. 'Your sketch of this was wonderful, but the real thing... it's just gorgeous. She was so beautiful.'

'They both were,' Abi said.

'Yes. I never realised Aunt Claire was so pretty.'

'She kind of hid it behind that abruptness of hers.' Abi took her phone out of her pocket and took a couple of photos of the picture and then Ellen replaced it on the sideboard.

'You have Mum's freckles,' Ellen told her.

'You have her smile.'

'Do I?'

'You do *when* you smile!'

Ellen stabbed her with an elbow. 'Funny!'

'You should smile more often, that's all I'm saying.'

Ellen walked to the window which looked out over the backyard. There wasn't a lot to admire in the view. It was mostly just other houses, but Abi joined her and gazed outside.

'Are you okay?' Abi asked.

Ellen sighed. 'I feel a little calmer now if that's what you're worried about.'

'Good. Things got pretty heated back there.'

'Yes. But they needed to, didn't they?'

'I suppose.'

'Are *you* all right?' Ellen asked.

'Yes. A little... tired.'

Ellen reached out and squeezed her shoulder. 'Ready to go, then?'

'I think so.'

The two of them left the room, looking in on Aunt Claire again.

'Is there anything we can get you?' Ellen asked.

Aunt Claire looked up. Her eyes still looked red and watery, but she shook her head. 'I'll be all right. I usually am.'

Abi paused, her hand on the door frame. She wanted to go in and hug her aunt again, but her body language clearly told Abi that that was the last thing she wanted.

'You'll call if you need us, won't you?'

'Yes,' Ellen chipped in. 'Call us.'

Aunt Claire looked genuinely surprised by this invitation and sniffed by way of an answer.

'And thank you,' Abi said. 'For today. For telling us.'

They left the house and got in the car, sitting for a moment without starting the engine.

'I can't believe that happened,' Abi said at last.

'Can't believe what?'

'That Aunt Claire broke down like that. She's human! She's

never shown any emotion before. Other than annoyance, that is.'

'Do you think she's changed? Do you think she'll want to see us in the future?'

'I don't know,' Abi said honestly. 'She seemed genuinely sorry, didn't she?'

'Yes. But – I don't know – it feels strange. I'm not sure if we can ever be close even if she made an effort now. You can't undo all those years that have passed, can you?'

'I really don't know,' Abi told her honestly. 'But, if she makes an effort, I think we should too, don't you?'

Abi was just about to start the car when Ellen grabbed her hand.

'What if I'm like Mum, Abi? What if I can't cope with life?'

Abi shook her head, hating the fear she could hear in her sister's voice. 'Ellen – you're *not* Mum, okay? You're your own person with your own decisions to make. Just because Mum...' Abi paused. She hated saying the words. 'Just because Mum chose to end things, it doesn't mean that you will. In fact, I'm pretty sure that's statistically very unlikely.'

'Really?'

'Truly.'

Ellen seemed relieved for a moment, but then her dark cloud seemed to descend again. 'I sometimes feel like she's inside me. All her sadness. All her pain.'

Abi leaned across the car and put her arms around Ellen and hugged her close. Sometimes, a hug was so much better than any words.

'You did so well today. That wasn't an easy thing to get through.'

Ellen sniffed. 'I couldn't have done it without you.'

'Nor I without you.'

They broke apart, each reaching for a tissue to dry their eyes, and then they smiled at one another in a moment that would bond them together forever.

'Shall we go home?' Abi asked.

Ellen nodded. 'Yes please.'

CHAPTER TWENTY

Abi couldn't settle at home. Although she felt emotionally drained from the visit to Aunt Claire's, and physically tired too after the drive, she also felt strangely restless. So, after a quick cup of tea and bite to eat, she grabbed her swimming bag and drove to the coast.

The sun was heading for the horizon and there was a cool breeze when she arrived and, for a moment, she wondered if she should just go for a brisk walk instead. But something compelled her to venture into the water. There was something cleansing and comforting about the sea and Abi felt that she needed it after that day and so she walked across the beach towards the water. There were so many haunting images that she wanted to wash away from herself. Her aunt's revelation about their mother's dependency on pills and alcohol. The mood swings her mother had endured. Ellen's rage at Aunt Claire, and their aunt's tearful apology. It had all been a lot to take in during the course of one day.

And then Abi thought of Ronnie. She hadn't yet got over the loss of her dear friend and was now processing the loss of her mother all over again too. She couldn't help remembering how she'd recently thought it so unfair that Ronnie hadn't lived longer, and yet he'd had so many more years, more *decades*, than her mother had had. How could that be right?

Abi dropped her bag onto the sand and disrobed. She was already wearing her costume and felt the chill of the evening air on her skin. Thankfully, there was still some warmth in the sun so she walked towards the edge of the sea, letting the water find her feet. She closed her eyes, feeling her toes sinking into the sand as she thought about the mother she'd known for so brief a time. If only she'd left a note or something to explain. It might have provided a little comfort and insight. But she'd left nothing. No, that was a lie, Abi thought, for Kristen Carey had left her smile to Ellen and her freckles to Abi.

Opening her eyes, Abi smiled, wondering if her mother had ever swum in the sea. Had she ever even visited the south coast? What would she have made of Winfield Hall? And what kind of grandmother would she have been to Bethanne and Rosie? There was so much life that she hadn't got to lead and Abi felt angry and sad about everything they had missed experiencing together.

The waves crashed against Abi's legs as she walked into the sea. It felt strange and not quite right entering the water without Edward beside her. Still, Abi waded in. She needed the cool water, the freedom, and to be held – even if it was just by the waves.

With one great gasp, she plunged herself in before she could change her mind and swam, keeping parallel to the beach and not venturing too far from the other swimmers who were there that evening.

She floated for a while, feeling the sea embracing her body as she gazed up into the sky. And there was that sensation again

– that strange oneness with the world where she felt like she might just be the very centre of the universe and yet so very small at the same time. And that was okay.

As she got out of the water, her skin lit up by the warm pink rays from the setting sun, she thought she should have invited Ellen to come with her. She didn't believe for one minute that Ellen would have accepted her invitation, but Abi thought it would be wonderful to get Ellen in the water, feeling that happy rush that the living sea gives you, watching the land from the water and gazing up into the infinite sky.

So often, when Abi called at Ellen's, she would spend time with her nieces rather than her sister, giving Ellen the break that she said she so often craved. They hardly ever spent time all together, but Abi determined that they should. In the future. Starting soon and starting with a trip to the beach together. It would do them all the world of good, she was sure of it.

Later that evening, once she'd returned to Winfield and had had a shower, Abi sat sipping a large glass of wine. She didn't usually drink in the evenings. Or much at all really. But she'd stopped off at a supermarket on the way back from the beach and had bought a bottle of rosé. The pinkness alone as she poured out a generous glass made her feel a little lighter and the warmth she felt a few moments later told her she'd made the right decision.

When her phone went a little after ten, she became instantly anxious, especially when she heard Douglas's voice.

'What is it? Is Ellen okay?' she asked quickly.

'Ellen's fine, don't worry,' Douglas assured her. 'In fact, she's the most chilled I've seen her in a long time. She's just gone upstairs for a bath so I thought I'd catch up with you.'

Abi smiled, glad that her sister had been relaxing after the stressful day. Abi had chosen the sea; Ellen had chosen a bath.

'Has she said much to you?' Abi asked.

'Not a lot. Just that Aunt Claire told you a bit about your mother. I'm so sorry, Abi. It's been quite a day, hasn't it?'

'You could say that!'

'And Ellen said she shouted quite a bit. Is that right?'

'Yes. She was quite scary!'

'Blimey!' Douglas gave a laugh that was full of nervous energy.

'I hardly recognised her.' Abi sighed as she remembered. 'There's been a lot of repressed emotions, I think.'

'I know,' Douglas agreed. 'And that's something I think we still need to address. In fact, Ellen mentioned it to me this evening.'

'What did she say?'

'She said she thinks therapy would be a good idea.'

'Really?'

'She's got the name of someone in Brighton. Comes recommended, she says.'

'Okay. That's good.'

'Ellen told me she's felt stuck. For years. Can you believe that?'

'Yes. I absolutely can. I could feel that with her,' Abi told him. 'Although I think some of the emotions she's been hiding from us came out today.'

She heard Douglas sigh. 'God, Abi! This is all so scary and I feel dreadful that I didn't realise much sooner.'

'It's not your fault, Douglas. Ellen's been very good at bottling everything up.'

'With just the occasional quip or bad mood to let us know something was wrong,' he added.

'I know. Perhaps I should've picked all this up years ago, but life has a way of distracting you.'

'And you had your own things to cope with,' Douglas told her.

'And you were busy with work.'

She heard him curse.

'It's okay, Douglas. We're here for her now and we will get through this.'

'You think so?'

'I really do.'

The therapist's home was a few streets back from the seafront at Brighton in a white Regency building that reminded Abi of a wedding cake. A flight of shallow steps led up to a glossy black door and Ellen pressed the intercom.

'I'm so nervous,' Abi confessed.

'Me too,' Ellen confided. 'Thanks for agreeing to do this with me.'

'That's okay. It can't be worse than our meeting with Aunt Claire,' Abi said with an anxious laugh.

'I hope not with what we're paying her.'

'Ellen – you must let me pay for these sessions, okay?'

Ellen shook her head. 'No. I've got it.'

'Are you sure?' Abi was surprised to hear this, knowing how expensive it was.

'Yes. I need to do this.' Ellen touched her arm and smiled. 'But if we go over ten sessions, perhaps you can pick up the bill!'

Abi laughed. 'Absolutely!'

Charlotte Simms answered the intercom and buzzed them in and a flight of recently-carpeted stairs greeted them. They climbed to the second floor where the door was ajar. It was a light, airy apartment with views towards a row of identical wedding cake buildings opposite. Abi could hear seagulls and the sound made her feel strangely at home, as if a little of the spirit of the sea was with her.

And then the session began. There was little preamble. Forms had been filled in online. But Charlotte, a kind-looking woman in her mid-forties, with a neat bob and a tailored suit, introduced herself briefly. She then gave free rein to Abi and Ellen. It was up to them. Where did they want to start? What were the issues that needed addressing?

Ellen began. She began with the meeting with Aunt Claire and then worked back to the night their mother had died. Abi sat and listened, learning so much not only about her mother, but about her sister too. Ellen seemed so in control. It was as if she'd been building up to this moment somehow, saving everything up and now she was ready to share it all and unburden herself.

The second session was scheduled for later that week and, once again Ellen began, this time with some of her memories of their mother. Abi listened, taking it all in. She asked questions too – the sort of questions that, not so long ago, would have sent Ellen spiralling into a rage had they been on their own, but the gentle presence of the therapist meant that Ellen kept her reactions in check. Indeed, she seemed ready to face any questions that Abi had for her.

One thing kept coming to the fore. Ellen and Abi were talking about themselves as if they were still those two frightened girls. It took Charlotte to point that out to them – that Abi was no longer that little girl on the stairs, half-way up, half-way down. And Ellen wasn't the protector anymore. She didn't always need to be in control of everything. It was too much to ask of anyone and it was time for her to cast that role aside. The relief of hearing all this was immense and Abi couldn't help thinking that they should have let go of these images of themselves years ago. But they hadn't. For whatever reasons, it had taken an outsider to give them permission to let go of the past.

After their second session had ended and they had made an appointment for a third, they found a nearby café and ordered drinks. Even though it was a warm summer's day, Abi wanted the comfort of a hot chocolate and Ellen thought that sounded wonderful.

'A hug in a mug,' Abi said as they wrapped their hands around their drinks a few minutes later.

They sat quietly for a little while, their thoughts settling.

'It went so fast,' Ellen said. 'Did that seem fast to you?'

'Yes. I feel a bit dizzy.'

'Are you okay?'

Abi sipped her drink. 'There's a lot to take in.'

Ellen nodded. 'And I don't think it's all going to suddenly be okay and that we'll wake up one morning and be free of it all.'

Abi glanced out of the window at the busy Brighton street and then looked back at Ellen.

'What you said in there – about taking the brunt growing up?'

'Yes?'

'I can see a correlation,' Abi confessed. 'You carried the burden, protecting me as the younger sister.'

'I saw it as my job,' Ellen told her.

'I know. But I see the same thing happening with Bethanne today.'

Ellen's eyes widened. 'What do you mean?'

'I mean, the way she absorbs everything you say and do – all your moods, all your fears. She takes it all on just as you did when you were her age.'

In the past, Ellen would have stood up and left, refusing to speak about such things but, now, she listened.

'I sometimes think it's too much for her, Ellen. I worry about her. She's a sensitive soul.'

Ellen nodded slowly. 'I've not done a very good job, have I?'

'I'm not saying that. I'm absolutely not saying that!' Abi stressed.

'No. I know you're not. But I am.' Ellen ripped open a packet of sugar and poured it into her chocolate. 'I know I've not been the best mother. Or sister. Or wife even. I *know*. Some days, it's all I can do to push myself through them. But I want to make things better. That's why this therapy's so important to me. I don't want to be stuck in the past or trying to process things from years ago. I want to be here, now! I want to be present for my girls and you and Douglas. And Pugly!'

Abi laughed. 'Pugly?'

'Yes! Even poor Pugly takes the brunt of my moods some days.' She took a deep breath. 'But I want to get through this without pills. I don't want to be like Mum. I don't think I am. Not really.'

'You're not.'

'I think I can cope.'

'I know you can.'

They smiled at each other.

'Ellen, can I ask you something?'

'What?'

Abi paused before answering. It was one of those moments in life where, once the words were out, you couldn't take them back. But she needed to ask.

'Did you ever resent me?'

'What do you mean?'

'I mean, all those swipes you've taken at me over the years – all the times you've called me "the lucky one" – it's all linked to that time, isn't it? All those hours you saw our mother in pain – all the stress and the trauma. You think I missed it all because I was that bit younger than you.' Ellen didn't respond. 'I'm right, aren't I?'

Ellen reached into her pocket for a tissue and wiped her eyes a moment later. 'I was trying to protect you from it all. You were so little, Abi.'

'But there's a part of you that resented that, isn't there?' Abi said as gently as she could even though her hurt was still raw.

Ellen turned to face her. 'You never saw what I did. Our mother – it was bad, Abi. I didn't know what to do. I felt really helpless. There was just me, you see. She used to tell me how awful she felt. I thought she meant a headache or something, but it was more than that, wasn't it?'

Abi could feel her tears rising again. 'Yes. I think it was.'

'So I tried to make sure you didn't see her like that. You often hated me for it. I'd push you out of rooms, telling you Mum wasn't feeling well and you'd accuse me of keeping her all to myself.'

'Oh, Ellen – I'm so sorry.'

Ellen sniffed. 'And I sometimes wish I'd been the little sister and you could have protected me from it all.' Tears were rolling down her face now and Abi reached across the table to hold her hand.

'I wish I could have done more for you back then.'

'But you're here now,' Ellen said.

'Yes. And we'll get through this – you and me,' Abi told her. 'We'll get through it and we'll be fine, okay? And, before our next session, you and the girls are coming swimming with me.'

'What?' Ellen asked in surprise, giving a loud sniff as she mopped her eyes again.

'No excuses – make it the weekend or after school. I'm picking you up and we're going to the sea. Plastic buckets, arm bands, towels, the lot! We're going to swim and paddle and look at the sky, and we can talk – or not. We can eat chips and ice cream...' Abi paused, waiting for Ellen to cry in alarm, but she didn't, 'and we can – we can just sit and be.'

Ellen closed her eyes for a moment and then nodded. 'That sounds perfect.'

CHAPTER TWENTY-ONE

The funeral wasn't the end of Edward's father. There was a lot of admin to get through, decisions to be made and bills to be paid. Oscar was hopeless. He passed everything on to Edward. Mind you, that's what Edward deemed best so he didn't complain.

Oscar was still living at their father's house and, as far as Edward could see, was keeping the place tidy. But Edward was dreading the moment when he'd have to tell Oscar the place was going to be sold. He couldn't foresee that going well as Oscar still believed that the old family home was his rightful inheritance.

Edward tried to put the stress of it all out of his mind. There was no point in worrying. He would just get through everything day by day, methodically, on his own. That was the sore point, of course – he didn't have anyone he could confide in. Other than Stephen. He was always good for a chat down the pub and at least he knew about the history between Edward and his family. It was a relief to talk to him occasionally, and yet it wasn't the same as talking to Abigail. That's what he really wanted. He missed her sweet company. He missed that warm smile of hers and her ability to laugh at life and see the joy in everything. Heaven only knew he needed a dose of that at the moment. But in order for that to happen, he'd have had to have been honest with her about everything – right from the beginning.

There was no coming back from this, was there? She'd told him how she'd felt and there was nothing he could do to change her mind. If he told her the truth, it would probably only upset her more and that was the last thing he wanted.

It had occurred to him, in the dark silence of nights at Winfield when he lay awake in bed, the breeze coming in from the downs, that he could leave, and perhaps he should. He could rent his apartment out and live elsewhere or he could even sell his half of Winfield. It wasn't what he wanted, but then he didn't want this awful half-life without Abi in it either. It was too painful, knowing she was just across the hallway and yet a world away. How could he go on living like that?

Another source of frustration that was seriously making him rethink things was the noise from Samantha's. He'd been round twice in the last week and she'd turned the volume down on her stereo, but he'd still been able to hear – to *feel* – the thump of the bass in the hallway. He'd clearly told her that things weren't working out but, before he could say anything about giving her her notice, she'd told him she was leaving at the end of the summer. The news had almost winded Edward; he hadn't known what to say so he'd merely nodded, trying to hide his relief.

He just had to endure his neighbour until then, he told himself. He hated confronting her and, if there was at least a time limit on this terrible form of torture, he could put up with it.

If only the situation with Abi was as easily resolved.

Abi was glad to welcome the weekend. It had been a long, emotional week with the two visits to the therapist. But today was going to be fun. She'd arranged an outing to the beach with Ellen and the girls and was picking them up later that morning.

She was just about to start packing her swimming things when there was a knock on her door. She hesitated. It wouldn't be Edward, would it? The thought made her feel uneasy. Things were still horribly awkward if ever they crossed paths. So Abi opened the door in trepidation.

'Tim!' she cried in relief a moment later, noticing that he had a sausage dog tucked under his arm.

'I'm sorry to bother you, but I thought I'd better let you know that I'm leaving.'

'What – for good?'

'Yes. It's my mother, you see,' he said with a roll of his eyes as if it was only to be expected. 'She's not well and I've said I'll move back in with her and take care of things.'

'Well, I'm sure she'll be very grateful to have you.'

He gave a funny sort of snort. 'I'm not sure about that. This happens every so often and she's never been grateful before, but at least I'll get my old room back so it'll save me rent for a while.' He gasped at his faux pas. '*Not* that the rent here was high!' he added quickly.

Abi smiled, putting him at his ease. 'So when are you going?'

'After the weekend, but I'll pay to the end of the month, of course.'

'We'll be sorry to lose you,' she told him honestly.

Tim gave a little smile and then kissed the top of the dog's head. 'Thank you for being such a great landlady. And for putting up with the dog-sitting.'

Abi stepped forward to stroke the little dog. 'It's been lovely being neighbours. Did Winfield inspire you to write?'

Tim sighed dramatically. 'I'm afraid I've been rather tied up with my doggy duties, and I haven't been able to write with *madam* and her music.'

'Oh, dear, I'm sorry to hear that.'

'To be honest, I've been trying to spend my time out and about with my dog buddies.'

'Maybe you'll have a chance to write at your mum's,' Abi suggested.

'I hope so,' Tim said.

'Well, good luck with it all and do come and say goodbye before you go.'

She watched as he returned to his apartment and it struck Abi that she was losing both her tenants this summer – first Tim and then Aura who would be moving into Harry's apartment after the wedding. Perhaps she'd better start thinking of advertising again. And maybe she should let Edward know that Tim was leaving.

Grabbing a notepad and tearing a page out, she scribbled a quick message to Edward, folding it in half and taking it across to his apartment and popping it under his door. It was the coward's way out, not facing him, but she told herself that she was going out later and didn't have time.

She was half-way across the hallway when she heard his door open.

'Abi?'

She froze, but then turned to face him.

'I've just put a note...' She motioned to the piece of paper he was holding, which he unfolded now and read.

'Oh, I see,' he said. 'Well, thanks for letting me know.'

They stood looking at each other awkwardly, their expressions hovering in that no-man's land between frowning and smiling.

'Are you well?' he asked.

'Yes. You?'

He nodded. 'Abi – I wanted to say sorry again.'

'It's okay. You don't have to.'

'I feel I do. I mean, we've not talked since...' he paused. 'Have we?'

Abi glanced down at the floor because it was too painful to look at Edward. There was a part of her that wanted to run towards him and hug him, which was ridiculous. He'd hurt her. And yet, she still loved him and she really missed him. She hated that he wasn't a part of her daily life anymore, and seeing him now and hearing his voice was almost too much for her.

'Edward, listen...' It was then that she heard her phone ringing. She glanced towards her apartment and then back at Edward. 'I've got to go.'

Edward nodded and turned to go and Abi did the same, the cloud of so many things left unsaid hovering over her.

It was Ellen on the phone with some reassurance needed about their day ahead.

'No, no – don't worry. I've got it sorted. I'll see you soon, okay?'

Abi hung up, glancing back out into the hallway as she'd left her door open, but Edward had gone.

～

Abi wasn't used to beaches at weekends, preferring to choose the quieter times during the week, but she and Ellen had decided it would be easier with the girls. Rather than racing after school on a weekday, they could spend the whole day together. And it was rather wonderful to get there in time for a picnic lunch and not to worry about the sun setting on them before they'd really relaxed into the day.

'It's a pity Douglas couldn't join us,' Abi said.

Ellen shook her head. 'He knew it was a girls' day. Anyway, he's going to see his brother. I think they're taking their mountain bikes out for a spin. He needs some time to just – you know – get out for a bit.'

Abi nodded, knowing how stressful the last few weeks must have been for Douglas. He deserved some downtime just like they did.

'How have you been?' Abi asked Ellen.

'Okay. You?'

'Okay. Mostly. There's a lot to process,' Abi confessed.

'I know.'

The two of them were sitting on stripy pink beach mats, sun hats on, legs bare, watching the girls playing with Pugly. Bethanne had quickly discovered that she wasn't too old to make sandcastles and she and Rosie had got to work collecting stones and shells for decoration.

'I'm glad we're doing this,' Abi said.

'What – the beach?'

'No! Therapy.' Abi smiled. 'Talking. Working things out. It feels good.'

'It's draining.'

'Yes, it's that too. I've never felt so tired, but it's a good kind of tired. It's a working-things-out tired, don't you think?'

Ellen nodded. She was wearing sunglasses and it was hard to read her expression.

'And you've been doing okay?' Abi asked again.

'I haven't locked myself in the bathroom again – if that's what you mean.'

'I didn't mean that!'

'No?'

'Well, I kind of did.'

Ellen gave a little smile. 'Is it crazy to feel this good after only two sessions of therapy?'

'I don't think so. If it's giving you what you need,' Abi said. 'I think it's giving us permission to process things – to see them perhaps for the first time – and to let them go. And I think, especially with you, that you've been carrying this on your own for all these years. I'm not surprised you're willing to let it go as quickly as you can.' Abi watched as her sister began drawing circles in the sand between them.

'I hope I'm letting go. What if I can't, though? What if it all comes back again and follows me around forever?'

Abi shook her head. 'I don't think it will.'

'You sound very sure,' Ellen said.

'Here's what I think: once you've made up your mind about something, that's it. You're committed to it – no going back. So make a deal with yourself – decide what you're going to do. After all, it's what you *want* to do, isn't it?'

'I wish I had your confidence.'

'Ellen – you *do!* You're more confident now than I've ever seen you. And you were far more confident than I was in those therapy sessions.'

'Was I?'

'You completely led the way. Didn't you notice? I was so

impressed! I'd have been totally lost without you. I probably wouldn't have even gone in!'

'Really?'

Abi reached across the space between them to hold Ellen's sandy hand. 'Truly,' she told her.

They went swimming after that and then for a walk, the four of them strolling and skipping along the tideline, skimming stones and pocketing pretty shells. Pugly barked at the sea, Rosie did gull impressions, shrieking loudly into the sky and Bethanne simply smiled at all around her. It was good to see her smiling, Abi thought. She looked relaxed, obviously picking up on her mother's improved mood.

'Abi? I wanted to say something,' Ellen said a little later as they turned around and made the slow walk back towards their beach mats.

'What is it?'

'I wanted to say sorry. All those years I had a go at you for...' she paused, stopped walking and stared out to sea.

'For being the lucky one, you mean?'

Ellen nodded. 'I shouldn't have said that. Not ever. I...' she paused and sighed. 'I was in a bad place. For a long time.'

'I know.'

'Feel free to yell at me.'

'I'm not going to yell at you,' Abi told her. 'I might push you in the sea!'

Ellen gasped and moved back from the waves quickly.

'I'm just joking!'

They grinned at one another.

'I feel horrible that I lashed out at you over and over again.' She took her sunglasses off and wiped her eyes.

'Don't cry, Ellen. It's okay – honestly. We're moving past all this now, aren't we?'

'I know.' She gave a sniff and put her glasses back on. 'I think I envied you, you see. You always had your art – even when you were small. You were always able to escape into it, grabbing your wax crayons or felt tip pens – you'd make this little nest for yourself. Then, when you left home, you had such a vision about what you wanted to do.'

'Did I?' Abi said, surprised to hear this.

'Yes!'

'It didn't seem like that to me.'

'Well, it did to me. I had no idea what I wanted to do. But it was more than that,' Ellen confessed as they walked on. 'You always had this drive. I don't know where it came from, but I certainly never had it.'

Abi frowned. 'You have drive! You knew you wanted a family and a home and you've always had a vision for how you wanted things to be.'

'I don't think that's the same thing.'

'What do you mean?'

'I mean, the things that I always wanted seemed so ordinary.'

'Ellen – a family and a home are far from *ordinary*! Just look at what you've got. Your girls are miraculous! And Douglas is an absolute gem.'

'I know. I know that *now*.' She gave a sigh. 'But I don't think I always did, did I? Not for the longest time.' She paused as if casting her mind back into the past. 'I always felt like there was something missing from my life. But I think I know what it was now.'

'What?' Abi asked, waiting patiently for Ellen to answer.

'Me!' Ellen declared at last. 'I think I've been missing from my own life.' She stopped walking again and Abi reached a hand towards her, giving her shoulder a squeeze. 'I think I've been so stuck in the past for all these years and I've not really been *here*, in the present.'

'But you're here now!' Abi told her and Ellen nodded, sniffing again and stuffing her tissue underneath her sunglasses.

The two of them stared out to sea for a moment, listening to the happy sound of Bethanne and Rosie laughing as Pugly tried to keep the waves back by barking at them.

Then they continued walking, returning to their spot on the beach and sitting down. The girls sat down too, grabbing some food from the communal bag and giggling as they fed titbits to Pugly.

'Listen,' Abi began in a whisper so the girls wouldn't overhear, 'while we're being really honest with each other, I just wanted to say something too.'

'What?'

'The time in London after... well, after my miscarriage.'

'What about it?' Ellen sounded concerned.

'I felt...'

'What, Abi?'

'You never really talked to me about it.'

Ellen frowned deeply. 'I thought talking about it would be the last thing you'd want to do.'

'Well, it was, but I needed to. I didn't have anyone else, you see. I mean, there were friends at work, but that didn't seem right. I was their boss and everything. It would have been odd and awkward.'

It was Ellen's turn to reach out to her sister and hold her hand now and she did just that.

'God, I'm sorry, Abi. I had no idea. I guess I was trying to help by not focusing on it.'

'Yes, maybe. I hadn't thought of it like that before.'

'Do you want to talk about it now?' Ellen asked gently.

Abi shook her head. 'No. All this stuff is in the past, isn't it?'

Ellen nodded. 'Yes.'

'So let's leave it there. That's what I'm learning at the moment. I think you have to face these things, certainly, and deal with them, but there comes a point when you've got to move forward and live your life.'

Abi felt Ellen squeeze her hand tightly. 'I agree.'

Rosie ran up to them both, her legs glittering with sand crystals. 'I'm hungry!'

'I'm starving!' Bethanne cried from behind her.

'But you've just been snacking!' Ellen said.

Abi stood up from her beach mat. 'I'll get chips, okay?'

Ellen bit her lip and her daughters stared at her, eyes wide as they awaited her decision.

'Okay. We'll have chips!'

'Hooray!' Bethanne yelled.

'Hooray for Mummy!' Rosie chimed.

Abi laughed and left the beach, returning with two big boxes a few minutes later. The four of them sat on the beach mats together, eating hot vinegary chips, the sound of the sea behind them. Abi had bought Pugly a sausage and he was enjoying that while sitting on his very own beach towel.

It was then that Abi remembered something.

'How's it going with the sewing machine?' she asked Ellen.

'Mum made me a tutu!' Rosie announced.

'Really?'

'Well, it's a skirt with frills,' Ellen said.

'I'll have to see it.'

'Actually, I've got a photo somewhere.' Ellen reached into her bag and pulled her phone out and scrolled for a moment. 'Here!'

Abi took the phone and shielded her eyes from the sun. 'It's lovely, Ellen!'

'Thanks! Swipe to see some other bits and bobs.'

Abi did so and gave a whistle when she saw purses, cushions, an apron and a dress.

'These are gorgeous!'

'You think so?'

'I *know* so. You could go into business.'

'Well, that's the plan. Nothing big. Not on your *Abigail Carey* scale or anything. But you know I've been thinking that an Etsy store might be doable.'

'Absolutely! I think it would be very popular.' She handed the phone back to Ellen. 'I'm sure Mum would be thrilled you're using her sewing machine.'

'I sure too. Thanks for getting it for me.'

Abi smiled, remembering the awkward visit she'd had to Aunt Claire's to fetch it. 'Do you think we'll ever visit her again?'

'Aunt Claire? I don't know. What do you think?'

Abi sighed. 'I don't like to write people off.'

'No, but she hasn't exactly opened her arms to us – like *ever!*'

'But I can't shake that image of her crying from my mind,' Abi confessed.

'Who's been crying?' Rosie asked, looking up from her chips.

'Aunt Claire.'

'Did you give her a hug?' Rosie asked. 'Hugs are good for people crying.'

Abi felt the sting of tears in her eyes at Rosie's sweet words. 'Yes, I gave her a hug.'

'And did it help?'

'A bit, I think.'

'Maybe you could give her another to make sure,' Rosie suggested.

'Yes,' Abi said. 'That sounds like a good idea.' Abi glanced at Ellen who gave a shrug.

'Maybe one day,' Ellen said. 'After a few more therapy sessions. When I'm feeling invincible.'

Abi smiled.

The tide was coming in and the colours in the sky were deepening. Abi's skin felt tight after a day of sun, sea and sand. It had been such a lovely day of sitting, swimming, playing and laughing. And talking and thinking. Abi had done a lot of thinking in between conversations with Ellen. Actually, she'd done nothing but think all week. Perhaps that's what therapy did for a person – it opened the mind a little to new thoughts and new possibilities.

'I've been thinking of talking to Edward and apologising,' Abi suddenly blurted out.

'You should.'

Abi frowned. 'But you don't even know what I'm apologising for.'

Ellen shook her head. 'Doesn't matter. Do it. Life's too short to hold grudges or to take the so-called higher ground. And you like him, Abi! You want him in your life, don't you?'

'Yes!'

'Then apologise. Whatever you've done or he's done – you can make it good and make things work.'

Abi stared at her sister in wonder. 'You sound like some kind of oracle!'

Ellen laughed. 'Me?'

'You're different. You're – you're *clearer*. Does that make sense?'

Her sister nodded. 'That makes absolute sense. I *feel* clearer and calmer than I have in years.' She smiled and Abi could sense this deep shift in her sister. It was sudden and miraculous and she was so deeply grateful to see it.

By this time, many of the visitors they'd shared the beach with had gone home and the temperature had dropped. Ellen and the girls were now sporting jumpers and cardigans, but Abi refused to say goodbye to the day yet.

'I think I'll just have one more dip,' she said. 'Anyone want to join me?'

Ellen shook her head. 'I'm just going to watch the sky.'

'Girls?'

Bethanne had her nose in a book and Rosie was busy filling the moat of her sand castle with water. So Abi ventured towards the sea alone. It was like walking into a painting and being absorbed by the colours. The peace of it all filled her and she gazed up into the sky, thankful for all that the day had brought her. And what was next, she couldn't help wondering? She'd told Ellen that she was going to make up with Edward and yet she'd barely been able to speak to him earlier that day. So what had changed? Had seeing the change in her sister inspired her? Or had spending a day at the beach made all the difference? Had the sea, sand and sky worked its magic, giving her a different perspective on things? Or did she just miss Edward too much to worry about whatever it was that had caused them to break up?

Of course, Abi hadn't forgotten why she'd broken up with him, but it no longer seemed to be a good enough reason to be apart from him. Now, when she thought about Edward, she felt a kind of softness in her heart. She guessed that she was learning so much from her therapy sessions and talking to Ellen, and something she realised now was that she'd been so very hard on Edward. Yes, he'd hidden the truth from her. Well, he'd lied, hadn't he? There was no getting away from that, and it had hurt Abi deeply, but he'd obviously had his reasons and she shouldn't just wipe a person out of her life. At least, not one who meant so much to her. And she missed him. That was the abiding thing. She missed him so very much.

Floating in the sea, her vision soft on the horizon as the sun began to set, Abi knew what she had to do.

CHAPTER TWENTY-TWO

It was the day after the trip to the beach and Abi was feeling wonderfully relaxed after her day in the sunshine with her sister and nieces. She'd taken a few photos on her phone and she looked at them now. Happy smiling faces. It had been lovely to spend the whole day with her family and Abi promised herself that there would be more days like that in their future. Maybe even with Aunt Claire too.

For a moment, Abi tried to imagine Aunt Claire sitting on a beach. It wasn't an easy image to conjure. Aunt Claire was such an indoors person. Abi couldn't ever remember being outside with her growing up. There'd been no walks, no bike rides and no trips to the park. But then she remembered the photo of Aunt Claire with her mother. That had been taken outdoors, somewhere beautiful like the top of a hill. Maybe that smile would return if Abi and Ellen invited her out with them.

Abi idly scrolled through a few more recent photos she'd taken. There were lots of the walled garden and her beloved sunflowers and, scrolling back further, there were photos of another garden too. Ronnie's. She paused, looking at the images, her vision blurring with tears. How she missed that garden and her dear friend. And now she cursed that she didn't have a decent photo of him. The only one she had showed him bent double in a flower bed, but the image made her smile for it was pure Ronnie – always tending to something. And there was the cottage – so perfect in its surroundings. Abi's heart ached for it.

And then something occurred to her.

Quickly, she switched her laptop on and logged in to a couple of online bank accounts. Then she checked her recent emails – something she'd neglected for a few days. There was one from Natalia, the jeweller she was working with. She'd had a lot of interest in Abi's recent designs and was proposing that Abi extended the range from brooches to pendants, earrings and bracelets. Natalia sounded very excited by the project and told her that, if Abi was happy to work on more pieces, the sky was the limit.

Abi sat back in her chair. This was unexpected, but wonderfully so. She'd never set out to design jewellery, but the opportunity had come her way and it excited her. It was the new direction she'd been looking for – giving her the chance to develop as an artist. It also meant she would be earning again and that meant she wouldn't be plundering her savings anymore.

'And that means...' She drummed her fingers on the table and then she picked up her phone and searched for a number, ringing it a moment later before she lost her nerve.

'Kenneth? It's Abigail – your uncle's friend. We met at his house. Yes, thank you. I'm fine. There's something I'd love to talk to you about.'

～

Later that day, when Harry had come home from work, Abi walked out into the garden. Aura was sitting outside on the lawn with her fiancé and Abi approached them with a smile.

'I hope I'm not disturbing you,' she said, sitting down on the grass beside them.

'Of course not,' Aura said. 'How are you?'

'I'm good. I've actually got something I want to run by you two.'

'Oh, yes?' Harry said.

'You know Ronnie's cottage? The one we talked about before?'

They both nodded.

'I'm going to buy it. I spoke to the owner today and he's happy to sell it to me in due course and avoid the whole process of putting it on the market.'

'Abi!' Aura cried. 'Does that mean you're leaving Winfield?'

She shook her head. 'No. I'm in the fortunate position to be able to buy the cottage without having to sell my share of Winfield. I'll be plundering my savings a bit, mind, but I've got some work coming my way and, well, I just feel it's the right thing to do.'

'Well, congratulations!' Harry said.

'Yes, I'm so pleased for you,' Aura told her. 'I know how much the cottage means to you.'

'Thank you!' Abi smiled. 'I'm really excited, but that's only half my news.'

'Oh?' Aura said, looking expectant.

'Well, as you know, I won't be leaving Winfield, but I think it would be lovely to rent out Ronnie's cottage and I was wondering if you guys would be interested in it.'

Aura looked at Harry. Her bright eyes were wide. 'Harry?'

Harry stared back at Aura.

'Listen, I don't mean to pressure you for an answer right away. I was just so excited to tell you.'

'So how would it work?' Harry asked.

'It would be an arrangement just like I have with Aura. Rent would be kept low, like my apartments here at Winfield.'

Aura looked delighted. 'It makes sense Harry. It has so much potential for us.'

'But I thought you loved Winfield.'

'I do. But this cottage – I think it's really us, don't you?'

'Yeah!' He grinned. 'I do. But I feel bad letting Edward down.'

'But it wouldn't be straightaway, would it?' Aura asked.

'Not at all,' Abi said. 'There's all sorts of things to sort out first. It's early days.'

'So we'd be here for Christmas, I imagine?' Aura said.

'It would be my guess you would.'

Harry nodded, taking all this in.

'But I really don't need a decision from you yet. You've got your wedding coming up and the last thing you need is another thing to worry about organising. Just give it some thought, okay?' Abi got up from the grass and was about to head back to her apartment when Harry stopped her.

'Abi?'

'Yes?'

'We'll take it!'

'Really? Are you sure?' Abi asked, noticing that Harry and Aura were holding hands, their faces flushed with excitement.

Aura looked at Harry and they both nodded in unison.

'Yes!' Harry said.

'Absolutely!' Aura agreed.

Abi laughed, clapping her hands together in glee before running across the lawn and hugging them both.

'I suppose we'd better take a look at it as soon as we can,' Harry added.

'Yes, of course!' Abi agreed.

'But I think we're pretty sure.'

'Oh, there's just one thing,' Abi added. 'One teeny *tiny* stipulation.'

'What's that?' Harry sounded slightly worried.

'That – just occasionally, I can come and paint in the garden,' she said. 'Would that be okay?'

Harry breathed a sigh of relief. 'That would be *very* okay!'

Harry and Aura were cuddled up on the sofa in her apartment. The French doors were still open, allowing a cool evening breeze into the room, refreshing after the heat of the day.

'Can you believe that?' Harry asked, stroking Aura's hair.

'Life is mysterious and full of wonders!' she told him happily.

'Our own home. Well, rented.'

'Our own front door,' Aura said. 'Not that I've minded sharing Winfield's fabulous front door!'

'And the garden's pretty amazing too. I mean, it isn't walled like Winfield's, but we'll have it all to ourselves.'

'Apart from Abi sketching there from time to time,' Aura pointed out. 'It'll be lovely to keep in touch with her that way. I wonder when we'll get the keys.'

'I think these things take time,' Harry warned.

'Well, we're not in a rush, are we? We're quite happy here.'

'Yes, we are,' Harry said, looking around Aura's apartment.

'What is it?'

'You've not started packing yet.'

'Harry, I'm not moving into yours until *after* the wedding!' She laughed.

'I know! I just thought you might have started putting things into boxes.'

'It won't take me long,' she assured him, 'and there are a few of my things in yours already.'

'I know.' He kissed the top of her head. 'It's just that I can't wait.'

Aura smiled and kissed him. 'Neither can I.'

Abi couldn't settle the next day. She felt like she was hovering and in constant motion. There were the ongoing therapy sessions, the plans she had for Ronnie's cottage, the upheaval with things changing at Winfield and, of course, her unresolved issues with Edward. Abi hadn't seen him around much. His car hadn't been in the driveway and she guessed he'd been away with work or else sorting things out to do with his father's estate.

She took herself out into the garden. The August sun was already warm at nine in the morning and Abi managed to lose herself in some work after giving her plants a good water before the heat of the day took its toll.

It was around mid-morning that she heard a car pulling up at the front of the hall, its tyres soft on the gravel. It was very likely to be Edward's car. Abi got up, leaving the sketchbook she'd been working in on her bench and returning to her apartment. She felt awkward and uncomfortable as she waited for the sound of the front door opening and Edward's footsteps crossing the hallway. But it couldn't be helped; she needed to see him.

Finally, after what seemed like an interminable age to an

anxious Abi, but was probably only two minutes, she heard him entering the hall. Without pausing to calm herself with a deep breath or worrying about what her hair might look like, Abi opened her door. Edward turned immediately at the sound.

'Abigail!' He looked genuinely surprised to see her.

Briefly, she thought of all the things she could say to him in that moment – the apologies, the explanations, the confessions – but none of them were good enough, and so she crossed the space between them and reached up, cupping his face in her hands and kissing him fully on the mouth.

'Abi!' Edward gasped when they finally broke apart.

'Hello,' she said.

He laughed. 'Hello! What did I do to deserve that?'

She could feel tears in her eyes at just being close to him again. 'Just being you.'

'But I thought you didn't like me very much.'

Abi shook her head. 'No, Edward! I – I...' her voice drifted away into the land of unspoken thoughts.

'Hey!' he said, placing a hand under her chin and lifting her head up. 'Are you okay?'

She nodded. 'I'm sorry,' she whispered.

'*You're* sorry?' Edward said, sounding confused. 'Abi – I'm the one who should be apologising to you – over and over again!'

'No. I was wrong. So wrong to behave like I did. I'm sorry, Edward. I shouldn't have pushed you away like that.'

'But I hurt you. I never meant to – but I did.'

'I know. But then I hurt you with my reaction.' She gave a nervous little laugh which was met by him kissing her.

'What you were going through – what you'd been through – it was none of my business and it was wrong of me to expect anything from you,' she told him.

'No. I should have told you. A relationship is about

openness and honesty. If I couldn't confide in you then what hope did we have?'

'But I want to be with you,' she told him, laying her heart bare to him.

'God, Abi! I've missed you so much!'

They kissed again.

'I've missed you too. It's been horrible not having you, well, just there,' she confessed. 'So many times during the day, I'll think of something to tell you or find something I want to show you, and you're not there.' She could hear the emotion in her voice.

'For me too. I was in London yesterday. I had some time to kill between meetings in South Kensington so I popped into the Victoria and Albert Museum.'

Abi gasped. 'That's one of my favourite places!'

'I thought it might be,' Edward said with a smile. 'I was thinking about you all the way round. Every time I saw something beautiful, I'd think of you. *Abi would love this*, I'd say to myself.'

'I've been swimming without you,' she confessed to him. 'It felt very strange.'

He chuckled. 'It feels strange when I make a cup of tea and you aren't there to have one with me.'

They both laughed, relaxing a little.

'I'm so sorry, Abi,' Edward whispered. 'I truly never meant to hurt you.'

'And I'm sorry I hurt you.'

'Does this mean we're good? That we're, well, together again?'

'Yes. We're good and we're most *definitely* together.' She smiled up at him. 'If that's okay with you?'

'That's very okay with me,' he replied, gently pushing her

hair out of her face. 'But, Abi?'

'Yes?'

'There's something I feel I should tell you.'

She shook her head. 'Edward, you don't need to. Not if it's too painful for you to talk about. I get that now.' She paused, resting her head on his chest and feeling that comforting familiarity. 'You know I've had a couple of therapy sessions with my sister?'

'Really?'

'There's so much I want to tell you, but there's something I've learned from the last few weeks. Not just in therapy but when talking to my sister and coming to terms with my own childhood, and it's that none of us lead perfect lives. We all have darkness and sadness and things we can't face or talk about. I get that. So please don't feel you have to tell me anything you don't want to. But, if you do want to then I'm here and I'll listen.'

She felt Edward's hands moving across her back, pulling her into the tightest of hugs, and she felt such relief and joy in that moment that she never wanted it to end.

CHAPTER TWENTY-THREE

When Aura woke up on the morning of her wedding day, the first thing she did was to grab her favourite piece of rose quartz which she kept on her bedside table and kiss it. The stone of peace, of healing, of compassion.

'Of love,' she whispered.

She got out of bed and unrolled her yoga mat in front of the French doors which she'd opened onto a glorious summer day. She took some deep breaths, finding her centre, her space, her calm. She then showered, washing her hair carefully. She hadn't booked anything fancy like a hairdresser. She didn't want the fuss of other people around her on her special day. But Maria was coming over to lend a hand with whatever was needed. It felt funny having Harry's mum volunteer for that role rather than her own mother but, even at this point in the proceedings, she wasn't sure if her mum was even coming to the wedding.

For a brief moment, Aura thought about her brother Johnny wondering where he was and what he was doing. He'd have no idea she was getting married, would he? And would he even care if he did?

Aura took a few more deep breaths, needing to exhale the stresses that could so easily threaten to ruin her day – if she let them. She had picked up her rose quartz in her left hand, the receiving hand, envisaging a day full of love and peace for her and Harry.

A few minutes later, she felt calm and happy and started to get ready, wondering how Harry was getting on in his apartment.

She picked up her phone and texted him.

Hope you remembered to get up today! x

A moment later, the reply came.

Still in bed. Why? Anything special planned?;) x

Aura giggled and replied.

Was thinking of getting married, but not sure now! X

She waited and his reply came.

I'm up. I'm up!! xxx

Aura smiled, picturing her tousled-hair fiancé leaping about his apartment. She couldn't wait to see him, but the ceremony wasn't until the afternoon which seemed an age away so she'd have to be patient and pace herself. She also couldn't wait to see Abi and Edward. Earlier that week, a rather breathless Abi had knocked on her door and told her that she and Edward had made up. Aura was thrilled because they were both very dear to her and deserved to be happy. She had to admit that she'd also been anxious about the atmosphere the pair might create at the ceremony and reception, but it was all good now.

It was after lunch when Maria arrived, looking wonderful in the pink floral dress that she'd bought with Aura. As soon as she saw Aura in her sky-blue lacy dress, her hands flew to her face.

'Oh, Aura! You look like an angel!'

They then got to work together, Aura sitting down and letting Maria fuss with her hair, fastening the little white rosebuds which the florist had delivered earlier along with the bridal bouquet. Aura couldn't have been happier with her bouquet. It was made up of white roses, and cosmos and Queen Anne's lace picked from the walled garden, all tied together with a sky-blue ribbon to match her dress.

'How's Harry?' Aura dared to ask, knowing that Maria would have called in on her son on arriving at Winfield.

'He's fine. A tad nervous, I think, but that's all good, isn't it?'

'Is it?' Aura wasn't so sure.

'It means he cares,' Maria told her.

Aura sighed in relief. 'And how's Leonard?'

'He's like a child at Christmas! I haven't seen him this excited since he ordered your angel wings!'

Aura laughed.

'Talking of which,' Maria said, 'we must make sure we get a photo of you all dressed up in front of those very wings. Leonard would love that!'

Aura smiled, feeling so very looked after. And loved.

The registry office ceremony was simple but perfect. Harry looked smart in his new navy suit and blue cravat, and Aura looked like a piece of summer sky in her dress, her red hair cascading over her shoulders, threaded through with the rosebuds Maria had helped her with. Harry and Aura held hands throughout the whole ceremony, exchanging their vows and their slim gold wedding rings.

Maria and Leonard both had tears in their eyes as Aura and Harry were pronounced husband and wife. As did Harry's Uncle Arthur, Aura noted. Edward and Abi had held hands throughout the ceremony too, and Aura's crystal colleagues,

Sylvie and Bella, were both wearing more crystals beads than you could shake a wand at. Aura's mother made a brief appearance, pecking her daughter on the cheek and leaving before anyone could ask if she was coming to Winfield afterwards. But Aura wasn't going to dwell on that because she was surrounded by people who truly loved her.

It was late afternoon when the small party returned to Winfield and Harry couldn't stop himself from sweeping Aura up into his arms and carrying her over the threshold of Winfield's front door, much to the delight of everyone else who clapped and cheered before heading out into the walled garden. A few moments later, the bride and groom appeared through Harry's French doors, Aura still in his arms. Abi made the most of the opportunity to throw her homemade rose petal confetti over them and everyone took photos.

The sun was out to bless them all and a large table had been laid with the food and the cake by the caterer, set up under a pop-up gazebo decorated with pretty pink and yellow bunting. And the garden looked resplendent. Not only was it full of the flowers Abi had grown, but Aura had made sure that the florist had decorated all the benches and the pretty little arches and statues which were new to the garden that summer, and they had all been threaded through with fairy lights which would twinkle prettily as soon as dusk fell.

'You look so beautiful,' Harry whispered in Aura's ear once they managed to find a quiet corner of the garden to be alone.

'And you're so handsome!'

'What – in this old thing?' He laughed as he patted his cravat. 'I might actually start wearing this to work.'

Aura giggled. 'You might start a new craze.'

'And you should wear rosebuds in your hair all the time.'

'You know, I think I might!'

They kissed. Immediately, the photographer pounced.

'Smile, please! And another kiss!'

'They kissed?' Maria cried. 'I missed it! Kiss again, you two!'

Harry obliged his mother and Aura didn't protest.

Afternoon embraced evening with open arms and the little party chatted happily, ate and drank, and danced among the flowers.

When the garden finally fell into indigo shadows and a bright crescent moon came out to watch over the proceedings, Harry and Aura began to say their goodbyes to the guests. Leonard and Maria had gifted the couple a night at a posh hotel deep in the Sussex countryside and it was from there that they were flying out to Naples for their Italian honeymoon the day after. It was all too exciting.

'I can't thank you all enough for coming,' Aura said as everyone gathered around her and Harry. 'You've made our day so special.'

'Yes, thank you, everyone!' Harry echoed. 'Mum, Dad – you've been brilliant! And a special thank you should go to Edward and Abi because, without them, I might never have met Aura.'

'Here's to Edward and Abi!' Leonard suddenly cried and glasses were topped up with champagne and raised to the owners of Winfield.

Hugs and kisses were then exchanged before Aura turned her back and threw the little bouquet of white flowers into the air. When she turned around, she was thrilled to see that it was her landlady, Abi, who had caught it.

❧

Finally, Abi and Edward were alone in the garden, sitting on a bench together. The moon had been joined by a thousand stars and the hot August day had cooled down.

'Samantha's been nice and quiet,' Abi said, nodding to the apartment at the back of the hall.

'Yes. I told her about the wedding and she decided to make herself scarce.'

'Oh, good. Well, I'm glad there wasn't any aggro. It would have been awful if she'd been blasting her music.'

'She's leaving, did I tell you?'

'No.'

'Pretty soon, actually.'

'Did you give her her notice?'

'I didn't have to. Thank goodness.' Edward sighed.

'And I've lost Tim.'

'He's gone already? I thought I hadn't seen him for a while. Or heard any dogs.'

Abi smiled. 'I'll miss him.'

'I won't miss Samantha,' Edward confessed.

'No. It's been a bit stressful being landlords, hasn't it?'

'But you're still going to be one with Ronnie's cottage.'

Abi nodded. 'I know. I don't mind that so much, though. You couldn't have better tenants than Harry and Aura.'

'I still think I should get a commission for you stealing Harry from me!'

Abi laughed. 'Yes, sorry about that.' She sat back on the bench, inhaling the sweet floral garland that had been wrapped around it.

'Can you believe it? Winfield's first wedding party!' she said with a huge smile.

'But maybe not the last,' Edward said.

She looked at him, wide-eyed. 'What are you saying?'

'I'm just saying you should be careful when you go around catching wedding bouquets!'

She laughed as she thought of the bridal bouquet resting in her kitchen sink. Edward picked up her left hand and kissed it and Abi felt a wonderful warm glow at being here in this moment with him.

'Listen, Abi,' Edward said and she felt that the mood had changed slightly. He looked serious now rather than playful.

'What is it?'

He was looking directly at her. 'I'd like to talk to you. Explain a few things.'

'Are you sure?' Abi said. 'You don't have to. You know that, don't you?'

'Yes, I know. But I think it's time. I think it's right.' He looked pale and awkward and Abi reached up to touch his face gently.

'Shall we go inside?' she suggested.

He glanced up at the sky and then out into the depths of the garden and shook his head.

'I think here's good,' he said, and Abi nodded, feeling the sweet peace of the garden around them.

And then Edward began.

CHAPTER TWENTY-FOUR

'The first thing I want you to know, Abi, is that I never meant to hurt you. That's the last thing I'd ever want to do,' Edward told her. 'It's one of the reasons I kept my past and my family hidden from you. It's all so ugly, you see. I couldn't bear to share it with anyone. But I can see how that hurt you and that I should've just been honest with you from the start. But it's been so hard to even think of broaching the subject because – well – I guess I've done a pretty good job of shutting it out over the years.'

Abi wanted to reassure him that she was okay with that now, but she kept quiet, fearing Edward might lose his nerve if she interrupted him now. His face was half-hidden in shadows and she heard him sighing.

'Frankly, I don't know where to begin. But, well, I told you my mum had died, didn't I? It was years ago and I still miss her. She was special. Very kind. The sort of person you could trust, and she deserved a better life than the one she led. A much better one.' He paused. 'It was a shame it wasn't just my mum taking care of me and Oscar. Things would have been okay then. But there was my dad. I told you he'd died. And, well, he has now. But the reason I told you that he already had was because he was as good as dead to me.'

Edward paused, his vision fixed on the middle distance of the garden where the fairy lights twinkled in the dusky depths. Abi waited for him to continue, wondering what he was thinking and anxious about how hard this was for him to share with her.

'Dad drank,' Edward said at last. 'A lot. And he wasn't pleasant with it. You know how some people can hold their drink – they have just enough to take the edge off life? Well, Dad didn't have those sorts of parameters. It made him nasty. Cruel. He'd lash out at my mum and me too. I don't know how she put up with him. She told me she loved him and that her role was to take care of him, but I could see she wasn't happy.'

Abi spoke at last. 'Oh, Edward, I'm so sorry.'

'And Oscar idolised him,' Edward revealed. 'He never saw his faults and Dad, of course, always encouraged Oscar. It started simply enough – giving Oscar a bottle of beer or a small glass of something. "The boys are having fun!" he'd say if Mum and I dared to challenge him. And that's something Oscar still accuses me of today. He says I'm not capable of having fun because I don't drink myself into oblivion. That's why it wasn't easy for me seeing you with Oscar. I thought I was going to go out of my mind with worry because I know what he's like when he drinks and safety isn't always his number one priority.'

Abi nodded, thinking of the day Oscar had nearly driven them off a cliff into the sea, and she felt the weight of guilt all over again. 'I'm so sorry I did that to you.'

Edward turned to face her. 'That we're both sitting here now is a miracle.'

'What do you mean?' Abi asked, seeing the frown deepen on Edward's face.

'I mean that you're not the only one Oscar almost killed in a car accident.'

Abi gasped. 'What happened?'

'It was about five years ago now, but I still have nightmares about it. Oscar had just bought a car. It was a bit of a wreck to be honest, but he loved it and couldn't wait to show it off. Anyway, there was this party coming up out of town. All our old friends were going. I'm not really one for parties, but it was the kind of party that – if you missed it – you'd never hear the end of it. So I came down from London and stayed in Lewes. Oscar and I went together in his car. The deal was that he'd drive us, but he wouldn't be allowed to drink. Of course, he wanted to show everyone the car so he agreed. No drinking.' Edward gave a hollow laugh. 'Well, you can guess how long that lasted. He managed half the night on soft drinks and he swore to me that he hadn't had alcohol, but I could smell it on him when we got in the car to leave. The trouble was, I'd had a couple of drinks myself and Oscar wouldn't have let me drive his precious car anyway. We fought for a bit about it. I said we should get the train back, but he wasn't having that. What was the point of having a car only to get public transport? It would have meant a hike to the station first too.' He stopped, gazing up at the crescent moon high above them and then he sighed before continuing.

'He was speeding. Of course he was speeding. And he didn't listen to anything I was saying. We got into quite a fight. I told him to pull over. I didn't feel safe and I didn't care if I had to walk the rest of the way back in the dark. It was better than being stuck with my maniac brother behind the wheel. I can't remember the details now. Time seemed to slow down and speed up at the same time.'

Abi nodded, remembering that sensation too that day on the

coast road.

'We were on a country road and thank god there was no other traffic. We approached a corner. I don't know. It was sharp and there was a country house with one of those long garden walls.' He closed his eyes. 'We hit it. The passenger side took the brunt. *I* took the brunt. Oscar had a few cuts and bruises. A bit of whiplash.'

'What happened to you?' Abi whispered.

Edward patted his left leg. 'This!'

She looked down at his leg and then she remembered all the times she'd seen him wince in pain.

'I sustained quite a few broken bones and was out of action for a long time. And there were complications afterwards. I was in rehab for eighteen months, and I've had four operations now.'

'Oh, Edward!'

'And my leg's never been right since then. You've probably seen me struggling and using a stick now and then.'

Abi nodded. 'And you're still in pain from it, aren't you?'

He nodded. 'I've got medication for when it gets bad. Swimming helps. It's about the only time when I'm totally pain-free.'

'I'm so sorry.'

'But that's not the worst of it, I'm afraid,' he went on. 'It's one thing to be nearly killed by your own brother and have him not remember exactly what he did, but it's quite another when your father doesn't believe what's happened.'

'What do you mean?' Abi asked.

'Dad blamed me. He couldn't believe that his beloved Oscar would do something like that even though it was obvious from the breathalyser test that he'd been drinking and that I was clearly in the passenger seat. I couldn't move because of my injuries. But all those facts meant nothing. Dad wouldn't have it. Oscar was blameless. It was a fault in the car, he said, or maybe I'd distracted him.'

'Oh, Edward! That's awful! Has Oscar ever taken responsibility for what he did?'

'You're kidding! I don't think he even remembers the accident. Not in any detail anyway. And he can't understand why I keep harping on about it.'

'He couldn't remember ours either. At least, that's what he said.'

'He'll never change, I'm afraid,' Edward said. 'I could see that in my dad too. And, like Dad, Oscar lives in his own reality and that's ruled by alcohol and chaos, I'm afraid. When I came back to Sussex and bought Winfield, it reopened all sorts of wounds with Oscar and Dad. I often wondered if I'd made a mistake coming here.' He turned towards Abi. 'But then I met you.'

Abi smiled at him. 'So it wasn't *all* bad, then?'

He grinned. 'No. I guess life has a way of balancing things out. At least, that's been my experience.'

'Do you think you and Oscar will ever be able to get along after all that's happened between you?' Abi asked.

'I don't think we'll ever be the best of friends,' Edward said. 'But he's still my little brother, and losing Dad has hit him pretty hard. He's at the family home now. We should be talking about putting it on the market, but I know Oscar's got nowhere else to go and I'm not sure what to do to be honest. He thinks the place is his as I've got Winfield. I don't know. Perhaps I'll let him keep the old place.'

'It would be very kind of you if you did,' Abi told him.

They sat quietly together for a few moments, the peace of the night-time garden holding them in a gentle embrace.

'Families can be tricky,' Abi said, hating herself for saying something so all-encompassing and non-specific, but feeling the need to say it anyway.

'Yes. Well, as you yourself know.'

'We seem to have that in common, don't we? Unusual childhoods!' She gave a nervous little laugh.

'That's certainly one way of looking at it.'

She reached across the bench to hold his hand. 'But we get through these things. Somehow, sometimes slowly, we get through them. And it's never *all* bad, is it? I know you had difficulties with your father, and my sister and I didn't exactly have an easy time of things being brought up by our aunt. But you have good memories of your mother, don't you? And I do of mine, even though she wasn't in my life for very long. I can only remember a handful of moments with her. But they were *good* moments, so I cling to those.'

'I know these last few weeks have been difficult for you,' Edward said. 'I just hope I've not made everything worse.'

'Of course you haven't,' Abi assured him. 'You mustn't think like that. You've had enough to cope with without worrying about me anyway. And we're together now, aren't we?' she told him, the conversation echoing one she'd recently had with Ellen. 'We're getting through all this and we're together.'

They sat for a few more moments and then Abi bent down and took her shoes off. 'Oh, that feels so good! I'm channelling Aura. Did you notice she took her shoes off as soon as she was back at Winfield?'

'I can't say that I did.'

'She was dancing barefoot with Harry. It was so cute!' Abi said. 'But the grass feels so crisp.'

'We've not had rain for a while now,' Edward said.

'Yes, everything's so dry. I'm having to water the garden constantly.'

'There are signs up on the downs warning of fire risks.'

They got up off the bench and slowly made their way back to the hall via Edward's apartment, his French doors open, allowing the rooms to cool after the heat of the day.

'Thanks for telling me everything,' Abi said once they were inside.

'Thanks for listening.'

They kissed and it was such a sweet, tender moment between them that Abi felt sure she was going to cry.

'Hey,' he said as she was about to leave. 'Want to go swimming tomorrow?'

'My nieces are coming over.'

'Oh, okay.'

'Would you be up for an evening dip?' Abi suggested. 'They'll be leaving around six.'

Edward smiled. 'That sounds perfect. It's going to be a hot one – we'll be glad of a cool down.'

'Night, Edward.'

'Night, Abi.'

Abi returned to her apartment, smiling as she saw Aura's bouquet of white flowers in the kitchen sink. She'd arrange the flowers properly tomorrow. Her heart was so full of emotion after the long day and a myriad images cascaded through her mind as she got ready for bed. Harry and Aura dancing. The garden so full of flowers. The hot shimmer of the downs under the August sun. Edward's face half-hidden by shadows as he'd told her about his past.

It had been quite a day. A day full of love and celebration. And revelations. And, as Abi slipped between the cool cotton sheets of her bed, she felt a wonderful peace filling her.

Perhaps, after all the stress and exhaustion of the recent weeks, things were finally calming down at last.

CHAPTER TWENTY-FIVE

Abi couldn't help wondering if it had been a wise decision to have her nieces over on Sunday. She was still exhausted from Harry and Aura's wedding the day before, to say nothing of hearing Edward's confession, but she'd promised Ellen she'd have them and she knew her sister and Douglas were going out for the day. And that was a much needed day together, just the two of them. It was good that they were learning to make time for one another again, Abi thought. After years of Douglas working away from home and Ellen's resentment at hardly seeing him, they were finally prioritising each other.

So when Ellen and Douglas dropped the girls off later that morning, Abi was thrilled to see just how happy her sister looked.

'I think Douglas's booked us lunch somewhere posh,' Ellen whispered to Abi as they were about to leave.

'Well, you both deserve it,' Abi told her. 'Go on – enjoy your day. We'll see you later, okay?'

Abi and the girls waved them off and then went inside. It was already hot in the garden and she thought it was best if they occupied themselves with something fun indoors and then see if it was cooler later in the day after they'd had lunch.

As usual, the girls wanted to paint and Abi was happy to oblige them, spreading paper out on the table. She made them all glasses of pink lemonade, chinking with ice cubes, and then got the paints out.

'What are you working on at the moment, Aunt Abi?' Bethanne asked as Abi sat down with them both.

'My jewellery designs. Remember I told you about the brooches? Well, I've been asked to do some designs for necklaces, bracelets and earrings too, isn't that exciting?'

Bethanne nodded. 'Will you include sunflowers?'

'I'm not sure I will,' Abi said, her hand flying to her silver locket. 'You see, it's good to branch out and do something different. I love my sunflower design, but I've already done it, haven't I?'

'Mummy said your sunflower was such an amazing motif,' Bethanne suddenly revealed.

Abi blinked in surprise. 'She said that?'

Bethanne nodded. 'And she wanted something strong like that for her new business. Something memorable. So she came up with this.'

Abi watched as Bethanne sketched a perfect heart on the piece of paper in front of her and, in its centre, two smaller, intertwined hearts.

'That's lovely!' Abi enthused, noting its simplicity and beauty.

'It's us!' Rosie cried. 'The big heart is Mummy and we're the smaller hearts inside her.'

Abi gasped. 'I love it!'

'Tell her the name,' Rosie said to Bethanne.

'Name?' Abi said.

'When I saw Mum's sketch of the heart, I said she could call her online shop 'Hearts and Crafts'.

'Bethanne – that's brilliant!'

'Do you think so?'

'I *know* so!' Abi bent to kiss her cheek. 'How clever you are.'

'Mum loved it too. And guess what? She's letting me join art club at school. I don't have to go to chess anymore.'

'Oh, Bethy! I'm so happy for you.'

For a few moments, the girls busied themselves with choosing the paints they were going to work with.

'Aunt Abi? Is what Mum does *art*?' Bethanne asked at length.

'I'd say so,' Abi told her honestly. 'Arts and crafts are very similar. You need an artistic eye to do what your mum's doing, don't you think?'

Bethanne nodded. 'Do you think she's letting me go to art club because she likes art too now?'

'Maybe. I think she's beginning to see how valuable it can be. And I don't mean in terms of making money, although that's obviously important. But it seems to be bringing your mum a lot of pleasure, don't you think?'

'She doesn't shout as much,' Rosie declared.

'Yes, she's a lot calmer now,' Bethanne agreed.

Abi smiled. The combination of art and therapy seemed to be working wonders for Ellen.

'She looks happy when she's making things,' Rosie said.

'Unless the thread snaps or gets knotted,' Bethanne added, 'then she says bad words.'

'That's perfectly understandable,' Abi told them.

'She showed us how to make a cushion cover,' Bethanne told her.

'It's lovely that you're all making things together.'

'Like we are now!' Rosie said.

'That's right,' Abi agreed and she watched her two precious nieces for a moment as they got on with the business of creating, and she couldn't help feeling so very happy that Ellen had discovered the joy of creating too and that it had brought a new closeness with her daughters.

It was a little after six that evening and Ellen and Douglas had picked up the girls and Abi was ready to call on Edward. As she crossed the hall and knocked on his door, she became aware of music coming from Samantha's apartment.

'Luckily, that's only just started,' Edward told her as he opened the door. 'But it's getting progressively louder. I think she's having some sort of farewell party. Her doors are open and it's spilled out into the garden.'

'Well, let her enjoy herself if she's leaving,' Abi told him.

'I can't wait to see the back of her.'

'What's that?' Abi said, nodding to a large bag he was holding.

'I've made us a little picnic. Thought we might be hungry after our swim.'

Abi beamed. 'What a lovely idea. So, where are we going?'

'How about our favourite spot on the river?'

'Perfect.'

Sometimes, in life, you don't want to try something different or have a new adventure. You want the comfort of something familiar, and Abi felt that as they parked in the little country lane and walked down the footpath, now overgrown with long summer grasses. Edward went first, swiping at nettles, and rescued Abi when she caught her dress on a fierce bramble.

They climbed over the stile into the field that Abi had come to love so much and laid their things out on the river bank, watching in wonder as a kingfisher darted downstream. Abi had lost count of the number of wild swims she and Edward had shared, but she felt like it was very much a part of her life now. Although, she had to admit that there was still that moment of trepidation when getting into cold water and Abi felt it once again as she left the river bank and submerged herself.

Edward was right behind her. 'Okay?' he called across the water as she swam a few strokes into the centre of the river.

'Glorious!'

She watched as he joined her, his smile full and his eyes bright in the evening light.

'You're right, it's glorious!'

Abi nodded bravely. Her skin felt cold from the water, but her heart was full of warmth for the man she loved more than she'd ever thought was possible and she swam towards him for a kiss.

They ventured downstream a little further and, when the water became too shallow, turned back to their spot on the river bank. A few minutes later, having dried and dressed, they sat on the picnic rug Edward had brought with him, eating the pasta salad he'd made, their limbs tingling after their swim. And they chatted about their day. Abi told him about Bethanne's growing confidence and how Ellen seemed so much happier these days. Edward told Abi how he'd been attempting to choose some wallpaper for his bedroom and had almost lost the will to live and was going to have to ask for her advice. She laughed and promised she'd help. They talked about Harry and Aura, imagining them enjoying the sunshine on the Amalfi coast. And they talked about Winfield and how the summer months had brought so many changes. And then they stopped talking and just listened to the sound of the river, watching the colours of the sunset reflected in its water.

As they walked back across the field a little later, a barn owl swooped low over the grass on silent white wings. They stood and watched as it turned and retraced its path before flying over an adjacent field.

'I read somewhere that barn owls are associated with strength and overcoming adversity,' Abi told Edward.

'Well, we could all do with more of that in our lives.'

'But others believe that they're a bad omen,' Abi added.

'What do you believe?'

Abi smiled. 'I believe they're beautiful birds.'

They returned to the car. It was beginning to get dark now and the drive back through the country lanes looked so different, the deep shadows from the trees turning the benign countryside into something a little eerie.

It was as they rounded the last bend that they saw the air was full of smoke above the village of Winfield.

'Where's it coming from?' Abi asked.

'Maybe there's a fire on the downs.' Edward glanced up at the flank of the hill above the church.

'No, it's coming from the valley, isn't it?'

'Is it?' Edward asked, looking again. The smoke was really billowing now, turning the evening sky a shade darker.

It was then that they heard the siren of a fire engine and its flashing blue lights appeared in the rear-view mirror a second later. Edward pulled over to let it by.

'Heavens!' Abi exclaimed. 'This looks serious.'

They waited a moment before pulling back out and then drove through the village before turning into the track that led to Winfield Hall.

And that's when they saw it.

'Edward!' Abi cried as fear flooded her body. 'It's Winfield!'

There were four fire engines in the driveway and flames were visible from the back of the hall.

Parking quickly, Edward and Abi leapt out of the car.

'Oh, my god! What's happening?' Abi's panic rose as they approached one of the firemen.

'We're the owners!' Edward yelled at him above the noise.

'You can't go in there!' the fireman shouted as Edward headed for the front door.

'What can we do?' Abi cried.

'Stand back!'

Abi's vision blurred with tears. 'How did this happen?' she asked.

Edward's face was white with anxiety.

'Is there anybody inside?' he shouted. The nearest fireman shook his head.

'Where's Samantha?' Abi asked Edward.

'I don't know.'

They looked around, but her car was gone from the driveway.

'I hope they're right and there's nobody in there!' Abi said, feeling Edward's arm around her shoulder.

'I think the fire's contained to the back,' Edward said after a moment.

'But it's spreading across the roof – look!' Abi watched in horror as the flames continued to rise into the night sky above Winfield. 'There must be *something* we can do?'

Edward took her hand and squeezed it. 'Abi!' It was all he could manage.

For a moment, Abi wondered if they should run up onto the hill above the hall for a better view, but she quickly dismissed the idea. It would be too upsetting.

They watched as another three fire engines arrived on the scene. After the peace of the river bank, the chaos at Winfield was hard to bear. Abi watched as plumes of acrid smoke rose in the air and flames shot up through the roof, wrapping around the chimneys. She was aware of a small crowd of villagers in the driveway, some with cameras, capturing the moment of horror. It felt so intrusive, but then she remembered that Winfield Hall was something of a local landmark and that it was natural that people should be curious and care about what was happening.

The House in the Clouds, she thought sadly. Now, the clouds were of thick, black smoke.

Abi felt so completely helpless. It was like the nightmare from her childhood with the flashing blue lights and the feeling that something was wrong – so *very* wrong – and yet she was unable to do anything about it. Standing there in the driveway now, she felt that same fear and anger surging through her again.

'We *have* to get round the back and help!' she told Edward.

'No! We can't go there, Abi!' He grabbed her arm to stop her.

'But what can we do?' she asked in desperation.

He shook his head, his vision fixed firmly on their home. 'I don't know. I don't think there's anything we can do.'

CHAPTER TWENTY-SIX

It was a solemn Abi and Edward who walked up the driveway to Winfield Hall the next morning. A kind neighbour in the village had let them stay the night at hers when it had become obvious that they wouldn't be going anywhere near their apartments that night.

The firefighters had worked into the early hours, not only putting out the fire but taking precautions to make sure that another wasn't likely to start in the dry conditions. Luckily, Edward had been right. The fire had been contained to the back of the house so only Samantha and Tim's apartments had been damaged. The others had been saved, but the smoky conditions would make it unpleasant inside the hall for some time.

Edward had talked to the fire investigation officer and had been told that a disposable barbecue had been found, left on the lawn in the walled garden outside Samantha's apartment. With the recent dry weather, it wasn't any wonder a fire had started. It seemed to have spread indoors quickly as the French doors had been left open. It was possible that a curtain had caught fire, but it wasn't known for sure.

'Someone made a call and I'm guessing it was Samantha,' Edward told Abi as they stopped at the front of the house. 'The man I spoke to didn't have much information, but I'm guessing the fire started when Samantha was still here and she just panicked and rang 999. It was probably too out of control for her to handle anyway and so she took off.'

Abi winced. It wasn't exactly the most responsible thing to do but, then again, Samantha had never really thought about anybody but herself.

'Let's just be thankful that nobody was hurt,' Abi said. 'And it's lucky that Tim had already gone and that Harry and Aura weren't around either.'

Edward nodded and they walked round to the back of the house.

Abi gasped as she saw the damage. The whole of the back had been destroyed. The roof had collapsed and they could see through to the hallway and the staircase.

'Thank god it didn't spread further,' Edward said.

Abi blinked her tears away. She had to keep reminding herself of just how much worse it could have been.

'I never told you this, but I initially bought Winfield as an investment,' Edward told her now. 'I thought I might live here for three or four years and then sell it. Maybe we should do that now. Just sell it.'

Abi's eyes widened in horror. 'Please tell me you're joking!'

He shook his head. 'I don't know if I can go through all this. We've only just restored it, Abi. Do you really want to do all that again?'

'Yes! I *really* do. And we *have* to, Edward! This is our home!'

Edward sighed. 'It's so much work.'

'But we're insured. We can fix this.' She took hold of his hand. 'Come on.'

They walked round to the front of the house and went inside. It was a shock to see a great gaping hole in the roof, the light of the sky coming in from behind the sweep of staircase. Abi swallowed hard. The thick smell of smoke was strong in her throat.

'Look – our apartments are still here. Sixty – no – *seventy* percent of Winfield is still good, isn't it?'

Edward looked around him, his expression filling Abi with fear that he was going to give up.

'And I've been thinking,' Abi said, keeping her focus clearly on the future. 'What if we don't rent apartments out anymore? What if we do something else?'

'Like what?'

'Well, I'd like to do some teaching and run a few courses. We could use the apartments for short-term accommodation. And there are other options like hiring the hall out for special events. Maybe even the occasional wedding party. That way, we get to choose exactly when we share Winfield. But we'd have it to ourselves at other times.'

'I don't know, Abi...'

They'd walked to the bottom of the staircase, the smell of the blackened beams and fallen rubble very strong now.

'We'll get it fixed. *Everything.* By next summer,' Abi declared.

'I don't know if that's possible.'

'But it has to be!' she told him.

'Why?'

'Because we're getting married here.'

A small smile began to spread across Edward's face. 'Did you just propose to me?'

Abi bit her lip to stop herself from giggling at his surprise. 'I did.'

Edward laughed, his eyes lighting up with sudden joy and then he kissed her. 'Well, if you did, I do!'

'You do?'

'I do! And right here too if that's what you want!'

She nodded. 'It is what I want. More than anything! But we'll need all this fixed up by the summer because, well, it *has* to be a summer wedding, doesn't it? All my favourite flowers are in bloom then. And your bride wants to walk down this staircase in her dress with her nieces scattering rose petals from the garden around her.'

'Oh, she does, does she?' Edward laughed again.

'She does! Can you imagine it? Can you see it – *really* see it?'

Edward looked up at the stairs again, and Abi could tell that he was trying to see through the devastation to a bright and clear future, and that perfect summer's day that they were heading towards together.

'Yes,' he said at last. 'I can see it.'

THE END

ACKNOWLEDGEMENTS

To the wonderful team who helped behind the scenes: Catriona Robb, Lisa Brewster, Rachel Gilbey and Roy Connelly.

Huge thanks to Heather Close who made the winning bid on my 'Name a Character' auction in aid of Young Lives vs Cancer.

And heartfelt thanks to my dear readers who have followed Abi and Edward's journey.

A NOTE TO MY READERS

I was in the honoured position of being able to hear your feedback on the first and second novels while I was writing the third – listening to what you loved and what you wanted more of, and I sincerely hope that *The Colour of Summer* lives up to your expectations. I've loved my time at Winfield Hall – it's a story I've long been wanting to write and I'm more than a little sad now that it's over, but happy that it's finally told and out in the world for readers to discover.

I have to admit that this wasn't an easy book to write. There is a certain pressure that comes with writing the last in a series – have you remembered everything, tied up all the knots, allowed each character their time and given the readers a full and satisfying conclusion? I'd also given myself the added pressure of having a title with the word 'summer' in it. I had deliberately set each of the trilogy's main action during the summer months, focusing on the beauty, lightness and joy of an English summer in the Sussex Downs. It would therefore be disastrous if I were to miss my deadline!

But, on top of these pressures were other ones. 2021 was a

very sad year for me. I lost my father in August – very suddenly and unexpectedly. Then we heard news that my husband's uncle had been killed in a road accident. We also lost a family friend, and another dear friend was slipping away after being diagnosed with a brain tumour five years before.

We also had to say goodbye to a much loved hen, Portia – a beautiful Buff Orpington so full of character. They say you should never have favourites, but Portia was our first mother hen, hatching a flock of chicks for us. Then, within a fortnight, one of her beautiful 'chicks', Mini P, died at just two years old. Sometimes, life can really test you.

Writing can be difficult when your heart is sad, but there were days when my story helped to release something in me, providing the same comfort and joy that I always try to give to my readers. Fiction is a dear friend at such times – whether you're reading it or writing it, and long may that continue!

With love to you all

Victoria x

ALSO BY VICTORIA CONNELLY

The House in the Clouds Series

The House in the Clouds

High Blue Sky

The Colour of Summer

The Book Lovers Series

The Book Lovers

Rules for a Successful Book Club

Natural Born Readers

Scenes from a Country Bookshop

Christmas with the Book Lovers

Other Books

The Beauty of Broken Things

One Last Summer

The Heart of the Garden

Love in an English Garden

The Rose Girls

The Secret of You

Christmas at The Cove

Christmas at the Castle

Christmas at the Cottage

The Christmas Collection (A compilation volume)

A Summer to Remember

Wish You Were Here

The Runaway Actress

Molly's Millions

Flights of Angels

Irresistible You

Three Graces

It's Magic (A compilation volume)

A Weekend with Mr Darcy

The Perfect Hero (Dreaming of Mr Darcy)

Mr Darcy Forever

Christmas With Mr Darcy

Happy Birthday Mr Darcy

At Home with Mr Darcy

One Perfect Week and Other Stories

The Retreat and Other Stories

Postcard from Venice and Other Stories

A Dog Called Hope

Escape to Mulberry Cottage (non-fiction)

A Year at Mulberry Cottage (non-fiction)

Summer at Mulberry Cottage (non-fiction)

Finding Old Thatch (non-fiction)

Secret Pyramid (children's adventure)

The Audacious Auditions of Jimmy Catesby (children's adventure)

ABOUT THE AUTHOR

Victoria Connelly is the bestselling author of *The Rose Girls* and *The Book Lovers* series.

With over a million sales, her books have been translated into many languages. The first, *Flights of Angels*, was made into a film in Germany. Victoria flew to Berlin to see it being made and even played a cameo role in it.

A Weekend with Mr Darcy, the first in her popular Austen Addicts series about fans of Jane Austen has sold over 100,000 copies. She is also the author of several romantic comedies including *The Runaway Actress* which was nominated for the Romantic Novelists' Association's Best Romantic Comedy of the Year.

Victoria was brought up in Norfolk, England before moving

to Yorkshire where she got married in a medieval castle. After 11 years in London, she moved to rural Suffolk where she lives in a thatched cottage with her artist husband, a springer spaniel and her ex-battery hens.

To hear about future releases and receive a **free ebook** sign up for her newsletter at victoriaconnelly.com